Dead Men's Harvest

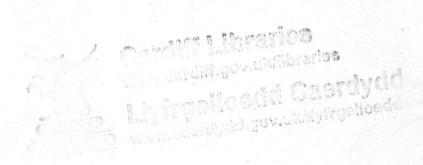

Dead Men's Harvest

Matt Hilton

W F HOWES LTD

This large print edition published in 2011 by
W F Howes Ltd
Unit 4, Rearsby Business Park, Gaddesby Lane,
Rearsby, Leicester LE7 4YH

1   3   5   7   9   10   8   6   4   2

First published in the United Kingdom in 2011
by Hodder & Stoughton

A CIP catalogue record for this book is available
from the British Library

ISBN 978 1 40749 343 5

Typeset by Palimpsest Book Production Limited,
Falkirk, Stirlingshire
Printed and bound in Great Britain
by MPG Books Ltd, Bodmin, Cornwall

MIX
Paper from
responsible sources
FSC
www.fsc.org   FSC® C018575

This one is for Alison Bonomi

'There is no hunting like the hunting of man, and those who have hunted armed men long enough and liked it, never care for anything else thereafter.'

Ernest Hemingway

Conchar is an ancient Gaelic term for those who admire the king of all hunters: the wolf.

To some, the wolf is a magnificent beast, the pinnacle of predatory evolution. To others, the wolf is a thing of nightmare.

Castle of the wolf: it was a good name for an Army Confinement Facility. Imprisoned within its walls were men and women who were ultimate predators and also, often, things of nightmare.

Criminals housed at Fort Conchar generally fell into four categories: prisoners of war, enemy combatants, persons whose freedom was deemed a risk to national security and, lastly, military personnel found guilty of a serious crime.

Occasionally it housed criminals who did not meet any of these criteria, but that was an extreme circumstance. Only once had it opened its arms to a man who checked all four boxes and then some. Designated Top Secret, his name was withheld even from those who guarded him night and day. Known only by a number – Prisoner 1854 – he was a cipher in more ways than one.

Mostly he refused to speak to his jailers. Some even thought him incapable of speech. But his mystery went much deeper than that.

He was a living dead man. According to official

records he had died, not once, but twice. And yet he still breathed.

If all went to plan, the dead man would, like Lazarus, rise again. And people would know him. And they would scream his name in fear.

CHAPTER 1

A breeze stirred and the susurration of foliage was like the whispering of lost souls. Frogs croaked. Water lapped. All sounds indigenous to the Everglades pine lands. Jared 'Rink' Rington ignored the natural rhythms of the Florida night, listening instead for the soft footfalls of the men hunting him.

There were at least four of them: men with guns.

From the cover of a stream bed, Rink spied back to where he'd left his car. The Porsche was a mess. Bullet holes pocked it from front to back and had taken out the front windshield. He'd wrecked the sump when he'd crashed over the median and into the coontie trees. A wide swath of oil was glistening in the moonlight, as though the Boxster had been mortally wounded and crawled into the bushes to die. Rink cursed under his breath, more for the death of his wheels than for his own predicament, but it wasn't the first time he'd had to consign a car to the grave.

Neither was it the first time he'd been hunted by armed men.

It kinda came with the territory.

The stream was shallow, almost stagnant. He used its steep bank as cover as he headed left. Above him someone stepped on a twig and it was like the crack of a gunshot. The insects grew still. There was a hush on the forest now. Rink crouched low, pressing himself against baked mud.

A few yards further on, another twig creaked beneath a boot.

Rink wormed himself out of the stream bed. A man moved along the embankment above him, periodically glancing down towards the water, but more often towards the road.

Through the bushes Rink saw another man was moving along the blacktop. This one held a Glock machine pistol, the elongated barrel telling him that it was fitted with a sound suppressor.

Frog-giggers want to do me in silence, he thought. Well, all right. Two of us can play at that game.

From his boot he pulled a military-issue Ka-bar knife, a black epoxy-coated blade that didn't reflect the light.

His options were few. He had to take out the men hunting him or die. Put that way he'd no qualms about sticking the man in front of him.

His rush was silent. His free hand went over the man's mouth even as he jammed the Ka-bar down between the juncture of his throat and clavicle. The blade was long enough to pierce the left aorta of the man's heart, killing him instantly. Rink dragged the corpse down to the ground.

The man on the road was unaware that his companion was gone.

From the dead man's fingers, Rink plucked free the Heckler and Koch Combat .45 and shoved it into the waistband of his jeans. There was no suppressor on this gun, so the knife would remain his weapon of choice for now, because the man with the Glock had to be done as silently as the first. Two other assassins were out there – possibly more – and he wanted to even the odds in his favour before exchanging rounds.

Rink was tall and muscular, built like a pro-wrestler. The man at his feet wasn't. But by exchanging jackets and with the man's baseball cap jammed over his black hair, he'd fool the other hunter for a second or so. Everything weighed and bagged, that would be all he'd need.

In the corpse's clothing, Rink moved through the bushes. For effect he pulled out the .45 so the disguise was complete. He held it in a two-handed grip, or that would be how it looked in silhouette.

The man to his right gestured; soldier-speak that Rink recognised. These men weren't your run-of-the-mill killers; they too must have had military training. Rink hand-talked, urging the man in the direction of a stand of trees. As he moved off, Rink angled towards him. Ten paces were all that separated them. The moon was bright on the road, but its light helped make the shadows beneath the trees denser. If Rink moved closer he could forget the charade.

The man halted. Something stirred in the foliage ahead. He dropped into a shooter's crouch, his Glock sweeping the area. Then a bird, disturbed from its roost, broke through the trees in a clatter of plumage on leaves. The man sighed, turned to grin sheepishly at his compadre.

Rink grinned back at him and he saw the man's face elongate in recognition. Charade over, he whipped his Ka-bar out from alongside the .45 and overhanded it at the man. Like a sliver of night, the blade swished through the air and plunged through tissue and cartilage.

The man staggered at the impact, one hand going to the hilt jutting from beneath his jaw, the other bringing round the Glock and tugging on the trigger. Rink dropped below the line of fire, the bullets searing the air around him, making tatters of the bushes and coontie trees. It was a subdued drum roll of silenced rounds, but no less deadly than if the gun had roared the sound of thunder. The man was mortally wounded, though not yet dead, but the Glock was empty and no threat. Gun in hand, Rink moved towards him.

Weakened by the shock of steel through his throat, drowning in his own blood, he couldn't halt Rink's charge. He was knocked off his feet and went down under the bigger man. Then Rink had a hand on the hilt of the Ka-bar. A sudden jerk sideways opened one half of the man's neck and that was that.

Dragging the corpse off the road, Rink concealed it amongst a stand of palmetto.

Two down, two to go.

Rink was beginning to fancy his chances.

Armed now with two reliable guns and his Ka-bar, he decided it was time to show these frog-giggin' sons of bitches who they were dealing with.

'My turn, boys,' he whispered.

A faint click.

'No, Rington,' said a voice from behind him. 'Now it's *my* turn.'

Rink swung round, his knife coming up in reflex, but it was too late.

Something was rammed against his chest and he became a juddering, spittle-frothing wreck as fifty thousand volts were blasted through his entire being.

CHAPTER 2

The headstone was the only feature that held any colour. Everything else was the grey of a Maine winter, with sleet falling like shards of smoked glass across the monochrome background. Even the trees that ringed the small cemetery were dull, lifeless things, their bare branches smudged by the shifting sky. The sleet was building on the ground, not the pure white of virgin snow, but slushy, invasive muck that filled my boots with a creeping chill that bit bone deep.

I hunkered over the grave and wiped the accumulation of icy slush off the headstone. The granite marker stood four feet tall, pinkish-grey, with a spray of flowers carved down one side and painted in vivid splashes of red and green. The name had been inlaid with gold leaf, as had the date of her premature death: almost a year ago.

I'm not a religious man, not in the accepted sense, but I still mumbled a prayer for her. Religion, or more correctly the effects of others twisting it, had been a factor of my professional life. I'd seen people murder one another for having a different faith, I'd seen people tortured and mutilated. I couldn't believe that if there was a God, then such a benevolent, loving figure would allow such outrages in His name – whatever that might turn out to be. For fourteen years I'd fought men whose minds had been poisoned by fanatical teachings; they all swore that they were doing His bidding. Made me wonder who was guiding me when I put the bastards down. I hoped that Kate Piers was in more caring hands than those of the god of war that must have propelled me.

I rose to my feet and folded my hands across my middle, looking down at the grave. The sleet stung my face, but it was small penance for failing to save the woman I'd fallen in love with.

'Are you ready, Joe?'

Lost in the past, I'd momentarily forgotten that Kate's sister was standing beside me. I looked at her, and her eyes shone with tears. Her sister had died protecting her life, and Imogen had never got over it. She felt guilty that it was her little sister lying cold in the grave and not her. But, more than that, I knew her tears were because she feared the man she loved was thinking the same.

I took one of her gloved hands in mine, pulled her in close so that I shielded her under my arm and placed a kiss on her cheek. 'Ready,' I told her. 'Come on. Let's get out of this cold.'

Imogen leaned down and placed a single rose against the headstone, then together we walked across the cemetery towards the gates. The cemetery wasn't large, just a half-acre ringed by a stone wall, and now almost overgrown by trees. The Piers family plot held five generations, including the body of my old army friend, Jake. This was where Imogen would come when her time on earth was over. Made me wonder where I'd end up. Nowhere as sanctified as this, I supposed; more likely an unmarked hole in the ground. Perhaps that would be fitting, because I'd sent plenty of others to such an ignominious resting place.

Imogen's house was perched on a rocky bluff overlooking Little Kennebec Bay, a short drive from Machiasport. The cemetery was situated on the Piers land, but even the five-minute walk was unpleasant in this weather. We clambered into the warmth of my Audi A6. I'd had the foresight to leave the engine running and the car was snug. I felt the blood rushing to my cheeks. Imogen struggled out of her gloves while I headed the car up the incline towards the house. In this half-light Imogen's home looked like something out of a Poe story, its pitched roof and steepled corners rearing against the slate sky. We didn't speak in the car, nothing beyond complaints about the weather anyway, and the transition from vehicle to house was done in a hurry.

There was a fire burning in the hearth and I stoked it, piling on logs, while Imogen prepared hot, dark coffee for me, cocoa laced with something stronger for her. I never did get to drink the coffee. In the next few seconds we were in each other's arms as we navigated the stairs to her bedroom. Survivors' guilt syndrome is a powerful thing, but I couldn't blame that for the surge of passion that rose up in the two of us. She just looked so damn ravishing, her cheeks pink with a flush of warmth, her hair slightly in disarray from having pulled off her hat. She looked fragile and vulnerable and in need of reassurance. I hoped that actions were more profound than words. All I did was put down my coffee, take her cocoa from her hand and place it next to mine. Then I pulled her into a kiss, one that I meant dearly. That was all it took for us to wrestle our way through the house, undressing each other as we went.

Imogen's original bedroom had been violated when she'd been attacked by a misogynistic killer named Luke Rickard. Rickard had wanted to kill me and had targeted me through Imogen. She steered me past that room and into the one she had now commandeered. It was a big house for a single person, and the master bedroom only accentuated that. The bed would be best described as super king-sized, but we made use of every square inch.

Afterwards we lay side by side, our bodies glistening with perspiration, Imogen's hair in even more disarray. She lay with one hand on my stomach, tracing lazy circles with her fingertips, enjoying for the moment the companionable silence. Perhaps there was more than that to the silence; there were things yet unspoken, but now was not the time or place. Beyond the windows night had fallen, and the sleet had turned to snow. It was like a shroud that blocked out the rest of the world. We were cocooned in our own little bubble and I wished that things could stay that way forever. But I knew they couldn't.

Some sixth sense in me had been anticipating the thrum of an engine and the squeak of tyres on the new snow. I sat up and looked through the window. The vantage didn't allow a view down to the parking area outside. Naked, I stood, and then stooped for my abandoned clothes. First thing first, I lifted my SIG Sauer P226 and racked the slide. After that I dragged on my jeans and then padded back to the window.

'Who is it?'

Without turning, I said, 'Don't know yet. You'd best get dressed.'

We weren't expecting visitors. On a night like this, with the blizzard driving in off the Atlantic, only someone very determined would be out and about. In my world that meant law enforcement officers or enemies. Experience told me neither would be good news.

A vehicle crept into view. It was a dark-coloured SUV, the windows tinted so I couldn't make out who was inside, or how many. The snow didn't help because it was swirling on the breeze, dancing a dervish jig between me and the vehicle. I watched until it pulled up alongside my Audi. No

10

one got out. Maybe they were running the tags on my car.

I quickly pulled on my T-shirt and a hooded sweatshirt. I shrugged into my leather jacket, still damp from earlier, even as I stepped into my boots. The clothes went on almost as frenetically as they had so recently come off. Behind me, Imogen had pulled on a robe and cinched it round the waist. She joined me as I took another peek out the window.

'Joe,' she said in a whisper. 'Who could they be?'

'I don't know, but I don't like it. I want you to stay up here until I find out. OK?'

This was Imogen's home. She shouldn't have to live in fear within its walls, but she did. Once already it had been invaded by a killer, and a cop had died on the threshold, trying to help her. Luke Rickard wasn't the one she feared now. I'd killed that piece of shit. But there were others who might still want to harm her. I met Kate after Imogen had gone missing, running for her life to avoid the wrath of a Texan mobster and his sadistic enforcers, the Bolan twins. I had found Imogen and then took the war back to its source, but that was when Kate had died. Imogen didn't have to worry about Robert Huffman or the twins: I'd killed them too. But the mob was far-ranging and had a long memory and she waited for the day they'd seek retribution. She didn't argue with my request for her to stay hidden.

I went down the stairs and threw on the spotlights

I'd fitted round the eaves. The light would momentarily blind those in the SUV. While they were blinking, I stepped out of the front door, the SIG hidden alongside my thigh. Enemies would do one of two things: reverse the car out of there, or come out with their guns blazing. I readied myself for either eventuality. Instead, the passenger door opened and a single figure emerged. He held his hands over his head, showing me that they were empty.

'Move away from the car.' I allowed the SIG to be seen, so he knew I wasn't taking no for an answer.

He nodded and took two exaggerated steps to the side. I left him standing there in the snow, his hands reaching for the heavens, while I angled for a look into the SUV. There was a driver, but no one I could see in the back. 'You as well, pal. Out of the car and show me your hands.'

These weren't men lost on the road and seeking directions, neither were they enemies. Their approach told me that quite eloquently. They showed they meant no harm by lifting their hands, without raising a fuss about their treatment. I waved the driver round the front of the car, ushering them both together. It was easier to keep an eye on them like that.

Both were alike the way men of military bearing are: strong and lithe, with short haircuts and hard eyes. They were dressed similarly in thick windcheaters, dark jeans and rubber-soled boots.

Bulges under their left armpits told me they were packing, both of them right-hand draws. The only thing that differentiated them was that one was missing a chunk of eyebrow, and the other, slightly heavier, had ten years on his friend.

'You're not cops,' I said. 'So I'm guessing you're with the government.'

The older man was the designated driver, which made me conclude that the first man to get out the car was the one who'd come to speak. I wasn't wrong.

'We should get out of the storm.' He nodded towards the house. 'Better if we talk inside, Mr Hunter.'

He used my name as a tool, couching his words so that they were more than a suggestion. He wanted me to know who was really in charge. It didn't work that way with me. 'My girlfriend is inside.' I left things at that. Let them think what they wanted.

'She knows all about you?' The man was wily, and he left the hint about my past unsaid.

'She knows that I'm not the type to let strangers inside without checking them out first. So . . . who are you, and what brings you here?'

The men lowered their hands. The younger of the two reached towards his armpit. Left hand, so I didn't flinch. He pulled out a leather wallet and flicked it open. He showed me an FBI ID badge. I smiled cynically at him. 'I've got one just like that. I bought it off eBay for five bucks. Who supplied yours, Charles W. Brigham? The CIA, I bet.'

Brigham chuckled. His mouth twisted, and the skin on his face puckered all the way up to his damaged eyebrow. Once he'd been very lucky that a knife blade hadn't taken off his entire face. 'As you know, CIA agents aren't in the habit of carrying badges. It's too much of a giveaway. But that's my real name. You have the ability to check it out.'

I did, but I wasn't going to bother. There was no reason for Brigham to lie. 'And who are you?' I directed at the older man. 'Your name will do, forget the Mickey Mouse badge.'

'Ray Hartlaub.'

'Brigham and Hartlaub? It sounds like an accountancy firm to me.' I smiled to show I was only fooling, but also that they held no fear for me.

'That would be Hartlaub and Brigham,' the older agent said. 'Seeing as I'm in charge.'

I'd thought as much. The one in charge never gets out of the car first. Not when there's an armed man waiting for him. 'So why are you here?'

'We were asked to come fetch you.'

I shook my head, more an act of derision than to dislodge the snow off my hair. There was only one person who could be behind this round-up. My old CIA contact from when I was hunting terrorists. 'Walter Hayes Conrad. What has that old goat got up his sleeve this time?'

14

'Nothing,' Hartlaub said. 'In fact, you can forget about SDC Conrad upsetting your life ever again.'

'So old Walt's finally retired then?'

'No, Hunter, Walter Conrad is dead. He was murdered a few hours ago.'

CHAPTER 3

Three days earlier . . .

It was undignified to run like this, but sensible under the circumstances.

Prisoner 1854 could feel the effects of eighteen months' confinement deep in his muscles and ligaments and it wasn't a sensation he liked. In his cell he'd exercised regularly, performing numerous repetitions of press-ups and crunches, interspersed with endless callisthenics. His body and mind remained strong, but running in the open, his lungs laboured under the uncommon strain of sucking in air through a constricted throat. It was one thing having the physique of an athlete when his cardiovascular system was severely impeded. But he pushed back the pain and kept running. Freedom was a far more exhilarating prospect to concentrate on.

He knew where he was – his confinement had come with some home comforts, including *unofficial* access to computers – but Google Earth was only part-way reliable. It was out of date, and it didn't include accurate topographical features.

A two-dimensional satellite image couldn't prepare him for the undulating ground, the closeness of the trees or the rocks that bruised his feet and threatened to turn an ankle every other step. But he ignored these factors as readily as he did the pain in his limbs and the burning in his chest. Speed was his best bet at present. Speed equalled distance, and distance meant a larger area for his pursuers to cover. Once he had them strung out in a broader circle the gaps between them and the opportunity to slip past them grew in his favour.

The MPs had dogs, but the dogs could only move as quickly as their handlers. He was more concerned with the helicopters buzzing in the sky behind him. They would come equipped with FLIR technology, seeking his heat signature. If they got a hit on his body heat they could direct men to surround and contain him. In his favour was the fact that they hadn't expected him to cover so much ground in such a short space of time. For now, he must keep his lead, get to some place where there were other people who would confound the heat-seeking technology. The only problem with that scenario was that his hunters would expect him to do just that. They'd have all the approaches to the nearest towns covered. But he wasn't over concerned with that either. Men were fallible; if he didn't want them to see him they wouldn't. And if he chose to show himself, then they'd end up dead.

A gap in the woods lay somewhere ahead. Light

was minimal, just a fingernail sliver of moon to offer guidance, but he knew the gap was there. He'd plotted the distance and the time it would take him to reach the glade. He had no watch or any other time-keeping device on him, but he was in tune with the rhythm of his pace and was confident that his first destination was close at hand.

He scrambled down a slope, grabbing at sparse brush to slow him down, his feet churning through loose earth, ankle-deep. He sloshed along a stream in an effort to confuse the dogs, made it about four hundred yards then clambered up out of the stream and on to a wide clay embankment. The clay had once been as viscous as treacle but had dried stone-hard many millennia before. The going was easier there, but he was exposed to the air and would be visible to the chopper pilots even without the aid of technology. He sprinted back into darkness on the far side of the clay bed, heading a few rows deep into the woods. He pushed through the thickets, thorns grabbing at his stolen uniform and at the flesh of his hands. But he let none of the discomfort slow him down. Unerringly he headed up and over the next rise and down into the glade he sought. There he allowed himself a few seconds. He fisted his knuckles into his sides, sucking in air as best he could as he scanned the glade for his marker.

Beyond the far trees rose the unmistakable geometrical shapes of civilisation. There wasn't much, just a peaked barn and a silo, but he'd singled out these structures when formulating his getaway plan. He didn't approach them, but turned west and ran another two hundred yards to where a wire fence cut across the glade. It was to dissuade cattle from straying, not to halt a fleeing convict, and he hurdled the fence with little effort. He then used the fence as a guide, following it back into the woods on this side of the glade. From nearby came the unmistakable yapping of excited dogs.

Damn those dogs! His pursuers had got closer than he liked. But it didn't matter. As long as everything was in place as he'd planned.

The fence ended at a sturdy tree, the wires hammered into the trunk. Bark had begun to grow around the wires, nature sealing the wounds, making of the tree a symbiotic creature of plant and metal. It was a minor detail, but he often noted the mundane and found the minutiae fascinating. He was always spellbound by what lay under the skin of the outer world. Yet he had no time to study this marvel; the dogs were getting close. Worse, he heard the pitch of one of the helicopters change and knew that it was extending the search in this direction.

At the back of the tree he found what he'd been searching for. A tarpaulin was draped over a shapeless form and twigs of brush had been piled over them both. He pulled at the corner of the tarp, smelled the tang of petroleum, and was filled with fierce joy.

He dragged the tarpaulin clear, uncovering an off-road motorcycle. He didn't know the make, and didn't care. It was enough that the bike was where he'd requested, as was the satchel containing a change of clothing and other items more important to him. He stripped out of the uniform, threw it from him like the reviled thing it was, and then slipped into jeans and shirt and leather jacket. His own shoes would have to do. There was a helmet, part of his disguise, and he settled it over his fair hair, pulling down the visor.

Light stabbed through the woods to the east.

Dogs barked frantically.

The helicopter roared close by.

To hell with them all.

He delved in the satchel and pulled out a gun. It was a Glock with spare clips of ammo. He secreted the gun in his waistband and stuffed his jacket pockets with magazines of bullets. That weapon was secondary to him.

Lastly he fished out the thing he desired most.

It flashed dully under the meagre moonlight, yet he still thrilled at the way the moonbeam caressed the blade as though it was liquid. In that second all his aches and pains, his minor abrasions, were forgotten.

He was back.

There would be no stopping him this time.

CHAPTER 4

Ray Hartlaub was a veteran with as many years' service with the CIA as I had with Arrowsake, the super-secret 'extermination squad' fielded by a coalition of nations including both the UK and the USA. I'd never personally come across the man, but had heard his legend over the years. Whereas I was always a soldier, Hartlaub had been one of the invisible men, the spooks, who went into disaffected areas of the world and fed us the information necessary to do our job. In many respects his had been a task even more dangerous than mine. As a rule I'd have been with a team, at the very least with one other man, whereas Hartlaub, by necessity, worked alone. He still came across as being of that mind. He could have pulled rank on Brigham, made him do the driving, but it struck me that he preferred to be in charge of everything. That was perhaps the only way he felt safe.

Charles Brigham was happy in the back, allowing us 'old guys' to sit up front as Hartlaub navigated the SUV towards the tiny Machias Valley Airport, which boasted a single runway. The snowfall had grown in volume, the hush that comes with a blizzard even dampening the thrum of the wipers.

The CIA is famed for its secretive ways, which possibly explained both men's reticence on Walter Conrad's death. All that either would allow was that he hadn't suffered. Well, that was a blessing, but I wondered about what he faced in his designated afterlife. If such a thing as Heaven existed, there'd be some major explaining to do before St Peter granted him access.

I was content with the silence. It allowed me room for my own thoughts. I wasn't dwelling on Walter's death. We were both engaged in a trade where death is the usual outcome. In many respects we had inured ourselves to how grief placed its debilitating hand upon us. We compartmentalised the loss of our colleagues, used that stored-up rage to exact retribution on their killers. I was saddened by his death – for God's sake, the man was like a father to me – but my sadness at that moment was outweighed by another death, one that I could not put aside: the death of my relationship with Imogen Ballard.

It was the thing that had gone unsaid as we'd lain side by side, slick with the perspiration of our lovemaking. We'd both been so eager to show our passion that it had gone beyond tenderness, and had become a purely physical thing. What we were doing wasn't *meaningful*. It was a conjoining of two people, and that was all. We had come together through our love for Kate. We had found consolation in each other's arms, but it had never been enough for either of us. Imogen was a beautiful, strong and giving person, and if circumstances had been different then maybe things would have worked between us. But not when Kate's ghost was forever in our memories. How could I ever get over Kate when Imogen resembled her so closely that it hurt just to look at her? How could Imogen move on when she would forever feel guilt over Kate's death? She couldn't when I was a constant reminder of that fateful day.

When I'd gone inside to tell her about Walter, her eyes had filled with tears.

'You're going with them, Joe?'

'Yes. There's nothing else that I can do.'

'But you won't be back.'

It wasn't a question. In any case I couldn't answer. I'm not sure I would've had the right words.

'I'm sorry about Walter. I know he meant a lot to you.'

A pang had dug its sharp talons into my heart, but not for Walter. Her words were loaded.

'So do you, Imogen,' I said.

She closed her eyes, trying to halt the flow of tears, but it was a battle she couldn't win. She sobbed and it was such a heart-wrenching thing that it racked her entire frame. I moved close and held her tightly. She cried against my chest. When she stepped away she looked a little stronger. She touched a hand to my face. 'Take care of yourself, Joe.'

'It isn't me I'm concerned about . . .'

'You needn't worry about me.'

'Easy for you to say.' I placed my palm over her hand, held it there. 'You'll always be *special* to me.'

'I know,' she said, her voice barely above a whisper. She gently took her hand away, and then tilted her lips to mine. Our kiss was dry, barely a buss of skin. Like a brother and sister chastely saying goodbye.

We didn't say anything after that. It was best that we didn't because we might have convinced ourselves that our relationship was right. I pulled my things together: not much, just a change of clothing, a toiletry pack and the fake documents I carried. I could have done with a shower, but that only meant prolonging the agony. The shower would have to wait. Bag of clothes in hand, I let myself out of the front door, closed it softly behind me. I felt Imogen's gaze on me as I crossed over to the CIA men's SUV. They didn't look put out by having to wait for me, but even if they had, then so what. Imogen had deserved much more, but at least I'd had the opportunity to say goodbye.

The Audi was a slight hiccup. It meant I'd have to leave it in situ. If it had been my personal vehicle, that could have been a problem. I would have had to come back to retrieve it, when really what I – or more correctly Imogen – needed was to make some space between us. I'd never cut all ties because she held a special place in my affections, but she required time to find herself another man, someone who'd give himself wholly to her. Luckily, the Audi was a rental. I'd picked it up after my previous car had been shot to pieces and then scorched by flames during a job over in Pennsylvania a few months ago. A call to the rental firm would suffice for it to be collected.

The Audi, the SUV, they were just vehicles to get us where we were going, inanimate things. They meant no more to me than the Cessna airplane in which we took off into the storm, despite the severe weather. The pilot deserved a medal, because he flew the plane against all odds and we touched down safely on a nameless strip in the Adirondacks, where we transferred to yet another government SUV. My shower remained on the back burner, because there was only one place we were heading to, with no stops in between. The storm wasn't as strong this far south, but it threatened us with gusts of icy wind and the snow couldn't be far behind. Hartlaub drove like he didn't want to contend with it a second time and we drew up to Walter Conrad's retreat in a little under a half-hour.

Walter was a sub-division controller of black ops. Simply put, he ordered the deaths of persons deemed enemies of his country. By its very nature, the job made him a morose fellow. One of the simple pleasures that Walter enjoyed was whiling away the hours with a fishing rod in hand; it was ironic that his way of finding peace was through further killing. At least, he always argued, the fish had a fighting chance. His love of the sport had always brought him out here to his cabin, with his own private stretch of water barely three hundred yards below the house. For someone with so many enemies this was not a good place to come alone. Not that that happened too often.

Ordinarily Walter travelled with a small retinue of bodyguards. I'd regularly been in the same room as his two most loyal protectors and it struck me that I'd never learned their names. I wondered if I'd do so now, on the roll-call of the deceased. If Walter had been murdered, then those two guys would surely have died alongside him.

Brigham led the way towards the back porch. A stern-faced duo watched our approach, men in dark suits and shades, ridiculous attire for this weather. Hartlaub mirrored my pace as we followed.

'It's not pretty inside,' the CIA man said.

'He's still here?' I was surprised. Walter deserved more dignity than to be left so long where he'd fallen.

'Walter has been moved, but . . . well, wait and you'll see what I mean.'

Brigham spoke to the two gorillas in suits and then waved us forward. One of the door guards stared at me through the lenses of his shades. Muscles bunched in his jaw as I stepped up on to the porch, and he averted his gaze. His action, waving me through the door, was a little rushed as though he didn't want to be under my scrutiny for too long. I went by, studying him in profile. He snapped his face away, staring ahead like the sentry he portrayed. I let it go at that and followed Hartlaub and Brigham inside.

The other times I'd been in Walter's cabin, I'd always entered via the front. I had never been in this rear section of the house. There was a kitchen, no frippery, no knick-knacks, just utilitarian equipment. There was also a bedroom, the door standing open to show a room as masculine as the kitchen. A bed, a dresser and a wardrobe was all the furniture Walter possessed, and there wasn't even a carpet on the floor. The rooms reminded me of a monk's quarters and made me wonder if Walter's reason for coming here was penance of a sort.

A short passage led to the large open space of the living area. The door was shut, but even so I could smell the stench from the room beyond. Hartlaub and Brigham had said that Walter had been killed earlier that day, so the stink wasn't that of decomposition. It was the kind of smell that lingers in a slaughter house: the sickly sweet fumes released from gutted carcasses. Hartlaub's warning rung in my ears.

Brigham pulled a small jar from a pocket and offered it around. It was a vapour rub, but not for anyone's aching muscles. When neither Hartlaub nor I accepted his offering he uncapped the jar and smeared some of the menthol gel under his nose. Cop trick, to keep the stench at bay. It

27

seemed that, like me, Hartlaub had been around enough dead bodies for it no longer to affect him.

Brigham opened the door and the warm rush of wind almost took my breath away. The overriding odour was the coppery tang of spilled blood. But worse than that was the gag-inducing putridity of voided bowels and spilled stomach contents.

Despite being inured to the after-effects of slaughter, I couldn't stop myself from pinching my nose. Beside me Hartlaub stood stoically, but his eyes were watering as much as mine. We moved tentatively into the room, squeezing past Brigham who looked content to remain at the threshold.

Investigators had been and gone, bodies tagged and shrouded and carried away, so only the aftermath bore witness to what had happened here.

It was like a maniacal artist had taken a couple of gallons of red paint to the walls and floor, with splashes and ribbons of blood everywhere. Other pools on the floor made nightmarish Rorschach designs, and there were hunks of skin and hair adhering to the carpet and furniture. Bullet holes stitched patterns in the walls. A chair had been knocked over, a settee thrown down on its back. I didn't have the expert eye of a detective, but even I could tell that at least three men had died here. Something else: this wasn't the result of a normal hit. This was the work of someone – or some*thing* – demented.

I turned from the scene of horror and met Hartlaub's eyes.

'You told me Walter didn't suffer.'

Hartlaub shrugged. 'He didn't. Most of the blood you see here was from post-mortem dismemberment.'

CHAPTER 5

Two days earlier . . .

Prisoner 1854 was reborn.

He arrived at his rebirth in a sleek, black limousine, and a flunkey reached down and opened the rear door for him, like he was an honoured guest. Stepping out of the limousine on to a driveway bordered by shrubs and tinkling fountains, he cast his gaze over a building that spoke of opulence rivalling that of movie stars and pop legends. He tipped a genteel nod at the servant who held open the door. The man grunted, then waved him forward with the barrel of a .38. So much for that illusion.

Behind him, two more guards took up position as he was marched unceremoniously towards the entrance of the mansion. Other guards flanked the doors, grim-faced men with hard bodies. Beneath their jackets, they wore automatic handguns in shoulder harnesses. Out in the sculptured gardens other men moved, some craning for a look at him. He returned their looks of disdain with a slight lifting of his chin.

Inside the foyer, a man waited. He was conventionally dressed in grey slacks, white shirt and a deep blue sports jacket, but that was where convention ended. His short dark hair was gelled and spiked, and he was wearing sunglasses that changed colour according to the strength of the light. Right now they were a yellowish green: the colour of decomposing flesh.

He held a semi-automatic pistol loosely by his side.

The prisoner held up his cuffed wrists. 'Do you think these could come off now? Either that, or you put away your guns?' His voice sounded like tearing paper.

'The cuffs stay on for now.'

The prisoner shrugged. 'Fair enough. But, just so you understand . . . I didn't trade one cell for another.'

'That all depends on what the boss decides.' The gunman, dismissing the others with a jerk of his head, led the prisoner through a sumptuous vestibule and into an equally lavish dining room.

Sitting at the head of a large table was a grey-haired man who watched the prisoner with eyes like slivers of Arctic winter. The prisoner looked back. His own pale eyes were a match for the seated man's. Killer's eyes. Well met, he thought.

'Please,' the grey-haired man said. 'Take a seat.'

The table was large enough that, when he sat down, the prisoner remained well out of grasping range of his host.

The man with spiked hair went around to the other side of the table and sat opposite him. He slipped off his sunglasses, hooking them in the top pocket of his jacket. He placed the handgun on the table, alongside cutlery that had been laid out for a meal.

The prisoner noted that his hosts had the best silverware, but on his side was a plastic spork, one of those utensils you get with a pre-packed salad from a delicatessen.

'You know who I am?' The grey-hair was a square-faced man, his features a natural swarthy tan, offset by the vividness of his eyes.

The prisoner placed his cuffed wrists on the table. 'Of course I do. You are my *benefactor*.'

The host smiled. He waved and his maître d' came forward pushing a trolley. The severe looking man began serving entrées. Around his feverishly working hands, the grey-haired man watched his guest. 'I admit to being surprised when you contacted me. I didn't think it would be possible from inside a prison as secure as Fort Conchar.'

'I had my ways. It's frightening how easy a prison guard's greed can be played upon, don't you think?'

'You were certain that I would help you escape,' said the host.

'You had the finances available. We both share a mutual hatred of a certain individual. It was a done deal in my opinion.' The prisoner lifted his cuffs. '*These* I did not anticipate.'

Giving his pursuers the slip by way of the off-road motorbike, he had made for a pre-arranged rendezvous. He'd expected to be picked up and shuttled eastward to this meeting, but he hadn't thought that he'd be treated like an animal. There were ten armed men in the party that had confronted him; they'd stripped him of his weapons and then cuffed him. He could have done for some of them at any time, but he wanted this meeting more than he desired to satiate his blood lust. That would come soon enough.

'You're a very dangerous man. I need reassurances before freeing you. After all, you murdered the guard I paid to help get you out.'

'I had to make my escape look genuine.' The prisoner smiled at his own cunning. 'We don't want the authorities realising that I had outside help. The guard would've squealed like a pig the first time he was interrogated. That would've caused us problems, would it not?'

'You have a point.' The host steepled his fingers as he studied the prisoner. 'All of this would've been pointless if I'd been implicated in your escape – or what you do next.'

The prisoner shrugged. 'So you agree that the guard's death was necessary?'

'As long as he's the last of my people you harm.'

The prisoner didn't reply. The maître d' placed a bowl of soup in front of him, unaware of how close he was to a man who could deal death whether his hands were chained or not.

'Am I expected to eat with these cuffs on?'

The host and his henchman exchanged glances.

The prisoner said, 'Five-star food with plastic silverware? Maybe you're afraid I'll assassinate you with an expertly thrown silver spoon?' He chortled to himself, a whistling noise that made a bellows of his scarred throat. 'Have you considered how dangerous a bowl of hot soup can be? Perhaps gazpacho should've been on the menu instead?'

The host lifted his glass and sipped the heady wine. He didn't immediately respond, savouring the prisoner's humour as much as the rich claret. Placing down the glass, he turned to his henchman. 'You can release him, Getz.'

Getz stood up slowly. He picked up his handgun. 'I'm not sure that's a good idea, sir.'

The host turned to the prisoner. 'Like I said, I need reassurances. How can I be sure I can trust you?'

'You helped me escape. In return I swore that I'd help you.'

'But is that enough? You're an indiscriminate murderer who has killed some of my employees before.' His eyes twinkled. 'What's to stop you doing so again?'

'Things were different then. Your men were going to take away someone very important to me. I had no option but stop them.'

'But you lost him anyway.'

'I did, and before I was through with him.'

Emotion played across the prisoner's face. 'But now you're offering me the chance to finish what I started. I'm indebted to you.' He arched an eyebrow, waited. Finally, the host nodded to Getz, and the henchman slowly made his way round the table. The prisoner held up his wrists.

'This man you seek . . . he is poised to bring me down.' The host used his glass to indicate the room, the house, his empire. 'He's about to give federal evidence in a trial that could take all of this away from me, quite probably my liberty, too. I don't want that to happen.'

'Release me, give me the resources we agreed and I'll guarantee he isn't around for the trial.'

Getz had arrived at the prisoner's side. From a pocket of his jacket he took out a key, but still he wavered. 'Are you positive about this, sir?'

'Yes, Getz. There's benefit to us all if we work together on this.'

Holding his semi-automatic close to the prisoner's head, Getz began unlocking the cuffs. As he did, he whispered, 'The boss might believe you, but I don't think you can be trusted. You're a psycho who should've been sent to the gas chamber. Give me the slightest cause and I'll put a bullet in your head. In fact . . . I'm looking forward to doing just that.'

The prisoner's grunt of laughter was as humourless as a block of granite. He nodded at the plastic spork. 'I'm just looking forward to the soup.'

Getz snorted at the bravado, but there was

wariness to his movement as he finished unlocking the cuffs.

'So?' asked the host. 'We'll work together on this? We have a deal?'

The prisoner rubbed the circulation back into his wrists. 'Of course we do, Mr Hendrickson. We're friends, OK? You have my word that I won't harm you.' The prisoner slowly swung his gaze up towards Getz who was still standing over his right shoulder. 'But just so we're all clear . . . I don't like it when a two-bit punk threatens my life.'

Getz sucked in air.

He should have pulled the trigger instead.

The prisoner's elbow rammed backwards and found Getz's groin. Getz folded forward, grimacing in agony. The prisoner snatched at his gun hand, hauling Getz down, so that he sprawled chest first, his right cheek braced against the table. The prisoner stood up, leaning over him, even as he reached for the spork. Then, with the bowl braced against his thumb, he jabbed the rigid handle into Getz's left eye.

Getz's reaction was to scream, to pull away in panic, his hands going to his blinded eye. He was unaware that the prisoner now held his gun. The prisoner reminded him by placing two rounds in his chest and Getz sprawled backwards on the carpet.

There was the sound of a mass charge, and Hendrickson's guards began spilling into the room.

The prisoner looked unaffected by their arrival, choosing instead to study the dead man at his feet. The bullets had pushed chunks of broken bone out of Getz's chest. He curled a lip in distaste, slinging the gun down beside the corpse. Guns, in his estimation, were for vulgar killers.

Seeing the gun thrown away, Hendrickson waved off his guards. They all began backing out of the room. The maître d' also had the sense to leave.

'That was a little unfortunate,' Hendrickson said. 'Getz was a good man.'

'He was an asshole.'

'I told you I didn't want any of my men harmed.'

'And I agree from here on. But if we do this,' the prisoner said, his ravaged throat pinching the words, 'we do it as partners. I won't be anyone's lap dog and *I won't take shit.*'

They stared at each other. Both men were under no illusions: if he wanted to, the prisoner could kill Hendrickson before any of the guards could come to his assistance.

'Deal,' said Hendrickson, moving forward and putting out a hand.

The prisoner took it, sealing the bargain.

'So, *partner*?' asked Hendrickson. 'You've gone by so many names in the past. What do I call you now?'

The prisoner thought for a moment. 'There's only one name I want to be known by,' he finally said. 'I am Tubal Cain.'

CHAPTER 6

Standing in the centre of the bloodbath, I tried not to ask the question, but I couldn't stop it: 'The bodies were mutilated, but were they whole?'

'By whole, you mean were all the parts accounted for?' asked Hartlaub.

I closed my eyes. 'That's exactly what I mean. Did the murderer take anything? You know what I'm talking about. Trophies?'

Hartlaub grimaced. It was all the answer I needed, but the last I wanted to hear. 'They had bones missing,' I said.

There were times in my soldiering career when I thought I'd seen the worst that humanity could inflict on another person. I'd seen people maimed, blinded, shot, cut, blown apart, but even those vivid images paled when I tried to imagine what Walter and his bodyguards must have endured. These murders hadn't been driven by simple expedience. Neither had the mutilation been down to punishment, or even plain hatred. Whoever had dismembered these bodies had delighted in the task and there was only one man I'd ever come across who could conceive of such barbarity. The problem was: the Harvestman was as dead as Walter was now.

In a cavern beneath the Mojave Desert I'd rammed a human bone through his throat and watched him bleed to death. I'd watched the light go out of his crazed eyes. Martin Maxwell, once a Secret Service agent, had been buried and the government had covered the shame of one of their own being responsible for his crimes. His headstone bore a different name. As far as the general public knew, it wasn't Maxwell but his stepbrother Robert Swan who'd masqueraded under the name of Tubal Cain. Outside of the establishment I was one of the few people who knew otherwise.

So had I been misled as much as everyone else? On more than one occasion I'd challenged Walter on the explanation for Cain being whisked away on a gurney. That first time, when I'd wanted to ensure the bastard was dead, Walter, in his usual enigmatic style had come back with the rejoinder; 'We don't bury the living.'

But that was exactly what he'd done.

'OK, Hartlaub. The charade's over. Take me to Walter.'

'Charade?' Hartlaub had made a career from lying, could come over as plausible even under the closest of scrutiny. But we weren't enemies and he allowed the corner of his mouth to turn up. 'Walter is dead, Hunter.'

'And so is Martin Maxwell, right? The son of a bitch . . .'

I wasn't sure who my final words were aimed at, whether Cain or Walter. I suppose that they were for Walter because they'd have been much stronger fired at the man who'd savagely tortured my younger brother, John. Walter had lied to me, sworn that Cain was dead and buried, and now he was adding to the lie by faking his own death.

'Where is he, Hartlaub? I don't want any more bullshit. Walter escaped this, didn't he?'

'OK, keep it down, Hunter. There are guys within earshot who are under the impression that Walter died alongside his guards.'

Taking in the splashes of gore, I counted where men had fallen. 'Looks like three men did die here. Walt's guys were killed, but who was the other unlucky bastard?'

'You know him, I'm told.'

I had an idea where this was leading. I did know a guy, a friend and fellow fisherman who often accompanied Walter to the cabin.

'You're talking about Bryce Lang?'

'Yes. Poor fucker must've been mistaken for Walt.'

I could see how that could have happened. Bryce had also been CIA. He was of an age with Walter, had the same air of the spook about him. Unlike Hartlaub and Brigham, who were active in the field, both of my older friends were the type who directed covert operations from offices at Langley and other institutions. They had the grey pallor and equally grey demeanour of men who spent their days cooped up in hidden places. Someone coming here with the intention of finding Walter Hayes Conrad could have assumed that Bryce was their man. Supposing that they had never met Walter face to face, that is.

If, and I was beginning to believe that I was right, it was Tubal Cain who was responsible for this carnage, he hadn't seen Walter when we were standing over him in the cavern at Jubal's Hollow. At the time Cain was so close to death that he must have been searing his optic nerves on the blazing flames of hell. But, if Walter had saved the man for some unknown reason, then there was the possibility that he'd visited with him since. And that begged further questions: what the hell had happened here? Why had Bryce been cut to ribbons? What had his killer been after?

Cain was looking for something.

My brother John.

'Walter is playing at being dead, that's it? He wants Cain to believe that he's dead. And he sent you to bring me in. There's only one reason I can think why he'd do that.'

'You've had experience with this man before,' Hartlaub said.

'So it is Tubal Cain? You're confirming that?'

'I ain't going to lie to you any longer. Cain was being held at Fort Conchar. There should've been no way for him to escape . . .'

'But he did.'

'Yes. Despite all the odds, he murdered one of his guards, used the uniform as a disguise. Once

41

outside he gave his pursuers the slip – we don't know how he managed that yet.'

'Fort Conchar is a super-max facility, yet he managed to walk out in a fuckin' guard's uniform! What about the checks and security points? I'd've thought that . . . Oh, wait. I get it. We're talking about Tubal Cain, aren't we? He took the body parts he required to get past the security.'

'Fingerprints and retinal scans are no problem to someone like him.' Hartlaub gave me a gentle shove towards the door where Brigham was waiting. 'C'mon. We'd best get going.'

'It'd better be to see Walter or we're parting company right now.'

'Let's move then.'

'Do you have a phone?'

'I do, but our orders are to maintain silence until we've joined Walter.'

I shook my head. 'There are other people involved in this. If Tubal Cain is out there, then they could be next on his list.'

'You're talking about Jared Rington?'

Rink had been with me when I'd taken Cain down, and was as likely a target of the deranged killer as Walter was. Harvey Lucas, too, though I couldn't see how Cain would be aware of his involvement.

'Can save you the trouble,' Brigham interjected. 'Walter asked for Rington to be brought in. The team sent to find him has come up blank. Rington's dropped off the face of the earth.'

CHAPTER 7

One day earlier . . .

'**M**y entire resources are open to you. Money, men, weapons. Choose whatever you want to get the job done.'

Kurt Hendrickson was a man of power. He was a significant figure in the criminal underworld of the Eastern Seaboard. He controlled the market in drugs, prostitution, pornography, extortion, and up until recently had been a major player in counterfeiting currency that he traded with terror groups intent on bringing down the mighty dollar. He wielded the kind of influence where he need only click his fingers to make people disappear without trace. However there was a specific man whose disappearance had nothing to do with Hendrickson. This man was under the US Federal Marshals' witness protection programme and, unusually, this was being overseen by agents of the CIA. Tracing him wasn't the main issue; killing him without being implicated in the murder was. It was bad enough that he was facing judicial trial; he didn't need the murder of the key witness laid at his door as well. It served his purpose that Tubal Cain had a vendetta against the same man.

'All I need from you is his location,' Cain said.

They were standing in a vault that Hendrickson had installed in the wine cellar of his house. The vault contained row upon row of firearms.

Hendrickson, it appeared, had a fascination with guns.

Tubal Cain wasn't that interested; his passion was for knives.

That stood to reason, considering his name was derived from the Biblical inventor of cutting instruments. But he was not averse to other weapons of destruction when necessary. He had a Heckler and Koch 9 mm in a shoulder rig. A Beretta 92F, a variation of the famous service weapon of the US armed forces, was in a second holster on his hip.

'I have a plan in motion. We will have his location within a couple of days.' Hendrickson picked up an ancient Colt and held it up to admire under the overhead lights.

'I want to get started now,' Cain said. 'I have an idea or two that might put us ahead in the game.'

Hendrickson nodded distractedly, lost in his fascination with the Colt. 'I killed my first man with this gun.'

Cain sniffed. 'I find guns so impersonal.'

'Maybe, but they get the job done. If you only desire a man's life, then a bullet in the brain will do it every time.'

'What if you desire more than his life?' Cain wasn't being sarcastic or enigmatic. He always liked to take something from his victims – bones in particular – as a reminder of his potency. He wasn't called the Harvestman for nothing.

'Death is enough,' Hendrickson replied. 'Kill this man for me, Cain. What you do to him afterwards . . . I don't care. In fact, it's probably best that you do take your trophy.'

'Oh, I intend to.'

'Good, good.' Hendrickson placed the Colt down, showed Cain the exit. 'I have men at my disposal. Use them as you will.'

'I work best alone.'

'Yes,' Hendrickson agreed. 'But there are others who may need dealing with.'

Involuntarily, Cain's hand moved to the scar on his throat. The lesion had never fully healed, a puncture wound that separated his trachea.

Hendrickson said, 'Don't worry. Like I said, I've a plan in motion and already have men on their trail.'

'They're good,' Cain pointed out. 'Send *plenty* of men.'

'It isn't so much the number as the quality. Rest assured, I have hired only the best in the business.'

Cain eyed him.

Hendrickson coughed low in his throat. 'They're not as skilled as you, but they're sufficient to kill a couple of out-of-practice soldiers.'

'Do not kill them,' Cain said. 'Take them alive. Once I'm finished with John Telfer, I want to reacquaint myself with Joe Hunter and Jared Rington.'

CHAPTER 8

Why Hartlaub and Brigham and, more pertinently, Walter, wanted to waste time showing me the horror wrought by Tubal Cain was beyond me. All Walter needed to do was pick up a phone, contact me at Imogen's house and tell me what had gone down. I'd have answered his call to arms in a heartbeat.

His reticence was possibly because the last time we'd met it had been on shaky ground. Walter had used Rink and me in a scheme spearheaded by our old Arrowsake commanders. We had been forced into a showdown with a group of white supremacists intent on bringing down the government. That sounds like a noble cause, but not when Arrowsake were prodding the group to action in the first place. They had planned to use the threat of domestic terrorism to raise funds and support for the intelligence community they served. It didn't matter to them that an innocent family were targeted, or that Rink or I might die, only that their ends were met. Coming clean about the entire plot, Walter had felt deep shame. We'd kind of cleared the air, but maybe there was still some residual embarrassment in Walter's heart. His lying about the eventual fate of Tubal Cain wouldn't be helping either.

Shit! The man had lied to me about the plot concerning Carswell Hicks and Samuel Gant, but that was because he'd been under orders to do so. Keeping Cain's survival a secret was his own doing. I'd be justified in telling him to go fuck himself, to deal with the problem on his own, but he knew I wouldn't turn my back now that I'd seen Cain's latest atrocity. I'd just lost one old friend in Bryce Lang, and I wasn't going to lose another.

Rink was more than a brother to me. We had both served Arrowsake, watching each other's back, and we'd done the same since leaving the forces, not simply through a sense of friendship or duty, but through a loyalty that transcended even the bond of blood. It's a terrible thing to admit, but his disappearance meant more to me than the danger my real brother faced now that Cain was back on the loose. I didn't doubt that John was under the protection of some of the best people Walter could field, but Rink was on his own. Rink was as tough as whalebone, and as capable a warrior as any I'd known. But he was also human and, unprepared for a sneak attack from a monster like Tubal Cain, he could be taken down as easily as anyone.

Rink can be a mother hen with me at times; he doesn't trust me to behave when I'm out from under his calming influence. Even when he knew I was spending a few days with Imogen he couldn't help checking up on me. I'd last spoken with Rink yesterday and he was his usual self. No concerns, just getting on with the day job. He was working on uncovering a low-key insurance swindle, nothing that would have forced him into deep cover. Unless he was purposely hiding, the CIA team sent to bring him in should have found him.

'Give me your phone.'

Brigham said, 'I already told you; they can't find Rington anywhere.'

'Maybe he doesn't want to be found by you.' My words were hopeful, but a gnawing sensation in my guts said otherwise. Unbeknown to even these guys, Rink and I had secret ways to communicate. Once we'd used the relay system set in place by Walter, but since the recent shady goings-on with Arrowsake, we'd deemed it necessary to have our own structure put in place. Harvey Lucas, our friend out in Little Rock, a wizard with computers, had built our very own network that piggy-backed various communication satellites without leaving a trace. In my haste, I'd thrown my mobile phone in my pack with my clothing and it was outside in the SUV. I held out my hand for Brigham's phone. The younger agent sought guidance from his superior, but all Hartlaub did was shrug.

I took the phone from Brigham and walked away from them, seeking a place where I wasn't stepping in blood. I keyed in numbers, listened, but as I feared the phone went unanswered. I pressed more buttons and left an encrypted message at a voice-mail box that only Rink could access. Then, on a whim, I decided maybe the most direct route was best and called Rink's office.

'Rington Investigations,' answered a voice with the slightest inflection of his Hispanic inheritance.

'Velasquez . . . It's Joe.'

'Jesus, man, me an' McTeer have been tryin' to get hold of you all day. We even called your girl up in Maine, but she told us you'd already gone.'

Velasquez and McTeer were ex-cops. Both men now worked with Rink at his private investigations business. They were hard cases, not the type to be easily ruffled. By the sounds of his voice though, something concerned Velasquez more than my apparently being incommunicado.

'Do you know where Rink is?'

'No, man. That's why we've been trying to get *you*.'

'He was working the insurance scam, right? Where was he headed when last you spoke to him?'

'Somewhere down in the Everglades . . . Pocahontas Swamp or somewhere. Shit, man, I had a deskful myself, didn't take much notice when he headed outa the door. I didn't even realise he was late back until some spook-types busted into the office and asked about him.'

'And he hasn't been in touch since . . .'

'We've been trying to get hold of him all day, too. McTeer is out driving around, scouting all the case's locations on the chance he'll find him. But I'm starting to think that's not going to happen. What the fuck's going on, Joe?'

I considered telling him about Tubal Cain, but decided against it. I presumed Walter wanted this kept under wraps at all costs, and that was why he'd brought me in quietly like this. Still, I wasn't prepared to put McTeer or Velasquez at risk.

'The shit has hit the fan, Velasquez. This is what you're going to do. Call McTeer in. Then shut up shop and go home. Don't come anywhere near the office until you hear from me or Rink.'

'What the fuck?'

'Trust me. You don't want to be linked to either of us, not while this is going on.'

'Rink's my boss, but he's also my friend. If he's in danger then—'

'Listen,' I cut him off. 'Just do as I ask, OK? You're both good men, and the last thing I want is for something to happen to either of you.'

'We can look after ourselves.'

Not against the thing that might be headed your way, I thought. I wanted to share my fears with him, but I simply couldn't. 'Just do as I ask . . . please. It's best for everyone.'

'Except Rink,' he said.

'Don't worry,' I said. 'I'll find him.'

The silence at the other end of the line was laden with Velasquez's fear. I got what he was thinking.

I would find Rink, but would he be alive or dead? That was the very thing I feared, and maybe he'd read as much in my voice.

'OK, Joe. We'll do as you ask. But as soon as you hear anything, and I mean *anything*, you let us know.'

'Deal.'

Velasquez was about to hang up, but felt he had to add, 'Bring Rink home, Joe. I've just put a down payment on a swimming pool. I need this job, man, or my wife will have my ass!'

It was gallows humour, but it made me smile. Not that I looked happy, it was a death's-head smile at most. 'I'll do my best or die trying.'

I hung up.

'Are we gonna get going now?' Hartlaub asked.

Ignoring him, I pressed buttons. My call was picked up on the third ring. 'Hello, Harvey,' I said.

'That you, Hunter?' Harvey Lucas is an African-American who reminds me of Samuel L. Jackson in the *Shaft* remake. He's as sharp as a tack and dresses the same. He's an ex-army Ranger, the best man with a computer I'd ever met, as well as a very good private investigator. More importantly than that, he was one of the few men I could fully trust.

'Have you heard from Rink?'

'Not for a couple of days,' Harvey said. 'There a problem, Hunter?'

'Yeah.' I told him everything. Harvey had been involved with us when Rink and I hunted Cain the first time. Because of that, he was possibly on the killer's radar screen and there was no way I'd leave him out of the loop.

'Doesn't sound good. You think that Cain might've got to him already?'

'Rink isn't the kind to get lost. I'm praying that he got wind of Cain's escape and has gone deep cover.'

'Not without warning us first,' Harvey said. He was right.

'Can you do a trace on his phone? See if you can pinpoint where it was before it was switched off?'

'Leave it with me. I'll get back to you ASAP.' He hung up.

I placed Brigham's phone in my jeans pocket. The young agent scowled. 'I'm gonna need it,' I snarled at him. He looked like he was about to argue but Hartlaub shook his head, and that was the subject finished with. I followed them to the SUV. Hartlaub drove, still neglecting to tell me where we were going. Then again I'd more on my mind to worry about, so didn't ask. Half an hour nearer our destination Brigham's phone rang and I fished it out of my pocket.

'What have you got?'

Harvey sighed. 'Not a great deal. The last co-ordinates for Rink's cell phone were logged at 04.43 hours this morning. They show he was kinda off the beaten track, out near to the Pahayokee Overlook in the Everglades National Park.'

Pahayokee Overlook? That would be Velasquez's Pocahontas Swamp, I assumed.

'Walter has some explaining to do first, but then I'll head down there.' My words earned me a dark look from Hartlaub, but I didn't care. Whatever Walter expected from me would have to wait. Rink was my priority.

'Where are you?'

'The Adirondacks. But if I have my way, I won't be here for long.'

'Meet me in Florida,' he said. 'I've access to a chopper so I can be there in five or six hours.'

I decided I could do with his help. I could head on down to the Everglades, but what was I going to do by myself? Beat hundreds of square miles of saw-tooth grass with a stick?

'I'll see you there.'

'Do you need me to bring anything?' Harvey asked.

My SIG Sauer P226 was a welcome weight in the back of my jeans. 'I'm good to go.'

CHAPTER 9

Flathead Lake was mirror-smooth, reflecting the evening sun where it peeked over the Salish Mountains. The water was burnished with fire, glinting highlights searing the eyes of the man who sat on the shore south of the Swan River tributary. He was dressed for the cool evening, with a scarf wrapped around his lower face, a cap pulled low so that only his eyes could be seen. Even his eyes had lens coverings, giving them an unnatural amber cast, which now was reinforced by the reflected water.

He wasn't local to the area. But then again, the nearby town of Bigfork was home to a large number of urban refugees who'd arrived during the last decade. Bigfork had fast become the leading arts community in Montana, attracting visitors from all over the world. The man's English accent wasn't uncommon, but neither was French, German, Swedish, Japanese or any other. In summer the population swelled exponentially, but even now, during winter, there were enough transients for the man to remain anonymous.

'Are you ready to go, Jeff?'

The man glanced to his right. Patricia was standing on a rock, hands jammed into her jeans pockets. The rock gave her extra height, accentuating her willowy frame. Her rat-chewed urban-chic hair was stuffed beneath a woolly hat – the type with ear flaps and tassels that wouldn't have looked out of place in Nepal.

'How about helping me up?' Jeff asked, extending gloved fingers to her.

'Come on,' she said, turning away and hopping off the rock. 'You can manage.'

Jeff shook his head. Patricia wasn't one for pity.

Standing up was always a problem, especially if he'd been in a certain position for too long. The scar tissue from the 'industrial accident' he'd suffered protested, doling out plenty of discomfort before he got moving.

His first few steps were achieved bent almost double. The sand under his feet didn't help, and it was only when he reached the hard-packed trail leading up to a lay-by on route 35, and he was able to grab handholds of the overhanging trees, that he straightened up.

Patricia moved slowly ahead of him. She'd a nervous energy about her, and she twitched every other step, as though she needed to burn some of it off.

Toby Callahan was waiting for them in the SUV. He was older than Jeff, and fifteen years older than Patricia, too. Patricia slid into the seat next to Toby, relegating Jeff to the back.

'Are you all done looking?' Toby's hair was going grey, the short bristles above his ears catching the final rays of light.

'It's a beautiful lake,' Jeff said. 'I don't think I could ever get enough of the place.'

Toby wasn't listening. His question hadn't required an answer. It was more a reminder that he had better things to do than play chaperone.

They drove north-west, skirting Bigfork and heading towards Jewel Ridge. The Mission Range loomed on their right, sweeping hillsides that dropped almost vertically from the heavens. The trees were on fire with autumnal colours as the day flared in a final goodbye and night was ushered in.

The cabin nestled on a hillside overlooking a rocky valley. A stream chuckled between boulders as it sought egress to the nearby Swan River. There was a grey sedan parked in front of the wooden porch where Jeff often sat watching the night sky. Standing by the car was a man in a black windcheater jacket, blue jeans and Timberland boots. His balding head was disguised by a denim baseball cap. As Toby pulled adjacent to the sedan, the other man ground a cigarette under his boot heel.

Toby wound down the window, and Brett Hanson leaned in. Jeff could smell his nicotine-laden breath. 'Flights are all arranged,' Brett said. He glanced into the back, catching Jeff's eye. 'We leave from Kalispell in ten hours. You'd better get your shit together, Jeff.'

'Yeah,' Jeff said, resigned. His family had been telling him the same thing for years.

The cabin in the woods had been his home for more than six months now. In some respects Jeff would be sad to leave, but in others he couldn't wait. It was five hours since Brett Hanson had announced that they would be going. It felt like five days. Ten hours to go and he'd be out of there.

He'd said earlier that he could never tire of looking at Flathead Lake, and yet he'd been lying to himself. He would be happy if he never saw the lake again if it meant he could go home. His *real* home. Wherever that was. He doubted he'd be welcomed with open arms at either place he'd once lived. Both the women he'd abandoned had moved on. They didn't even know who Jeffrey-fucking-Taylor was, for Christ's sake!

Home would have to be a new place of his own making. This cabin certainly wasn't home. It belonged to the US Marshals Service. Supposedly a safe house, it was as much a prison as any made of stone and steel bars. It defined him as a prisoner.

Patricia Ward was beautiful. She'd been his companion through the last six months. She had walked with him, hand in hand along the lakeside. She'd strolled with him among the booths and stalls at the summer fair, sat in cafés and restaurants, laughed at his jokes. They'd even once engaged in tentative sex on a blanket under the spreading boughs of an oak tree. But she would never be his lover. She would always be his jailer. She was as much a part of the lie that was Jeffrey Taylor as everything else.

The strolling, the laughing, the sex: all part of his cover story.

Patricia was his bodyguard. She was there to see that he stayed alive for the day he was called to give evidence in the trial against the crime syndicate he'd once worked for. It was her duty to keep him alive, before delivering him into the hands of new jailers at an appointed time and place. Ward by name, warden by nature. It'd be funny if it wasn't so fucking ironic.

Toby Callahan and Brett Hanson were also US Marshals.

It was their duty to look after Jeff, too. But they made no bones about their relationship. To them, he was a thief. He was a scumbag who'd turned against the scumbags he'd worked for, making him even more of a scumbag in their opinion.

It was odd then, that Jeff preferred both men to the woman who only *pretended* to be fond of him.

CHAPTER 10

To look at him you wouldn't believe that Walter was supposed to have been cut to ribbons by a deranged killer. In truth he looked better than he had for some years, with a little colour in his usually pallid features and some of the unhealthy weight gone from around his middle. Giving up on those cigars and junk food must have finally paid off for him. The only dead thing about him was the fish-eyed stare he shot my way as I stepped into his temporary living quarters on the eastern shore of Tupper Lake in the Adirondacks National Park.

'I guess that I deserve the ass-kicking you're about to give me,' he said.

'Let's not go there, eh?' The son of a bitch did deserve a mouthful of abuse, or worse. Actually, I could have wrung his fucking neck, but I didn't have it in me. Right then I didn't see him as the lying piece of crap he was, but an old man mourning the loss of his best friend. So, I wrapped an arm around his shoulder. 'I'm just glad to see you're OK.'

The old man shivered in my embrace, then he

pulled away and I let him go. He turned his back on me and I followed, allowing him the moment to gather himself. I made a silent bet that when he finally met my gaze there would be more moisture in his eyes.

His temporary quarters were in a large lakeside house, an almost square block formed of beams and planks all painted a uniform red and a slightly pitched shingled roof that angled down towards the surface of the lake. A porch led to a jetty where there was a cabin cruiser moored in the shallow water. He led me through the house, along the planks of the jetty and on to the boat. Behind us, Hartlaub and Brigham waited on the decking.

Walter ushered me into the cabin and sat in a plush leather chair. A bunk opposite him indicated that Walter had taken a nap, but judging by the twisted blankets it had been an uncomfortable forty winks. I sat down on the bed, fisted my hands on my thighs, waited for him to speak. He delved in a cooler box and came out with bottle of sour mash, No 7 brand.

'JD?' he asked.

I declined and watched as he took a swig directly from the bottle. He wiped his lips with the back of a wrist and I zoned in on his fingers, which were trembling. The healthy flush in his cheeks must have come from this bottle. I had no desire to watch him get drunk, but he'd lost an old friend today, and even someone who'd been around death for most of his adult life wasn't immune from its touch. Maybe the alcohol would help him steady himself, so I wasn't about to get on my high horse about his drinking.

'I'm sorry about Bryce,' I offered.

'Me too, son,' he said. 'But more than that, I'm sorry that you were lied to. It must have been a shock when you were told about my . . . my demise?'

'It was. But I see now why you did that.'

He blinked then finally looked up at me, his eyes now glassy. 'You do?'

'You wanted your survival to be a secret. When Hartlaub and Brigham came to find me, you feared that I'd tell Imogen the truth. That would've put her at risk. It was good of you to think of her.'

There could have been a morsel of truth in my theory, but I guessed the genuine reason he wanted people to think he was dead was to rule out a second attempt on his life. He possibly read my face because he looked away. 'I must have put you through hell, son.'

'I'm all right. But I wish you'd told me what was going on instead of wasting so much time. You know that Rink's missing?'

'I heard. It spoils my plans somewhat.' He lifted a consoling hand, knowing that his words offended me. 'My intention was to bring you both in, ask you to help me stop the Harvestman before he could organise himself. But I see that by doing so, I've made a real error of judgement. Cain has moved much faster than I ever expected.'

'What about John?'

'John? Uh, he's fine. He's surrounded by a team of marshals and I've arranged for him to be moved to a place of safety.'

'So my priority is to find Rink.'

'No, Hunter. Your priority is stopping Tubal Cain.'

I held my breath. There was nothing conscious about the act, simply a bodily response as I studied the face of my old friend. He took another chug at the neck of the Jack Daniels bottle. I lct out the pent-up air, reached across and took the bottle from him. I placed it on the deck next to my feet. 'You've some explaining to do – why you spared that evil bastard – but right now I'm not interested. It's enough to know that he's out there and up to his old tricks.' An image of Bryce Lang being carved like a Christmas turkey came to mind and I had to slow blink to clear my mind. I jerked my head, an indistinct motion, but it conveyed my meaning as I indicated Walter's colleagues outside. 'You have your own resources to hunt down Cain. I'm going to find Rink.'

He leaned down and placed his head in his hands. 'Last time we spoke, you advised that I distance myself from Arrowsake. I did that . . . to the best of my abilities. But they wouldn't let me go. Tubal Cain was *their* project, Hunter. It was they who briefed me at Jubal's Hollow, who told me that I should contain him at all cost. You thought that you'd killed him, well, you almost did. When I realised he was still alive I had him transported to a medical facility where his life was saved. After that he was transferred to Fort Conchar to be held for . . .' He paused, seeking the words.

'Future use?' I offered.

He shook his head. 'Further study.'

I didn't have time for a convoluted explanation, but now that Walter seemed poised to offer one curiosity won out. I looked at him questioningly.

'You've heard of MKUltra?' he asked.

Of course I had. It was a CIA experiment conducted during the Cold War; one that had sought to turn out brainwashed assassins who could be used to target those deemed enemies of the USA. It had been fictionalised by Hollywood on more than one occasion, most famously in the movie *The Manchurian Candidate*. What I believed Walter was hinting at was that Arrowsake had recognised Tubal Cain as a potential future weapon. They had kept him alive in order to mobilise him when it became necessary.

'Arrowsake again,' I grunted. My old masters were fast becoming my nemesis.

Walter shook his head, then finally lifted it from his cupped palms. 'No, Hunter. They are responsible for keeping him alive, but they had no part in his escape. If they wanted him out to do their bidding, they would've simply had him moved to another facility, then released without the hullabaloo that surrounded his escape from Conchar.'

'You're saying that someone else helped him?'

'He couldn't have escaped without external aid.

Everything was too easy for it to have been left to chance. Tubal Cain has the backing of someone with money and resources, that's obvious.'

'How long has he been out?'

'Only a few days.'

'He's resourceful. He probably had a series of secure drops set in place before he was imprisoned. Documents, money, weapons, everything he needed to move around the country at his leisure.'

'A likely assumption,' Walter agreed. 'He must've got his hands on fake identification and such, because it's apparent that he's flying here, there and everywhere. He couldn't have been in the number of places he has been otherwise. But, still, he needed help from someone to set up his escape in the first place. He had a getaway vehicle waiting, and quite probably was picked up and transported out of the state by someone later on. I think the plane he's using belongs to whoever is helping him.'

'You have your suspicions?'

'I do. I believe that Cain contacted his benefactor, offered his services, in exchange for assistance to get out of prison.'

'Only one person I know who'd benefit from such a thing,' I said. 'You're talking about Hendrickson.'

Walter acknowledged my accurate assessment. 'A month from now, Kurt Hendrickson, Sigmund Petoskey and other members of the Hendrickson organisation are facing judicial trial. As you well know, your brother John is our key witness in the case against them. It would suit the Hendrickson organisation if John doesn't make it to trial.'

'And it will suit them even more if John's death can be blamed upon an escaped convict with a vendetta against him,' I finished. 'With John out of the way, the trial will collapse, they'd be exonerated, and free to continue where they left off.'

'Of course it would be a simple matter to show their hand in this, but for one thing.'

I snorted. I'd already seen it coming, but it still made me sick. 'To implicate them, it would mean coming clean about Tubal Cain.'

'The scandal the government wanted to avoid the first time around would be magnified tenfold.'

'That's why nothing has made the news about his escape? Cain is supposedly dead, so how could he be on the loose again? And that's why you've brought me in . . .'

'We have to do this quietly, son.'

'I can't guarantee that,' I said.

'You must. It's imperative that Cain is silenced, without the government's inclusion being a factor in any of the fallout. You will have our full backing, but only on our word. Nothing will be recorded anywhere, we *will* exercise full deniability. In the past I've influenced the decisions of the other agencies, I've had your actions covered up. On this occasion the consequences are way too big to do so again. If you don't cover your own tracks this time, well, you might have to pay the consequences.'

'So if things go wrong I'll be vilified? Painted as

the crazy vigilante I'm suspected of being? It's some deal you're offering me, Walter.'

'It's why you must do things quietly.'

There was no question that I was going to become Walter's bloodhound. That was a given. But I was certain he hadn't realised the enormity of the beast he was letting loose. I hated Cain; he was a monster who shouldn't be allowed to exist. But Walter had just aimed me at other enemies, too. The Hendrickson Organisation. If it proved that they were behind Cain's escape, and were sponsoring him against my brother John, then they had nothing to worry about concerning an upcoming trial. If I had my way, none of them would be around to make their day in court.

'For the time being Hartlaub and Brigham are at your disposal. I'll have them take you anywhere you want to go, but then they will have to withdraw,' Walter said.

'They can take me to the nearest airplane. I'm going after Rink.' Before Walter could argue, I added, 'I've a feeling that when I find him, I'll also find Cain. And God help *anyone* who gets between us.'

'Just remember, son . . .'

'I know, Walter. I have to do it quietly. You say John's safe. You can guarantee that?'

'He's safely out the way.'

'Keep things like that and I'll do what you ask. But if anything happens to him all bets are off.'

CHAPTER 11

His trip to the Adirondacks had proven more a distraction than a step in the right direction. Tubal Cain had never seen the man responsible for saving his life that day in the cavern at Jubal's Hollow, but he had heard his name whispered during frequent visits by doctors who conducted their studies upon him while he was confined at Fort Conchar. He didn't feel that he owed Walter Hayes Conrad a thing: the man's apparent magnanimity hadn't been born from humanity. He had tracked the CIA man to his retreat in the woods, before news of Cain's escape forced him into deep hiding. He'd ambushed the two goon-like bodyguards, shooting both of them before moving on to the older man. Give the old bastard his due, he'd held out even when Cain dismembered his bodyguards in front of him. Only when Cain turned his ministrations to the CIA man himself did he elicit any answers. Shame that he hadn't mentioned sooner that he wasn't the one Cain was looking for. It would have earned the man a quicker death than the one that followed.

Still, he wasn't complaining. The distraction had proven quite enjoyable. Just like old times. Cain left the Adirondacks feeling rather nostalgic.

With Conrad apparently aware of his escape, he would be untouchable for now, so Cain had moved on to another avenue that would lead him to his prey. He found Michael Birch easily enough.

Birch thought he had made it when he'd landed the job with the Virginia State Attorney's Office. He was only an underling to the state attorney himself, but so what? He was moving in the kind of circles he'd always aspired to. Securing the job, he'd expected a new lifestyle that included big money. As a top analyst in his field, he'd attained the rewards befitting his position, but had avoided the media interest that occasionally made the state attorney's life unbearable. He rested easy in his obscurity, just took the remuneration and left the accolades to his boss. He'd thought himself safe from the men and women that his office prose-cuted. Untouchable. But he hadn't vectored the Harvestman into the equation.

Cain – once an agent with the United States Secret Service – knew how the Federal Witness Security Programme worked. He also had insider knowledge of the creation of new identities for those placed into the safe keeping of the US Marshals Service.

The idea was to create total anonymity for the witness, to help them relocate and blend into a new community. Jobs, housing, subsistence payments and identity documents were all laid on. In a country of over three hundred million people the witness should be untraceable. Since its inception in 1970, no person under the WITSEC programme, who'd followed the strict security guidelines, had come to harm. But there was always a first time.

It was a system in which Cain saw too many flaws.

For one, there was no such thing as a fresh start when it came to criminals. Notification of past transgressions was often passed to the local law enforcement community. A thief of John Telfer's magnitude would be on someone's database.

Second, and most important, although witnesses were given new names, they were encouraged to keep their first names, or select a new name with the same initials. There couldn't be too many JTs on the Marshal Service's books.

Then there was the reason why Cain had sought out Michael Birch. Although a secretive process, there was always a trail back to some lowest denominator. The attorney general made final determination based on the recommendation of the state attorney assigned to the federal case, but it was always the lackeys of said attorney who wrote up the accompanying reports. Birch was one such lackey.

Birch wasn't a brave man.

Not when Cain was standing over him with a knife in his hand.

He soon gave up the codes to enter the database on his laptop computer. As well as the fingers Cain took as a memento of their meeting.

Cain would have liked to have spent a little more time with Birch but he had to get from Virginia to Montana fast.

He worked best alone, but wasn't averse to a little assistance on occasion. He touched down at Glacier Park International Airport north of Kalispell and alighted from Kurt Hendrickson's Challenger 604 private jet only a few hours later. The jet was of the type employed for executive travel and could carry up to nineteen passengers, a flight crew and steward. It had a full galley with the capacity for gourmet catering, stereo DVD, satellite phones, the business. It was sheer indulgence for one man. But Cain would have it no other way.

A rented Ford Explorer was waiting for him.

Cain was extensively travelled, but he'd never been to Montana. He'd formed the impression that the state's topography was primarily grassland, but in this north-western corner near the Canadian border he was surrounded by towering, snow-capped mountains. He had his own take on the veneer of reality that surrounded him, but even he could appreciate the beauty of the mountains. The tree covered slopes offered plenty of opportunities for the concealment of corpses.

Tapping coordinates into the sat-nav, he picked up the route south towards Somers at the head of Flathead Lake, before turning east towards

Bigfork – the aptly named 'village by the bay'. On the drive down he made a point of studying the vehicles passing in the other direction. Jeffrey Taylor could be in any of them.

Michael Birch's laptop had offered up three names with the initials JT. Joanne Theriault was a no-brainer, and it didn't take much digging to find that Jonah Thexton was a fifty-eight-year-old African-American. Jeffrey Taylor and John Telfer had to be one and the same.

Something else that Birch's computer had given up: Telfer was due to be moved within the next few hours. Cain could have waited for him at the airport, but there was also an Amtrak depot in the nearby Glacier National Park, where he could board a train to Seattle or Chicago. If Cain missed him, he might never get another chance at finishing what he'd begun at Jubal's Hollow. So too, at remote Jewel Ridge, the likelihood of taking Telfer away from his protectors would be greater than at either an airport or rail terminal. There was less chance of outside intervention.

WITSEC normally leave their charges pretty much to their own devices. They don't offer a round-the-clock bodyguard service, not until the witness is being returned to give evidence at trial. Still, Cain knew that Telfer would have been afforded more than the norm. Not only was he the key witness in the trial of the Hendrickson/Petoskey counterfeit currency ring, but he also knew the secret of the Harvestman.

Official records said that the Harvestman was Robert Swan, Martin Maxwell's estranged half-brother. The government said that Swan had murdered Maxwell, along with his wife and children, before going on his four-year killing spree. Cain found that most insulting. Swan, a hopeless musician, could barely pick a tune out of a guitar, never mind pick the bones from a body. Nevertheless, the story served the government well, considering they did not want a scandal erupting that *one of their own* was a psychopath. John Telfer knew otherwise, so the CIA, Secret Service and others would want to ensure that he kept that knowledge to himself. Likely he'd have twenty-four/seven chaperones so that he didn't get too loose in the lips.

Cain and Telfer shared a common bond.

Both were living dead men.

According to the government records Telfer had been the Harvestman's final victim and, like Cain, he hadn't survived Jubal's Hollow. It was time to put a final exclamation mark on that statement.

CHAPTER 12

'I'm glad I caught you, Harve. Florida's probably a dead end. There's been a change of plan. I'm going to come to Little Rock and reacquaint myself with an old friend.'

Hartlaub and Brigham had dropped me back at the airstrip where the small plane that had brought us from Maine awaited my return. I was predictable in that sense, so it was no surprise to find that the plane had been prepped to take me on to another location. The pilot was your typical 'ask no questions' type employed by the CIA and our sole interaction was him telling me to strap in, then he took us west towards Arkansas. Hartlaub and Brigham watched us swoop into a sky the colour of ashes; neither man felt the need to wave goodbye.

As soon as we were in the air, I called Harvey on my phone, after first checking that Rink hadn't left a reply at the voicemail box I'd used earlier.

'You're talking about Sigmund Petoskey?'

'Yeah,' I said, recalling the last time I'd seen the sanctimonious piece of shit. Sometimes I regretted not putting a bullet through his skull, but I didn't have the proof that he had anything to do with the danger John was mixed up in until much later. Occasionally I'd thought about a return trip to Little Rock with the intention of righting that wrong, only I'd been busy with other more urgent tasks in the past year or so. I told Harvey about Walter's suspicion that the Hendrickson organisation was behind Tubal Cain's escape and, more than likely, Rink's sudden disappearance. Sigmund Petoskey was Hendrickson's man out in Arkansas. 'I think that Siggy is a good starting point.'

'I'll get on it and see if I can locate him. His old haunts have been shut down, and now that he has an impending court case he's playing at being lily-white for the media. Chances are he's laying low somewhere the cameras can't see the sweat on his brow.'

'That suits me fine.'

When I first met Harvey, he'd been reluctant to help. Siggy Petoskey was the local gangster in his neighbourhood and he'd worried that he'd feel the man's wrath after Rink and I left town. As it happened, something had thrust him directly into the middle of the war we'd waged against the Hendrickson gang. It culminated in Harvey shooting dead a hit man who was chasing my brother John. The fact that the hit man chose to beat up Louise Blake, my brother's ex, had snapped something in Harvey and he'd forgotten all about his fear. Since then, Harvey had kind of joined my club. I knew that I could rely on him to back me up all the way.

'How is Louise?' I asked.

Having saved her life, Harvey had taken it upon himself to look after Louise. She'd welcomed his company, but in the interim I sensed that they'd drifted apart. Harvey hadn't mentioned her in the last few months. Their relationship, in part, wasn't so unlike mine and Imogen's.

'You think that she could be in danger?' Harvey asked.

'With Cain out and Hendrickson behind him, I don't want to take the chance. They might get the wrong impression that she's a direct line to John again.'

'Soon as you hang up I'll call her, get her somewhere safe.'

'You two aren't an item any more?'

'No, Hunter. It was a short-lived thing. Louise moved on, has herself a new man, a new job and a new home. Not sure how she'll react when she hears me on the other end of the phone.'

'There's only one way to find out. Speak to you later, Harve.'

I hung up, letting him get on with the job.

Then I settled down to catch a nap while we crossed the country. Sleepless nights were a factor in my life, but like many soldiers I'd developed the skill of catching a few minutes at every opportunity. In my game you didn't know when next you'd eat, sleep or shit, so you did so whenever you could. Only on this occasion the sleep wouldn't come. Too many things were playing through my mind, a parade of horrors that wouldn't let me rest.

Bryce Lang's face appeared, and I conjured the fear he'd been in when he thought that Luke Rickard was after him. It would have been nothing compared to coming face to face with Tubal Cain. That segued into an image of my brother strung from a wall in Cain's ossuary in the Mojave, the flesh stripped from his back as Cain had tried to whittle the living bones from his ribcage. I watched in detached horror as John turned his face to mine and let out a bleat of terror, except this time it wasn't John but Rink who was squirming under the maniac's ministrations. The sight of my best friend chewing his lips in agony forced my eyes open and I blinked around the cabin of the plane. Beyond the windows the clouds pressed close, huge towers of cumulus as steel-grey as the phantom blade that had dug into Rink's body.

Maybe I'd let out a moan because the pilot was staring at me over his shoulder. I nodded him back to the controls. As verbose as a brick, he offered a grimace then returned to guiding the plane. I closed my eyes again, scrunched down in the seat and tried to get comfortable. That wasn't going to happen, of course. My heart was hammering in my chest and the distinctive flutter of an adrenalin spike caused my extremities to shiver.

Growing up on the streets of Manchester in the north of England, I recall nothing remarkable about my early days. My father, Joseph, died when I was young, and shortly after that, my mother, Anita, remarried. Bob Telfer wasn't the man my dad was, and maybe that was why we never seemed to gel. He was a good enough person, but he wasn't the ambitious type and was happy as long as there was food on the table and a tin of lager in the fridge. He didn't deem spending time with a boy a worthwhile pursuit. That was OK by me; I just roamed the streets, or immersed myself in comic books or pulp fiction novels, dreaming of being like the heroes on those dog-eared pages. When my little brother was born I was shoved even further away. I wasn't jealous of John, but it seemed that he could do no wrong in Bob's eyes. I distanced myself even more, becoming involved in the skinhead scene that was rife at the time; as a result I ended up in scrapes with other groups. Arrested twice for fighting, I almost got myself a criminal record, but there was one cop who took me to one side and put me straight on a thing or two. He was an old-school copper, the type who'd take you down an alley and smack some sense into you, but on this occasion he only gave me some good advice. *You think you're some sort of tough guy, huh? Well, why don't you prove it? Go join the army, lad. They're always looking for tough guys.*

His words stayed with me, and as soon as I was old enough I enlisted. To prove something to the cop, I tried for the elite Parachute Regiment and made it through the rigorous selection process, and I stayed with 1 PARA until I was drafted into the specialised unit codenamed Arrowsake. It was round about then that I realised I wasn't as tough as I thought. The training was hellish, but I thrived on it and came through the other end alive and more or less intact. I'd found direction, and a sense of unity that I'd never known with my own family. Walter Hayes Conrad became a surrogate father figure, but my greatest gain was someone who I truly felt was a brother. Jared Rington.

We were an unlikely pairing, I suppose. I was a northern English grunt, he was a half-Japanese, half-Scottish Canadian raised in the Midwest of the USA, but our differences were outweighed by what we had in common. We formed a bond that was unshakeable, and that bond had only strengthened over the years. I could always rely on Rink to be there to watch my back, as I would always be there to watch his.

That was what was bothering me most. When Rink needed me there, I'd been up in Maine with Imogen. OK, so I deserved a life of my own, but I felt that my selfishness had helped place Rink in mortal danger. Christ, Rink would laugh at that. He was no shrinking violet, in fact he was one of the toughest warriors I'd ever known and not the type to need a chaperone. But still, I couldn't help feeling that this was my problem and it shouldn't be Rink who was going through hell . . . again.

From the front my taciturn pilot made a noise I took to mean that we were going down. Then the plane was buffeted and jostled as he banked it through the clouds. It was dawn over the Midwest, and the storms that were hammering the Eastern Seaboard had been left hundreds of miles behind, so as we broke from the cloud cover the rooftops of Little Rock twinkled back at us under the breaking sun. The Arkansas River snaked through the city, a ribbon of fire, and the pilot followed its course before banking again out towards Adams Field, Little Rock's airport.

I checked to see if anything looked familiar, tried to pinpoint the area where last I'd assaulted Sigmund Petoskey's lair, but couldn't. I didn't care; he wasn't going to be in a dilapidated building this time. It wouldn't matter where, I would find him and make him tell me where Rink was.

Walter had guaranteed John's safety. It was time for me to look after my other brother.

CHAPTER 13

Much further to the north-west day hadn't yet broken. Jewel Ridge was in darkness but there were lights on behind the cabin's shutters. They were too bright to be a single night light, so it was likely that the occupants were up and about. Maybe the people inside were going through their early-morning ablutions, or perhaps cooking up a calorie-laden breakfast in anticipation of the long day ahead. They'd be moving in slow motion, their bodies not yet revved up to full throttle. It was a good time to surprise them, Cain decided.

Minds that should be sharp and alert would still be foggy from the lingering effect of sleep. These were the least industrious hours on the clock and it didn't look like anyone had been out the cabin yet. The vehicles parked outside hadn't been loaded. Morning dew had begun collecting on the windscreens, pine needles blown from the nearby trees had gathered on the hoods.

Cain had parked his own vehicle a mile away. He'd jogged in, arriving at the cabin fully awake, his body energised for what would follow. He paused, studying the cabin, allowing his beating heart to calm. When he went in it would be cool-headed and loose-limbed.

He checked his weapons. Both the H&K and the Beretta would be brought into service, but it was the Recon Tanto knife with its epoxy-coated blade he'd prefer to use. Sticking someone with a knife was far more personal – and satisfying – than blowing them away at a distance. Cain enjoyed the proximity of death when delivered with a blade; it allowed him to see his victims' initial shock, the cold realisation that their life was his to take, the final dimming of their eyes.

But he wasn't going to be impetuous.

He had no way of knowing how many protectors were inside the cabin. This wasn't a mission simply to kill with abandon. At any other time he'd relish walking into that cabin, taking the odds as they came, and, if he didn't happen to kill them all, well, such was the chaotic nature of life. In the here and now, though, there was a precise target and he couldn't allow his personal desires to get in the way of a successful result. John Telfer had to die. But to get to Telfer, he had first to take out those who would try to stop him.

Cain was dressed for the occasion. He wore dark clothing and high-top boots, a cap pulled down low over his fair hair. He felt like he was back in the game again. With the tree-lined hillside as cover, he approached the cabin. Using the shadows to his advantage, he moved to the parked

SUV. Holstering the Beretta, he pulled the Tanto out of its sheath. A quick jab of the blade split the tyre and the SUV sank at one corner. Not totally disabled. He jabbed the next tyre. Now it would be difficult to drive.

He quickly slashed the tyres of the sedan, then, happy that the occupants of the cabin would have no means of a quick getaway, he moved towards the porch. Putting away the knife, he drew the Beretta, advancing with a gun in each hand like some fabled Two Gun Tex.

The planks on the porch looked reasonably sound, but he couldn't take the chance that they'd creak under his weight, giving away his position. Whether or not the people inside were at a low ebb, hearing furtive movement on the porch would galvanise them into action. Cain didn't want that. He had to maintain the element of surprise. Get Telfer: that was all that mattered.

From within the cabin he could hear muffled conversation. Two voices, those of a man and a woman. But were there more?

He made his way around the side of the cabin. There was a window at that end, too, which like all the others had shutters. Moving up close, he found he could peer through a narrow niche between two slats. The cabin was open plan at this end. The living quarters were kept to a minimum, with a couch, a TV, and table and chairs. There was a kitchen area at the back of the building with a wood-burning stove that doubled as a cooking range. Stairs led up to a mezzanine-type gallery where a bed occupied most of the space. Beneath the gallery were two doors. Likely one was to a bathroom, the other to another bedroom.

Through the chink in the shutter, Cain watched a slim woman wander across the room. She pushed hands through her cropped hair. She had a gun holstered on her hip. She said something, a low murmur. A man answered her from the bed on the raised gallery. He sat up. He was fully clothed, appeared to have been merely killing time.

Under the gallery, the door on the left opened and a stocky man with a greying brush cut came out, rubbing his face with a towel. The woman lifted a mug off the range in the kitchen, handing it to the man, before taking her turn in the bathroom.

Cain frowned. Neither man was John Telfer.

Swinging off the bed, the man clumped down the stairs, hitching his jeans to a more comfortable position. He had a shoulder rig, but it was empty. Cain glanced around and saw the man's sidearm lying on the table. Now that the woman was in the bathroom, only the guy with the brush cut was armed. He had an impressive-looking Desert Eagle strapped to his waist.

Now would be a good time, Cain told himself.

Prudence, though, prudence.

First he circled the back of the building. He passed the back door, moved round the corner. The bathroom window was shuttered, but would

84

have given him a look inside through the slats if he had the desire. No distractions, though.

The final room didn't have a window.

The man inside was as much a prisoner as Cain had been at Fort Conchar.

Happy that Telfer couldn't make a break for it, he returned to the front. Cat-footed, he stepped up on to the porch. From inside came the clump of boot heels, enough to cover his own movements as he moved to the door. Elbows braced to his ribs, he held both semi-automatic weapons ready. Then he rocked back, lifting his heel.

The door opened.

There was a split second while Cain stared into the eyes of the older marshal. The man had slipped into a jacket. He was holding a small knapsack in his left hand. Getting ready for the off.

'Shit!' the man whispered. He dropped the bag, at the same time slapping his other hand towards the Desert Eagle on his hip.

Cain fired, both his guns pumping rounds through the marshal's chest. This close they met little resistance. The man barely moved even though significant portions of his lungs and heart were projected across the room.

Cain's heel was still partly raised. Economy of motion dictated he follow the movement through. He kicked the dead man to the ground, stepping over him and into the room.

Already the second marshal was on the move. He was still two steps from the table when Cain shot him through the neck. The man spun, beads of scarlet making a dervish whirl in the space he vacated. The marshal caromed off the far wall. He turned towards Cain, his mouth opening to shout. Cain shot him again, punching a hole through the balding spot on the man's forehead.

Two men dead in as many heartbeats.

The woman was still a dangerous adversary. So might John Telfer be. It was highly unlikely that he'd been armed by his protectors, but Cain remembered that Telfer was one sly son of a bitch.

Concluding that the woman – an armed and trained protector – was by far the greater threat, Cain quickly moved towards the bathroom door. He unloaded the entire H&K clip through the door and walls. A bullet punched through the door in an attempt at return fire, but Cain heard the unmistakable grunt of someone mortally wounded.

Shoving the H&K back into his shoulder holster, he drew the Tanto with his left hand.

From inside the bathroom came a crash of breaking glass. The bitch was trying to escape!

He kicked open the door, expecting to see the woman wriggling out the window. Instead he almost lost his face as she fired. Only his super-charged instincts saved him. Wood splinters from the door frame jabbed at his right cheek, but other-wise he went unharmed.

'Run, Jeff!' the woman yelled.

Cain studied her in the time it took to swing

the Beretta towards her. She was wounded low in her gut – her childbearing days history, if she managed to survive. She had a second bullet wound on the mound of her right forearm. Blood slicked her wrist and made her grip on her weapon tenuous.

Stepping directly into her space, he jammed the Beretta to her forehead. Her lips writhed in a grimace. But that was more to do with the seven inches of steel he'd rammed below her ribcage.

The woman blinked slowly and Cain watched as her pupils dilated. He moved his face very close to hers, his lips trembling a hair's breadth from hers as he inhaled her final breath. It smelled of peppermint mouthwash and the coppery tang of blood.

As she sagged, Cain supported her on the length of his knife. Lord, but she was pretty, he thought. If only he had more time.

Allowing her to slip off the steel, he backed away. A quick glance to his right told him Telfer hadn't come out the bedroom. The woman's final words had gone unheeded, which was good.

Cain tapped on the door with the barrel of his gun.

'Knock, knock. It's the big bad wolf. Are you there, little piggy?'

From behind the door he heard the frantic gasps of a terrified man.

'It's been a long time, John,' Cain said. 'Hope you didn't forget me while I was gone?'

Inside the room, furniture was being scraped across the floor.

Cain booted the door and went inside.

A bed had been upended, the mattress concealing the cowering figure behind it.

'Aw, come on, John. Don't go all shy on me. Come out and say *hello* to your old friend, Cain.'

The mattress quivered, the man hiding there was shaking so hard. 'Please!' he yowled. 'Dear God in heaven, please don't kill me!'

Cain frowned.

'Please. Can't you just let me go? I promise . . . I swear to God I won't say a thing to anyone. I'll disappear. Tell Mr Gambetti, I swear I won't testify against him.'

Mr Gambetti?

Cain leaned in and with the barrel of his gun he forced the mattress to one side.

The man cowering against the wall shivered uncontrollably.

'You're Jeffrey Taylor?' Cain asked.

The man nodded slowly, unsure of what was expected of him.

Cain slow-blinked at him.

He didn't like swearing or profanity. It was unbecoming to a warrior-poet like Tubal Cain. But under these circumstances he allowed himself a little slip of the tongue.

'So where the *fuck* is John Telfer?'

88

CHAPTER 14

I'd heard much talk of Russian oligarchs: those billionaires who reaped the benefits after glasnost and the fall of the Berlin Wall, who were famous in my country for purchasing soccer teams, amongst other things. Most of those mega-rich men were upstanding and honest, very savvy in business, but then there were a few others. Following the collapse of the USSR the Russian mob had flourished throughout the world, and in particular had targeted the USA as a new home for their schemes. Whenever a Russian name was tied to a mobster, it struck fear in people's hearts. But Sigmund Petoskey didn't quite hit it for me. As Rink eloquently put it, Petoskey was a half-assed punk with delusions of grandeur. He wasn't even a real Russian, his only claim to the Motherland being a great-grandfather who had moved to the States at the turn of the twentieth century. Give him his due, he'd managed to claw himself out of the gutter and become a successful businessman. But he was still white trash whatever way you looked at him. He could have the fanciest of homes, talk in that plummy accent, and move in the same circles as the elite of Arkansas society, but when all came to all, he was still the same piece of crap that had scrabbled in the gutter for scraps. Or, as Rink said, who went frog-gigging for meat for his mother's stew.

I didn't fear Siggy Petoskey, and I sure as hell didn't respect him.

Which wasn't necessarily a good thing.

Healthy respect for an enemy is a prerequisite to the successful outcome of any mission. Underestimating an enemy can lead to your own undoing. With that in mind it was important that I approach him with a clear head and correct intent. It had been a busy night and I could feel the burr of fatigue at the edges of my consciousness. I needed to sleep, to recoup my senses, to take Siggy Petoskey with all cylinders firing.

The problem with that tactic was that Rink would have to endure further hours at the hands – and *ministrations* – of his captors. If he was still alive. I refused to accept that he was dead. If Rink had been killed, then we'd have found him in the same state that Bryce Lang and Walter's bodyguards had been discovered in. He'd have been displayed as a warning, not hidden away somewhere. Rink had been taken for one reason: to control me. While I was seeking Rink, I would be too distracted to thwart Tubal Cain's plans for my younger brother. I was being manipulated, but that was OK. I was determined to find Rink whoever pushed and prodded me along.

Instead of sleep, I made do with that shower I'd put off last night. In a stall at Harvey's ranch-style home I practically scalded myself under the blasting water, before turning the nozzle to freezing to rinse off and reinvigorate myself. After shaving and brushing my teeth, I changed into the spare set of clothing from my bag. The black T-shirt and black jeans were wrinkled and carried a faint smell of must. My black leather jacket and boots finished off my funereal attire. My fashion sense didn't generally extend to bright and cheerful, but I'd been dressed in more lugubrious attire than this when conducting night-time assaults on enemy territory.

Harvey served up a heart-attack-inducing break-fast of eggs and crispy bacon with rounds of toast dripping in butter. He'd also had the presence of mind to brew a two-litre jug of strong coffee that I put a massive dent in. These days I didn't smoke, rarely imbibed strong alcohol and tried to eat healthily – Harvey's breakfast notwithstanding – so caffeine was my only guilty pleasure. When I was done, I carried my dishes over and Harvey placed them in his dishwasher. He looked efficient in his handling of the machine. He had the bachelor thing down to a tee.

'So, there's no woman in your life right now, Harvey?'

'Nothing serious,' he said. 'Couple of ladies I see now and then, but none that I'd want to set up shop with. I haven't found the right one, yet, Hunter. I'm not as lucky as you.'

I pinched my lips round an answer, offered only a nod. I hadn't told him of my decision regarding Imogen, but maybe he'd read something in me. Perhaps this was his way of telling me I was a fool for letting her go.

Harvey reached into his trouser pocket to pull out an item smaller than the last joint of his pinkie finger. Handing it over, he said, 'Keep that safe.'

I tucked the item into a hidden change pocket under the waistband of my jeans.

'I'm not happy with the plan, Hunter. Just so you know, man.'

I shrugged. 'What's the worst that can go wrong?'

Death would be the least of it, for certain.

Harvey said, 'You and Rink. Sometimes I can't believe either of you. How can you be so blasé about dying?'

'We all die, Harve. Sooner or later.'

'I'd rather it was later, thanks. I see myself in my nineties, tucked up in bed with a pretty nurse mopping my brow.'

'What are the chances, huh?'

'For you? About the same as a jelly doughnut making it to the final of America's Biggest Loser.'

I laughed, then glanced at my watch. 'C'mon. It's time to get moving.'

Harvey had an old Chevrolet pick-up truck that he occasionally used when conducting undercover operations. It was white, but was splashed with trail mud, rusted around the wheel arches, and there was a big dent in the front fender. It looked clapped out, but under the hood it was finely tuned. Not unlike my friend, I thought: Harvey had affected a disguise in direct contrast with his usual sharp look. We climbed into the truck and Harvey set it rolling towards Little Rock. It would take a quarter-hour to reach the city, another to get to the building where we'd find Siggy Petoskey. As we headed over, I checked in with the voice-mail box but found it still empty. I called Velasquez and McTeer, got them both at their respective home numbers, but they had nothing new for me, apart from further exhortations to find their boss. Hanging up the phone, I said, 'It looks like we're still on.'

Harvey sucked in his cheeks. He'd neglected to shave this morning and fine grey bristles winked in the reflection of the sun through the wind-screen. 'I still think it's a crazy plan.'

'I always was too impulsive for my own good,' I retorted. That's what my stepdad Bob Telfer used to tell me, as did my ex-wife, Diane. More recently Rink had been saying the same. 'But short of torturing Rink's location out of Petoskey, I can't think of a quicker way.'

'I vote we torture Petoskey.'

'We could do that, but there's always the chance he doesn't actually know where Rink has been taken. This way, at least we get a shoe in Hendrickson's door.'

'Unless you're killed,' Harvey pointed out, 'which will kinda fuck things up for us all.'

'Hopefully that won't happen. I've been thinking about that pretty nurse of yours mopping my brow too . . .'

I checked my weapons and the spare ammo I'd jammed in my jacket pocket. My old SIG Sauer P226 had been exchanged for one that Harvey kept in a strongbox at the ranch. I had left mine with him for safe keeping. Likely this one would be taken away after the shooting I was about to commit. Harvey had wondered why I chose to carry the SIG when he had a couple of cheaper models lying around. Frankly, I preferred the SIG to other handguns. It had an unusually heavy stock, but instead of it being an impediment, that made for a great bludgeoning weapon when the fighting got so close that a clean shot wasn't an option. The poundage necessary to depress the trigger on the first shot was always greater than the next – a safeguard against misfiring a round – the resulting snatching action throwing off the aim of those unfamiliar with the gun. But I'd been using a SIG since my training in Point Shooting way back when and knew how to compensate. My other weapon was a standard issue military Ka-bar knife. The knife was in an ankle holster inside my right boot, the gun I carried in a shoulder rig under my left arm. That was unusual for me: usually I carried my adapted gun in my waistband at the small of my back, but this gun still had the sights and safety lever intact so could easily snag in my clothing.

'Cocked and locked?'

Harvey's words were clichéd, as was my answer. 'Ready to rock and roll.'

He pulled the Chevrolet into a parking lot alongside a municipal building. The old truck would have stood out against the sedans and minivans favoured by the public servants inside the building but for the fact the Department of Works and Sanitation held offices here, and ours wasn't the only battered pick-up in the lot. We weren't interested in this place, but in another building across the road. This was a fleapit cinema showing a season of comedy movies from the black and white heyday, and it appeared that Sigmund Petoskey was a huge fan of Abbott and Costello's zany antics. He was a regular at the matinée showing – all part of his plan to look like a normal law-abiding citizen. The show was about to end.

And another was about to begin.

We waited in the lot. Harvey powered up his notebook computer and logged in. Harvey was good with many weapons, but none as powerful as the laptop he carried. He rattled off codes and clicked on to a site that would look no different from Google Earth to a casual observer. Of course, this was not a programme in the public domain, and was very much up to the second. I didn't bother looking, that was his territory. I watched the exit from the cinema. Some people were already beginning to trickle out, blinking as they walked from subdued lighting into the glare of day. It looked like Abbott and Costello didn't have that many fans keen enough to attend this early showing as there was little more than a handful of people leaving the cinema. That was all the better for me.

Stepping out of the truck, I gave Harvey a wink, then headed across the lot towards the road.

Another small group came out of the cinema. They milled momentarily in place, three men in windcheaters and cargo pants surrounding one other man. Something instantly apparent was that these three weren't the cauliflower-eared fools who had been Siggy's protectors the last time we'd met. These men had the cool aloofness and sharp eyes of professionals. I had to be wary of them, but my attention was focused on the other. It was the man in the middle I'd come to see.

Siggy Petoskey was a large man, though not in the way that Rink is large. He was soft-featured, with rounded shoulders and a paunch that came from excess. He was dressed for business in a tailored charcoal suit, cream shirt and red tie, but to stave off the winter nip he had donned an overcoat that reached to his knees. A flat cap covered his bald pate, and he wore leather gloves. On his face was the sour sneer I recalled from last time.

We were on the fringes of the Downtown Convention District here. Traffic was quite busy and there were plenty of pedestrians on the sidewalks

96

and waiting at the nearest crossing. So many eyes that I hoped that it would temper the response of Petoskey's guards long enough to do what had to be done. I speeded up, saw a gap in the traffic and rushed across the road, receiving the honk of a horn from a motorist who deemed my brash move injudicious. I angled quickly towards Petoskey's group, who were to my left and no more than twenty yards away. Already I'd caught the attention of one of his guards. Hearing the car horn he'd turned my way, seen how fast I was approaching, and maybe even read the intent in the stern set of my features. His eyes narrowed in recognition.

He moved, and true to form it wasn't to pull a gun, but to warn his colleagues and to cover his mark. They responded instantly, closing in a box around Petoskey, two of them shielding him from my approach as the third covered him with his arm and side and began ushering him towards a limousine parked near the kerb. I snatched a glance that way, saw a fourth man was out of the car and had the door open to receive their charge. I couldn't get Petoskey without first shooting one of the two men in front of me. I pulled out my SIG, continued forward, but then lifted the gun to the sky and discharged a round.

All around us, pedestrians reacted to the sound, some shrieking, others racing for cover. Birds broke from their roosts. I yelled something wordless and animalistic, adding to the panic, before firing off another round into the sky. Two rounds down, that was all I was prepared to waste, just in case things went to pot, which was always a possibility.

I was only yards away now and the close protection team had Siggy in the car, one of them throwing himself on top of his boss while the fourth man slammed shut the door. The car began to pull away and I raced forward, causing the three still on the pavement to turn to cut me off. Thankfully they hadn't yet drawn their weapons. They each grappled me, and my SIG was knocked from my hand and clattered on to the floor. I swore and struggled with the guards, butting my head into a face that came too close.

As the limousine sped away, the guards both sighed with relief that their mark was safe but also steeled themselves to deal with the maniac in their midst. They were, however, conscious of the number of witnesses on the street, and now that I was disarmed they weren't prepared to shoot me. Thank God.

They did swarm on me, though, grappling my arms. I kicked the legs of one of then from under him, them stamped on his chest to keep him down. Another got a stranglehold around my throat, looping me under his elbow, and he bore me forward while the other tried his hardest to trip me. I thrashed and struggled, bit at the side of the man holding me. My teeth sunk into his windcheater ineffectively, but the man realised what I was doing and shouted in anger. His friend doubled his efforts, lifting my legs by hauling up my knees. The man on the floor rolled out from under me and came to his feet, pushing down on my back so that between them they forced me face down on the pavement. I tried to grab for the SIG, but couldn't reach it. One of the guards snatched it up, placed it to the nape of my neck.

'Stop struggling or I'll shoot,' he whispered savagely in my ear.

'All right! All right!' I shouted. 'You've got me. I give up.'

All three were shouting commands, to me, to each other, but also to another party. I heard the vroom of a racing engine and a vehicle bounced up on to the kerb dangerously close to us.

Please don't be the police, I prayed.

My plea was answered. The van was a plain blue Ford with a side door. The door was hauled open in the same instant that I was snatched off the floor by my three captors and I was thrown face first into the back compartment. Two of those holding me piled on top, and there was another man already inside. They began frisking me and found the Ka-bar and spare ammo almost immediately, plus my cellphone. The final man scrambled inside and the door slammed. The engine raced again and I felt the jolt as the van bumped down off the kerb and roared away at speed.

I wondered about Harvey. I hoped that he had stuck to the plan. I suspected that Rink would've come running regardless of what we'd agreed.

But Harvey hadn't come.

CHAPTER 15

Twice Cain had hunted and twice he'd followed the wrong trail.

The first time was when he'd launched the attack on Walter Conrad's cabin only to find that the CIA boss wasn't among those he'd slaughtered, and now there was a similar situation at the cabin on Jewel Ridge.

After his initial outburst of fury he could see the funny side of things. What was the point in being annoyed? The interlude had given him an opportunity to spend some quality time refining skills that he'd seldom employed while locked in his cell at Fort Conchar. The three US Marshals had died with little fanfare, but here he had someone on whom he could really practise his art.

'What's your real name, Jeff?'

Jeffrey Taylor was lying on top of the dining table that Cain had cleared with a sweep of his forearm. Cain had found three pairs of handcuffs among the property belonging to the marshals and had made good use of them. Taylor was chest down, both wrists secured to the legs of the table. With only one other set available, Cain had snapped the rings around the man's ankles. He was going nowhere.

'My name *is* Jeff!'

'So it's your second name that is fake?'

'You know that already.'

Cain studied his knives. Back when he'd been collecting trophies to be used in his ossuary at Jubal's Hollow he'd favoured a descaling knife. The slightly curved blade with a serration along the back edge had been useful in both slicing and sawing, and could fillet a human being as easily as a fish. Here his choices didn't hold the same finesse. Tanto or Bowie, both knives were man killers, but not much use for delicate procedures. He decided on the Tanto, the wieldier of the two.

He sank the diamond tip into Jeff's right calf muscle and the man screamed.

'I don't know,' Cain said, 'and that little bit of pain is for assuming I'd know anything about you.'

'Dear God! It's obvious that I'm not who you're looking for. You said you were looking for someone called John. That's not me!'

'I know that, Jeff. But I still want to know your full name.'

'Why? Why is it important? I'm not the person you're after.'

'Names hold power, Jeff. They're magical, don't you know that?'

'My name isn't magical . . . it's . . . it's nothing but *dirt* these days.'

Cain smiled, but Jeff couldn't see his face. Cain

wondered what it was about characters like Jeff Taylor and John Telfer and how they could be so frank about their worthlessness. It was something that he found both naive and endearing.

'If it's so dirty you shouldn't mind telling me.'

'My name is Jeffrey Thompson, OK? Is that what the Gambettis wanted, that I come clean about my identity before you killed me?'

'You mentioned these Gambettis before. They're the people you are hiding from? They're obviously not to be feared, because if they were any good they'd have found you by now.'

'You work for them, don't you? There's no reason to torture me like this if you don't.'

'I don't work for them.'

'Then let me go . . . please!'

'I'm not finished with you yet.'

'Why are you doing this?'

'Because it's in my nature, Jeff.' Cain ran his blade up the back of Jeff's shirt, slitting it all the way to the collar. His flesh was a puckered mass of scar tissue from his right hip up to his shoulder blades. 'I noticed when I led you from the bedroom that you had trouble straightening up. These scars on your back . . . what caused them?'

'The Gambettis. They tried to kill me once before.'

'Like I said, they aren't to be feared if this is all they achieved. What did they shoot you with? Was it birdshot?'

Jeff didn't reply. He closed his eyes and Cain knew that he was recalling the day he was wounded. Cain jabbed Jeff's opposite calf with the Tanto. 'When I talk, you answer.'

'Dear God! Whatever I say or don't say you're going to kill me. Why don't you just get it over with?'

'Because it's much more fun like this.'

Cain stood close to Jeff's head, leaning down to whisper in his ear. 'I mentioned that names are magical. Some names hold power. Do you know my name?'

'How could I?'

'My name is Tubal Cain.'

'Cain? What . . . like in the Bible? The one who murdered his brother?'

Cain snorted. 'Not *that* Cain. I am *Tubal* Cain. Brother of Jubal and the father of cutting instruments. You know me now?'

'No.'

'Yet you often call on your *dear God* for help. How can you expect Him to help you when you haven't even taken time to read His good book?' Cain traced the scars with his fingertips. His expert touch detected where the scar tissue was tightest and caused Jeff the most discomfort. 'Like I was saying, some names are magical. My name is magical. It has the power to alleviate your suffering.'

Cain inserted the Tanto into a bundle of scar tissue and sliced.

'There! Doesn't that help to free you up a little?' Jeff screamed.

'Dear God,' Cain mimicked. 'You sound like you doubt me, Jeff.'

He selected another point on the man's back and dug deep through the flesh. Jeff screamed even louder and strained against the cuffs holding him spread-eagled over the table.

'It's a shame, Jeff, but you don't seem the type to waste my time on. You're obviously ungrateful. When I did the very same to John Telfer he barely made a murmur of complaint? And to think I could have confused you with him.'

'Pleeeaaasssseee . . .'

'It makes me realise how much I want to reacquaint myself with my old pal, John, and how you're getting in the way of that. Goodbye, Jeff.'

Cain jammed the blade deep this time, all the way through the ribs and into Jeff's heart. It was a quick kill and didn't engender the same visceral thrill he usually experienced when murdering, but every second spent here was another second away from finding John Telfer. Catching and spending time with Ol' Johnny Boy was what he truly coveted.

Freeing the knife, he wiped it clean on Jeff's trousers. He looked down at the trussed man and shook his head.

'I wish I could say it was a pleasure meeting you,' Cain said as the man settled in death. 'But it wasn't. That doesn't mean I won't recall our time together fondly. In fact, I intend taking something with me so that I never forget you.'

Readying his knife, Cain reached for Jeff's nearest hand.

CHAPTER 16

I was in for a rough time.

The back of the van became not only a container but also an entertainment centre for those who were my jailers, particularly for the man I'd headbutted. He relished getting a little payback for the lump I'd put on his forehead. He punched me twice, once in each kidney, while the other three guards held me prone. I had steeled myself for a beating, but it doesn't matter how ready you are, a dig in the kidneys always hurts like hell.

They were all swearing, at me, at each other, their professionalism slipping now that we were out from under the disapproving gaze of the public. One of them grabbed my hair and forced my face hard against the ribbed floor of the van. Someone punched me between my shoulders, causing a flash of pain that went all the way to the tip of my coccyx and back again. Then my arms were twisted round and another of them cinched my wrists with plastic ties. When that was done, I was hauled over so that I could see them as they threw punches down at my guts. Their faces were twisted with glee and hatred.

Considering that a minute or two before they believed I was a nut job intent on killing them and their mark, I could understand why they would want to hurt me. I was pleased in a way that they were using their fists, because if one of them thought to use a gun I might never see daylight again. Another thing that pleased me: while they were punching the shit out of me, they'd forgotten about continuing a more thorough search than the one that had already turned up my weapons. To motivate them to further fury, I spat a gob of saliva at them. My spit hit one of the men flush in his face, and he paused only to wipe it away before slamming his saliva-smeared palm down into my forehead. I suffered a double whammy. His palm rammed my head down on one of the ribbed spars of the floor. I almost blacked out. It didn't stop them hitting me again.

Finally the beating subsided, though it wasn't because my captors were any less furious or tired of hitting me. The driver was shouting at them through an open hatch. My blood was pounding in my ears, and there was too much bumping and banging as they shifted about to hear clearly, but I got the gist. The man in the front was shouting that the boss wanted me unharmed. Thank God for small mercies.

'Think this is your lucky day, asshole? Well, guess again. We aren't going to kill you. Not yet, but I don't fancy your chances once the boss is finished with you.'

I squinted up at the voice to find the man I'd headbutted leaning over me. He was a guy in his mid-thirties, fit and strong-looking. Nothing distinctive about him apart from the raised welt I'd put on his forehead.

'You can't kill me,' I said, trying to sound confident. 'There were witnesses. They saw you snatch me off the street. The cops will be looking for me. What do you think will happen to you if I turn up dead?'

The men all laughed at my naivety. My tormentor pressed a knuckle into my breastbone, digging at a nerve bundle. 'The cops will turn a blind eye. Mr Petoskey owns the cops here . . . didn't you know that?'

One of them lifted a gun and I recognised it as the one I'd come armed with. He pointed it at my face. My tormentor said, 'See, this is the way things will happen. Once the boss is finished with you, you'll be gut shot and left lying in the road. We've plenty witnesses here who'll swear we were delivering you to the police when you made a break for it, snatched one of our guns, and we had to shoot you in self-defence. We can do anything we want to you.'

'No one would believe that . . .'

'They would if they were *told* to.' The man held out his hand and his friend slapped the SIG into his palm. The man carefully slipped the safety on. Then off again. It was all for show. He checked there was a round in the chamber. Then he jammed the gun under my chin. 'In fact, there are enough of us here now, that if we told the boss that you got your hands on a gun and we had to kill you, well, he'd believe us too.'

I screwed my eyes shut, made a whimpering sound.

The man laughed and the others joined in like the pack of hyenas they resembled.

'I thought you were supposed to be some sort of tough guy?'

'You don't know me,' I said.

'Oh, but I do.' He tapped the gun on my forehead. 'We heard that you might make a try on the boss. How'd you think we were ready for you coming? Did you think we just happened to have a van sitting around on the slightest off-chance that some random lunatic had a go at the boss? My problem is this . . . I don't know what anyone was fucking worrying about. You're a goddamn pussy who can't even shoot straight.'

Again a round of laughter.

'Joe Hunter. We've heard all about you. Fuckin' Brit coming over here, thinking he's the hardest fuck in town. Well, I got news for you . . . you ain't fuckin' nothin'. You just made the biggest mistake of your life, buddy. You just came up against someone who isn't afraid of your type.'

'Jesus,' I sighed.

'You a praying man, Hunter? Well, get praying, 'cause you're gonna need all the help you can get.' The man lifted the SIG. Like I've already said, the stock is heavier than on most other handguns, so when he brought it down hard against my skull it put me right out of the picture.

How long I was unconscious I couldn't say, because when next I gathered my senses the van had stopped moving. The side door was open and only two of my captors remained inside. The others were standing outside the van, their figures indistinct against a gloomy backdrop. They were talking hurriedly, but I couldn't make out was being said. I lay there, gathering my wits as I started to assess my injuries. My entire body felt like one large bruise, but I couldn't detect any breakages. It took me a moment to realise that my hands were now in front of me. The plastic ties had been removed and rigid-cuffs snapped on instead. My feet were free, and in kicking range of the two men keeping guard. They had guns out, so I didn't fancy my chances. Anyway, I'd come to see Sigmund Petoskey, so I wasn't about to spoil my prospects by attempting an audacious escape.

One of the guards outside moved towards the van. When he leaned inside I could make out the welt on his forehead. 'Bring him. And if he tries anything shoot him in the knees.'

The two men grabbed me and pulled me to a sitting position. I recognised the one on my right as the recipient of my saliva earlier. He said, 'You heard the man, try anything and I'll kneecap you. We have to keep you alive for now, but that doesn't mean we can't put you through hell.'

There was nothing gentle about the way I was hauled from the van and dumped on my feet. Blood rushed to my head and I was a second or so away from blacking out again. Only the flash of agony from where the SIG had torn my scalp kept me galvanised. The two men hooked an elbow around my arms and then propelled me forward, following the other two. To make things more difficult I could have dragged my feet, but we were heading in the right direction. Stumbling along, I just kept my mouth shut.

We were inside an empty warehouse, a large open space bordered on either side by huge stacks of pallets laden with sacks and boxes of all shapes and sizes. The floor was smooth concrete, swept clean, with yellow markers indicating pathways for forklift trucks. Other yellow chevrons alongside the paths marked out danger zones, possibly where it was unsafe to turn the trucks due to the proximity of the stacked goods. It was dimly lit, only the occasional overhead strip light penetrating the gloom. We passed through pools of contrasting shade and light as we moved towards the back of the building. As we neared the far end, I could detect a sour tang and guessed that the warehouse was one of many next to the banks of the Arkansas River. With a building this large and well stocked, I was surprised that there weren't more people around. Maybe they'd all been given the rest of the day off while their boss conducted his more nefarious brand of business.

There was an office at the left corner of the building, next to a roller door that was currently closed. Just inside the roller shutter was parked the limousine that had spirited Sigmund Petoskey away from the cinema. As we approached, a man clambered out the front, came round and opened the door for Siggy. Petoskey climbed out languidly, tightening his gloves over his fists like some gangster from a *noir* movie. He sneered at me, said, 'I wondered when we would meet again. I've been looking forward to this for a long time.'

Me too, if only he knew it.

One thing that was apparent: away from the ears of his business associates, Siggy Petoskey had lost the ridiculous accent that made him sound like Dr Watson from an old Sherlock Holmes flick. But he was still the same supercilious fucker I remembered with distaste.

Here, where the surroundings were better illuminated, I got a look at the product names on the boxes. I had to smile. Petoskey had gone from organising dog fights to shipping pet supplies. Another attempt, I guessed, at cleaning up his blackened image. He misconstrued my smile.

'You have nothing to be happy about, Hunter. In fact, I think this is about to become the worst day of your life.'

'I knew that the second I missed killing you earlier,' I said.

The man with the welt on his forehead spun quickly, backhanded me across my mouth. 'You

113

need to show a little respect when speaking to the man in charge of your destiny.'

I stared directly into the man's eyes, as I allowed a trickle of blood to seep from between my lips. 'Respect for *him*? Sigmund Petoskey's so full of shit he gives sewers a bad name.'

The self-elected disciplinarian lifted his hand again, but he was halted by the opening of the office door. A slight, unremarkable-looking man stood etched against the glare of a bright lamp. 'Enough, Charters.' He directed his words at the man with the welt, then turned an insipid stare on Petoskey. 'We have no time for pissing competitions, Sigmund. Let's show Hunter we mean real business.'

This newcomer was a stranger to me. He looked pretty bland with his watery eyes, his slight frame dressed in slacks and canvas jacket and a pair of suede boots, but I guessed that there was nothing commonplace about him. The way Charters jerked at his command and Petoskey nodded in acquiescence told me who was in charge here.

Directly in front of me the door to the office was pulled open and a silhouetted figure stepped forward. Framed in the lamplight from within was the last person I expected.

'Louise?' I asked. 'Is that you?'

Louise Blake should have been warned to lie low, but it seemed as if she hadn't taken Harvey's warning seriously.

For one brief moment I considered the possibility that Harvey was involved in Rink's disappearance.

But I quickly discarded the notion. Louise Blake had always been a wilful person, and had probably chosen to ignore the warning at her peril. She had been brought here for the same reason that Rink was missing. It was all a set up. And all along, I was the real target for this plot.

Betting that she wasn't a willing party, I searched Louise for any sign of deceit. Her face was in shadows, but I could still tell that it was swollen and sore. I couldn't blame her for being wilful; every time that I'd featured in her life it seemed she ended up bruised.

'Louise?' I said a second time. 'Are you OK?'

The woman sobbed.

The little man with the watery eyes flicked a hand at Petoskey. 'Show him.'

Petoskey stepped up behind Louise and I saw him lift something to the back of her head.

'No,' I started to say, my body going rigid. On each side my guards strained to hold me back, while Charters grabbed at my hair, holding me so I'd no option but to watch.

CRACK!

Petoskey fired a single round into the medulla oblongata at the base of Louise's skull. All motor function failed instantly, and Louise died without ever realising her face now decorated the front of my jacket and shirt.

She flopped to the ground, her hand outstretched towards me like a broken lily. In reaction I jerked forward, but Charters yanked back on my skull, bringing me to a squirming halt. Petoskey grinned, holding a semi-automatic handgun pointed at my chest.

'You murderous bastard!' I yelled.

Petoskey looked down at Louise's cadaver, and there was something decidedly unhealthy in the way his eyes lingered on the swell and curve of her backside. Then he snapped his eyes up to mine. 'Perhaps now you'll fully understand how serious we are.'

'You shithead,' I said. 'I'm your enemy, why did you have to kill her? She had nothing to do with me, for God's sake!'

From my left-hand side, the little man interjected. 'Charters, I stopped you before, but please ensure that Hunter learns a little courtesy when speaking to us.'

'With pleasure,' Charters said releasing my hair. He stepped in front of me, smiling as he studied my face. Then he backhanded me, his knuckles raking across my jaw. It left my skull tolling like a bell, and fresh blood invading my mouth. Judging by his smirk Charters was mildly pleased with his handiwork. 'Watch your mouth in future,' he said.

'You watch your arse,' I told him right back. 'Because I swear to God I'm going to kill every last one of you.'

His next backhander slackened one of my teeth.

'That's enough for now, Charters,' said the little man. 'But if he shows any further disrespect, you have my permission to chastise him as you see fit.'

'Here,' I said, and spat a mouthful of clotty blood on to Petoskey's overcoat. 'How's that for disrespect?'

Charters and his friends all got their digs in this time, leaving my kidneys screaming in protest. To my dissatisfaction, Petoskey appeared unfazed by my uncouth gift. It was obviously why he'd worn a raincoat.

'Take him inside,' the little man ordered.

Petoskey stood to one side as my jailers forced me into the office. It wasn't the largest of spaces, and wouldn't accommodate all of my captors, plus me. The only concession to furniture was a single wooden chair and a small desk, upon which lay a large envelope.

'Please be seated, Hunter.'

I sat facing the door, but only because four meaty hands pressed me into the chair.

Charters hovered by the door, but his friends had to wait outside. Charters loosely aimed the SIG he'd taken from me. Petoskey and the newcomer took up positions so they were both facing me but neither would impede the aim of their guard. I looked from one to the other.

'So let's get things straight. Who's the biggest arsehole out of the two of you?' I asked.

'I'm growing tired of your disrespect, punk,' Charters offered from the back of the room.

I paid him no mind, searching the faces of my two immediate captors. 'Well?'

'I'll allow you one concession,' said the little

man. 'Our principal owes someone a final say on your fate, but if it comes to it, I don't mind killing you and taking the consequences.'

'I guess that means you're the one that I have to kill first,' I told him. 'Then again, I owe Petoskey big time for what he did to Louise. Maybe I'll save you for later.'

'Such bravado from a man in chains,' Petoskey laughed. 'Should I show it to him now, Baron?'

Baron? That was the name of the little man. Just like his bland face, his name meant nothing to me, other than it was now marked for death.

'I'll do it.' Baron picked the envelope off the desk. 'Let me open this for you.' He slipped out a black and white photograph and placed it in front of me.

Despite myself, I flinched.

The glossy shot was of my best friend.

Rink was slumped in a chair. He was tethered. His face was a patchwork of cuts and watery blood was spattered down the front of his bared chest. A wound gaped high in the meat of his right shoulder. Only the seething hatred burning from behind his swollen eyelids told me he was still alive.

'Jared Rington is alive,' Petoskey said. 'But one more wrong move out of you, Hunter, and believe me, he *will* die.'

Baron stepped forward. 'You do believe that we are capable of Rington's murder, Hunter?'

Beyond Charters, I could see where they'd left Louise lying on the ground. Steam was rising from the ruin of her skull. 'I believe you.'

'Good, but just in case, listen . . .'

From his coat pocket Baron pulled out a digital recorder. He flicked it on and held it close to my ear.

'Hunter.' Rink's unmistakable voice issued from the device. 'Frog-giggin' fuckers got the drop on me, man. I'm sorry I got you into this, buddy.' He laughed humourlessly. 'They say that they'll hurt me if you don't do as they ask. Tell 'em to go screw themselves.'

There was a static buzz, the sound of Rink being introduced to a Taser.

Baron flicked the 'off' switch.

'When your buddy said that we'd hurt him, he meant *even more* than we have already. The only way you can stop that is to give us what we want.'

Petoskey leaned in close. 'So . . . do we have your *cooperation?*'

What choice did I have?

A maxim of counterterrorism: you don't make bargains with terrorists. You refuse to negotiate. You show the demented bastards that you aren't prepared to back down. Not ever. Show them a weakness and they will exploit it, exponentially growing the problem.

I opened my mouth to speak, but my words weren't those of an ex-counterterrorism soldier. They were those of a best friend.

'What do you want from me?'

CHAPTER 17

Baron took another turn at the envelope. From inside it he drew a second photograph, which he placed on the desk in front of me.

'Don't know him,' I said.

'You don't?' Baron said. 'Now that is strange. But no problem; I'm going to explain everything about John Telfer that you need to know.'

I took a second look at the photo. It was the same photograph that had been splashed all over the newspapers and TV newscasts when John had been mistakenly identified as the Harvestman.

'John Telfer?' I tasted his name on my tongue. 'Sounds familiar.'

'It should,' Baron said. 'Considering he's your brother.'

'Half-brother,' Petoskey added. 'If we want to be precise. You were looking for John when you attacked me last time, remember?'

'You know all about him then?' I asked. 'You should also know that he's dead. He was murdered by a serial killer out in the Mojave Desert last year.'

'We know the story,' Baron told me. 'But that's all it is. John Telfer survived. As did *others*.'

'There were no survivors,' I said.

'You survived,' Baron pointed out, 'as did Jared Rington.'

Shaking my head, I said, 'No. You've got it all wrong. We weren't there.'

Of course, they were having none of it, because they had inside information from a man who had been there. It was apparent to all that John had survived; otherwise the impending court case would have no legs to stand on. None of this would have been necessary.

Baron tapped an index finger on the photo. 'Where is he, Hunter? Tell us and we will let Rington go free.'

I pasted a look of astonishment across my face. 'You want me to give up my brother? Are you totally insane?'

'Not insane, Hunter,' Baron pointed out with a nod towards Louise's corpse. 'But we are supremely motivated.'

Petoskey leaned a fist on the desktop. For a second he was within grabbing range, but I didn't go for it. What would that achieve? Maybe I'd get to snap his neck, but it wouldn't help me find Rink. Reading something in my face, Baron touched Petoskey's elbow and he pulled back as though avoiding a lunging viper. It told me something about Petoskey: he was a murderous fuck when it came to innocent girls, but he wasn't as perceptive a killer as Baron was.

Regaining his composure, Petoskey tried again. 'John Telfer is a dead man, Hunter, either now or later. At least this way you get to save the life of your best friend.'

My laugh was short and brutal. 'As Rink so eloquently put it, go fuck yourselves.'

Petoskey's face darkened. 'It would serve you well to remember what else your friend said.'

'Don't you worry . . . I haven't forgotten.' My words were a threat, and there was nothing subtle about them.

'Perhaps you require another demonstration of our power?'

'Harm as much as a hair on his head, and I swear to God I'll rip your throats out.'

Baron clapped his hands slowly. 'Very good, Hunter, that's just the passion and drive we require from you. Maybe you can put it to helping us find your brother.'

If my hatred was a flame it would have scorched him to his very soul, though I doubted the bastard had one. 'Let me repeat myself. Go fuck yourselves.'

Petoskey smiled at my audacity. 'John Telfer *is* going to die. Tell us where he is. I'll see to it that his death is quick and painless. However, if his death is left to our *associate*, then I'm afraid I can't make the same promise.'

'Your associate?' I stared pointedly at Baron.

'As much as I'd like to confirm it, I'm not the

one Sigmund is referring to. Like I said, Telfer wasn't the only one who survived what happened at Jubal's Hollow.'

I knew where this was going but wasn't about to admit it.

'You're lying.'

'Am I? Is that a chance you're prepared to take?'

'I killed the bastard. I rammed a broken bone through his throat and watched him die.'

'You saw him die?' Petoskey laughed. 'You're sure of that?'

I concentrated on the picture of my brother. All I could hope was that Walter's promise to keep John safe was being honoured, because I still had a more urgent task. 'I want to see Rink,' I said. 'I want to see him alive and well, or I don't tell you a thing.'

The two men shared a knowing smile, like they'd both just won a private bet. Baron drew a syringe from his pocket.

'Unless that's Novocaine to fix my slack tooth, you can keep it,' I hissed at him.

'Just a little sodium pentathol,' he told me. 'You need to be moved and I don't trust that we'd reach our location intact if I allowed you free rein.'

'You have my friend hostage. Do you really think I'm going to try something stupid?'

'Desperate times call for desperate measures,' Baron quoted. 'I'd rather not take the chance.'

'Believe me,' I said, without any trace of irony, 'if I was going to do something stupid, I would've done it by now.'

My cuffed hands were resting on the table, mere inches from the photographs. Rink was alive but one thing was obvious: if I died now, Rink would follow soon after.

They wanted to see how stupid a desperate man could be?

'OK, bring it on, Baron,' I said.

Baron watched me with an unwavering gaze. A single droplet of what's sometimes referred to as 'the truth serum' shivered from the tip of the needle. In one motion he jabbed the needle directly through my clothing and into my shoulder, pushing down the plunger.

'I don't care much for your bedside manner,' I told him.

'Did it smart a little? I am sorry.'

'I just fucking bet you are.'

Already the edge of my vision was getting fuzzy. Sodium pentathol was a drug I was familiar with. It's not the wonder drug portrayed in espionage movies where a person will divulge their deepest secrets, though it does loosen the inhibitions to a point where they are chattier and more open to suggestion than normal. A slightly higher dosage acts the same as any other anaesthetic. I must've received the higher dose.

Blackness fell like winter's dark shade.

CHAPTER 18

Over the years I've been subjected to the effects of drugs – a prerequisite for one trained to resist torture – but there wasn't much I could do to fight the dosage given to me by Baron. The drug took hold of me but its effect was dulled slightly so I didn't experience the absolute oblivion that comes on a surgeon's table; at the extremes of my consciousness I was aware of movement. Nothing that I could define, simply hands lifting me into the back of the van, followed by an interminable rumble and shudder as I was driven along uneven roads. At some point I must have been transferred to a helicopter, as even through the fog I recognised the thrum and slice of rotor blades cutting the air.

Baron administered further doses of sodium pentathol throughout the journey and I remained in a hazy state until he jabbed me with another needle. Whatever antidote I was given, the effect was instantaneous.

I came to, fully awake, feeling strangely invigorated, propped between Charters and the one who'd slammed my head on the floor of the van earlier. The cuffs remained in place. Baron was sitting next to the pilot but Petoskey was nowhere to be seen. Probably he'd crawled back under his rock.

'Where's Siggy?' I had to shout to make myself heard over the roar of the rotors. No one answered me, so I changed tack. 'Where are we?'

From his place in the co-pilot's seat, Baron nodded across fields swept by moonlight. Beyond were trees, silvered by the winter moon, and it struck me that I'd been unconscious for most of the day. The trees bordered a river valley. We were looking to the east, and by the mild tang of brine, and the emptiness of the sky beyond the trees, I gathered that we were somewhere on the Eastern Seaboard.

Baron wasn't one for hints but that didn't matter as, by now, I'd put two and two together.

'You're an ex-spook,' I said to Baron. Now I knew how Hendrickson had the intelligence available to find Walter's hidden cabin in the Adirondacks. 'How did you wind up working for a couple of punks like Hendrickson and Petoskey?'

He had to lean towards me so I could hear his reply. 'Money. Simple as that.'

'I didn't think it was from a sense of duty.'

'Duty doesn't pay as well as Hendrickson does. Anyway, you've got a nerve. You've agreed to give up your brother for the sake of a friend. Where's the duty there?'

'It's not something I want to think about,' I told

him. 'Even if I tell you where John is, there's still the possibility he'll get away. The way things are Rink has no chance.'

'Even so,' Baron said, 'you surprise me.'

'I love my brother. But we're not *that* close.'

'How much do you value the life of your best friend?'

'Why do you even bother asking? He'd die for me.'

The helicopter took us north along a rugged coastline that alternated between dense woodland and open bays dotted with beachfront houses. The sea was as smooth as stretched silk, inviting a skimmed stone to pock the surface with concentric circles. On any other occasion I might have appreciated the beauty. Now my mood was too foul, engaged as it was in contemplating the bloody and violent deaths of my fellow fliers.

As I'd been deliberately wedged between Charters and the other, my view to the front was limited to snatches through the partially opened partition that led to the crew cabin. Baron had turned away, conversing over a satellite phone, but I had no hope of hearing anything above the thrum of the blades and whistle of wind. To my gruff chaperones, I said, 'So where are we heading, boys?'

Charters grunted, touched the lump I'd given him on his forehead. He adjusted himself in his seat, none too careful about where he placed his bony bits. When I didn't respond, he nudged me again as he jiggled into a more comfortable position.

Looking him up and down, I asked, 'Are you always such an arsehole, Charters, or do you feel you need the practice?'

'Practice makes perfect.' He lifted his elbow and slammed it across my forehead, taking payback in full. My skull felt like a well-whacked piñata, but it was worth it. Before his arm dropped back to his side, I'd slipped a Swiss-army knife I'd dipped from his pocket into my waistband.

Having no need to goad him now, I lapsed into silence. My guardsmen took my silence as a sign of being chastised and Charters in particular looked pleased with the result. Let him gloat, while he had the opportunity.

The helicopter banked to the right, throwing the three of us together. Charters now experienced a little of the discomfort that I'd had to put up with. As the helicopter levelled out he pushed me away none too gently, with another dig in the ribs for good measure.

'I think you've had all the practice you need.'

My words won me a grunt of laughter. The concept of one man's misfortune being another man's pleasure was often a by-product of the mercenary lifestyle these men followed. Someone like Charters was only happy when making another person's life a misery. I'd met many of his type throughout my lifetime. The years I'd spent as a soldier ensured I made the acquaintance of

128

such beasts. Except then I usually ended up killing the miserable bastards.

Baron twisted round and called back to us, 'We're going down. You might want to grab a hold of your seats.'

No sooner had he said it than the helicopter banked to the left. We appeared to be in a nose dive, rushing towards the unforgiving earth. At the last possible second the pilot adjusted the controls and the nose went up and the skids touched ground with hardly a bump.

Charters opened the door to show a wide expanse of verdant lawn. He climbed out, then lifting a handgun for emphasis, he said, 'Out, Hunter.'

I clambered out, my feet sinking into the spongy lawn. Over my head swooped the whirling rotor blades. Behind me came the thud of the second guard stepping out the helicopter. He pressed a hand to my shoulder, ushering me before him. Baron brought up the rear. His mobile phone was ringing but he ignored it.

Charters was in the way, but he wasn't big enough to block my view of the house we approached. It was a huge colonial edifice, the kind of house that often serves as a backdrop to glossy adverts for luxury cars, though you wouldn't expect to see the trimmings on this house in *GQ* magazine.

On the balustrade at the top of the building's façade there were men with guns, also searchlights and CCTV cameras. Behind bullet- and blast-proof windows guards stood as stoic as sentries at Buckingham Palace. Other men with machine guns patrolled the grounds. I wondered how likely it was that the lawn and perimeter walls were sown with heat- and motion-sensing devices. If they were, then nothing larger than a mouse would get inside the compound uninvited.

Sigmund Petoskey waited for us at the front door. He must have travelled via a different craft. He held a mobile phone in a loose grip, and I guessed it was him who'd been ringing Baron a moment ago, eager for our arrival.

'Glad you could make it, Siggy. It'll save me another trip to Little Rock to kill you.'

Charters' slap to the back of my head sent flashes of silver across my vision. Giving him the evil eye, I made him a silent promise. He curled a lip.

Turning to Baron, I said, 'I hate what you're forcing me to do, but I'm gonna tell you where John is as soon as I know Rink's safe.' Then squaring my shoulders before Charters, I said, 'But I swear to God, if this piece of shit lays one more hand on me, I'll fucking break his arm.'

Charters laughed but behind his hard gaze I noted a worm of trepidation, like he'd just figured out that perhaps I wasn't joking. He glanced at his superiors for direction. An insidious smile flicked at the corners of Baron's mouth as if the threat was something he'd like to see enacted.

Maybe it was a sense of duty, maybe it was false

bravado, or that Charters felt my challenge made him lose face before his superiors. Whatever motivated him, he said, 'I don't like your tone of voice, asshole.' He prepared to backhand me across the face.

'I'm warning you,' I growled.

But he wouldn't be told.

His curled fist whipped towards me.

My response wasn't to take the blow stoically. Neither did I step back to avoid it. I came forward, pivoting so that both my palms accepted the blow. Fingers curling over his forearm, I pulled it with me as I pivoted a second time, taking his outstretched arm under my armpit. Pulling up on his wrist, and forcing down with my body, it was my entire weight versus the fragile make up of his elbow. I heard the twang of rupturing tendons. Not that the matter could end there. I'd promised I'd break his arm. Retaining his wrist, I rammed a knee hard against his hyper-extended elbow. It was like snapping a green stick. Not bad for a man in handcuffs.

In the telling it sounds a lot, but it was a moment's work. Before Charters could even register that his arm was shattered, I'd already moved away from him. The other guard gave a strangled gasp, and he started after me before faltering and grabbing instead at the gun in his shoulder holster. If I'd desired to, I could have speared my stiffened fingers into his eyes, or grabbed his chin and twisted his head a hundred and eighty degrees on his spine, except I'd still to see Rink alive.

Instead I turned my gaze on Baron. Finally I'd got a rise out of the man, even if it was only a momentary widening of his eyes. He lifted a hand towards the guard. 'That's enough, Drummond. I think we'd all agree that Charters asked for what he got.'

Drummond swayed in place. His hand drifted from his gun. Charters was still down on one knee, cupping his broken elbow in his opposite hand, gasping and squeezing tears from his sphincter-tight eyes.

'I did warn him.'

'Are you finished?' Baron asked.

'For now.' The way I said it must've reminded Baron that I'd promised to kill him first. His fingers tickled the butt of the gun wedged in his waistband: the SIG taken from me earlier. We were like gunfighters in Dodge City, facing off, awaiting the slightest twitch that'd herald imminent death for one of us.

It was Petoskey who ended the stand-off. He directed his words at Baron in an almost conspiratorial whisper. 'Now who's having a pissing competition? Let's get inside, now. Hendrickson isn't the most patient of men, remember.'

Baron slowly drew away from the gun and scratched an itch on his jaw. It was all for show, a touch of the disdain he felt for my skills. In the next instant his oily smile was back in place and his hand made a sweeping gesture indicating that I follow Petoskey up the steps and into the house.

From behind me, Charters swore loudly. I glanced over my shoulder at him and his face was a picture of hatred. Saliva stitched a pattern between his widely splayed lips. 'You broke my fucking arm!'

'Yes,' I said, ensuring Baron heard my words. 'I promised you I would.'

CHAPTER 19

Rink and I had been in many precarious situations over the years. But never had we faced a predicament like the one we'd gotten ourselves into this time.

Forget the fact that there were five armed men in the room with us. Or that I was cuffed, and Rink was strapped to an 'Old Sparky' type chair. We also happened to be in the basement of a fortified mansion with twenty or so armed mercenaries prowling the grounds overhead.

The odds of us surviving the next few minutes were about the same as falling out of an airplane, tumbling thousands of feet, then landing on your feet and walking away. Still, I'd heard urban legends about just such a miracle, so I wasn't about to give up. Rink was relying on me, and so was my brother, John.

Despite my promise to the contrary, I would never give up my brother. Yes, I loved Rink like a brother. But Rink was also a soldier. Like me, he knew the risks. John was a civilian. A foolish, misguided civilian, who had allowed greed to get in the way of good sense, but he shouldn't have to suffer the kind of enemies Rink and I had lived with all these years.

Petoskey and Baron were going to be pissed off when they found out I'd no idea where John was. I'd always been worried that a situation like this could present itself and for that reason hadn't pushed to know where Walter had hidden him.

Rink was awake. He'd certainly taken a beating at some point, but he'd been cleaned up and a rudimentary dressing had been applied to the wound in his shoulder. His face carried a few scrapes and bruises that were in the final stages of swelling, but he didn't look *too* bad, for all that.

'How are you, Rink?'

'Good to go.' He smiled.

Giving him a slow smile of my own, I turned to our captors.

'Release him. Rink walks out of here. Then I give you what you want.'

Petoskey shook his head slowly. He was like a dorm prefect denying a hall pass, smug and super-cilious. 'You give us Telfer first. Once we have him, then Rington will be released.'

'No offence,' I said to him. 'But I don't believe you.'

'Then we're on the same wavelength.'

There were four guns pointed at me. My hands were cuffed. Under the circumstances Petoskey was safe from me.

'So what happens now?' Purposefully, I turned

to Baron. 'You're going to have to wait a little longer for your big pay day.'

'We could always force Telfer's whereabouts from you,' he said. With a flick of his jacket tail, he showed me a Taser clipped to his belt.

My eyes went large, fear flaring. His smile flickered, telling me that he wasn't buying the act. But that was OK. I'd made him pause. He was thinking. But I was already acting.

The obvious play was to go for Baron. The only thing was, as I went towards him, one of the others would shoot me dead. So, I stepped back. My cuffed hands were raised, as though to fend off a blast of his Taser. Then I shot forward at an oblique angle, and rammed the cuffs' rigid spacer into Drummond's face. His nose crunched, and blood spattered. His shout of alarm had the desired effect. Instead of anyone shooting at me, they reacted by recoiling in defensive reflex.

I slewed to one side, the penknife I'd dipped out of Charters' pocket in my fist. My arms dropped over Petoskey's head, and I squirmed behind him, using him as a shield before anyone in the room could make a move towards me. Next second, the blade was against his throat and I could feel his super-amplified pulse throbbing along the blade and into the handle.

'Anyone moves and this piece of shit is dead!'

Petoskey stiffened, and I smelled a waft of fear rising off him.

There was a moment's confusion as Baron, the

two other guards and bloody-faced Drummond lifted their guns. I dragged Petoskey backwards, placing him between Rink and the others.

'Do you want Petoskey to *die*?'

All four guns wavered. I'd have preferred to pull Petoskey's gun free of his shoulder holster, but that meant giving up the advantage of the knife at his throat. While I tried to pull the gun out, one of them could easily put a round in my head.

Adding potency to my threat, I pushed the tip of the knife into Petoskey's flesh. Blood beaded out. Petoskey screamed like I'd almost sawed his head off, yanking his face aside. As he did so, my own face made a momentary target for Baron. As fast a shot as anyone I'd seen, he lifted my SIG and fired.

The retort of the gun reverberated around the cellar, the sound amplified by the domed confines. Tatters of a paper wad sifted in the air, coming nowhere near their target. Uninjured, I smiled at Baron before tucking in behind Petoskey.

'Fucking blanks?' Baron shook his head in disbelief.

'You didn't think I'd risk firing real bullets with so many members of the public around?'

'You had this planned from the start? You son of a bitch!'

'Have to admit to winging it a bit,' I confessed, 'but I always intended killing this prick.' I jabbed Petoskey with the blade and he howled. 'You want me to do it now?'

Baron allowed the gun to drop, and he lifted his other hand, tried to wave me down. 'Easy now, Hunter.'

'You don't get paid if he dies? Is that it, arsehole?' I jabbed the knife a little deeper. 'I'll kill this murdering motherfucker in a heartbeat. You got that?'

Baron's eyes pinched, and I swear, other than cruelty, it was the first genuine emotion I'd seen crossing his features. Greed was a strong motivating factor with the insipid bastard.

'Now,' I said, 'this is how it's going to play out. All of you put your guns on the floor. Do it now or I'll take Petoskey's head off.'

'I don't think so, Hunter,' Baron said. 'Or you and Rington will be dead in the next second.'

'We were going to die anyway. At least we'll have the satisfaction of seeing Petoskey die first.'

Petoskey was done waiting for Baron to take charge. 'Just do as he says!' he shrieked. 'Baron! I swear to God, if I get injured . . .'

Baron placed my SIG on the ground. Both hands came up empty.

'The Taser, as well,' I said. 'And don't think you can use that thing to get me. I'll likely stick Siggy with my first convulsion.'

Baron unclipped the blocky weapon, dropped it at his feet. Then he nodded at his companions to drop theirs.

'Kick them away, boys,' I said.

Reluctantly the three of them did so. 'Good,' I

said. 'Now, you . . . Drummond? Get over here and undo Rink.'

The bloody-faced man moved towards me, and I edged round so I could keep tabs on what he was doing. Just for effect I dragged the blade down Petoskey's throat, smearing a trail of blood that began pooling in the hollow below his Adam's apple.

Drummond glanced at Petoskey, and I could only assume he read dire threats in his boss's eyes, because he quickly began pulling free the straps from Rink's wrists. Rink swiped blood and sweat from his flesh, flexing his arms, promoting circulation. It was too early to move. So I waited. Drummond ducked down and undid the straps from around my friend's ankles.

Rink booted Drummond in the chest, knocking him sprawling on his backside. 'Stay down,' Rink told him. 'Get up before I say and I'll snap your goddamn spine.'

Baron and the other two men were itching to do something, but indecision made them falter. So did Petoskey's headshake. Rink stepped up beside me, his hand dipping beneath Petoskey's jacket and coming out with a handful of semi-automatic, the same gun with which Petoskey had executed Louise Blake.

'Which of you punks has the keys to Hunter's cuffs?'

Baron indicated with a raised finger.

'Sling them over here,' Rink said.

The keys sailed through space and Rink snatched them out of the air with his free hand. Then, stepping towards the others, he passed them back to me. It was awkward undoing the cuffs. Luckily they'd been placed on me with the locks towards my hands or it would've been impossible. I freed my knife hand first, wriggling free of the metal hoop, but never taking the blade from Petoskey's neck. I left the cuffs hanging from my left wrist.

Using him as a shield, I propelled Petoskey over to the nearest dropped gun. It was the SIG. I racked the slide, ejecting the next round. That was all the blanks I'd fed into the gun; the others were the real deal.

If I was that airplane passenger I mentioned, I was currently in freefall without a parachute. I was sailing on the breeze now, but still had to land on my feet and walk away. Falling isn't the problem, it's hitting the ground at speed that can test your mortality. The hardest part of our escape was yet to come.

Petoskey wasn't a willing hostage, but what could he do? I had a gun under his chin, and Rink watching my back, as we fled up the steps from the basement and into the house. He cried out to his minders, yelling at them to give way, threatening them with instant death with more venom than I could have mustered.

There's always one in the bunch who thinks they know better than their boss. One man, a swarthy-faced guy who reminded me of the last time I'd fought Hendrickson's men, thought that I'd be intimidated by the Uzi sub-machine gun he lifted to halt our progress. Under those circumstances, it was a *spray and pray* gun. He wasn't going to shoot his boss to get at us.

'You were ordered to give way,' I snarled over Petoskey's shoulder. 'Maybe he's a complete prick but you should still show more respect.'

I shot the man between his eyes and he crumpled on the hardwood floor.

'You can't get the staff these days,' I said. Petoskey cried out, possibly at the realisation that I was indeed prepared to kill.

Out of the front door, we charged across the grounds. Men milled around us, shouting in confusion. Above them all Petoskey's strident screams demanded obedience. Up on the roof, a would-be sniper swung his sights on Rink. Rink fired first, and blood sifted like cherry blossom on the wind.

I'd lost track of the time, but by now it had to be the early hours of the morning. It was still dark but the spotlights on the roof made the grounds stark. Beyond the spill of light the shadows were dense. Through the darkness, the helicopter looked like a giant-sized hornet crouching on the lawn.

Harvey Lucas had piloted choppers during Desert Storm.

He hadn't come to my assistance back in Little

Rock, but had stayed back as we had planned. My hope was that the tracking device from Harvey secreted in the waistband of my jeans had done its job, and that Harvey was in position now. Just in case our plan had gone to pot, I said to Rink, 'You think you can handle that thing?'

I didn't doubt his ability, because Rink had also piloted a chopper or two in his day. My concern was that Rink had suffered torture for the past two days, and had a wound in one shoulder, so I didn't know how he was holding up. It was one thing running around and killing snipers when the adrenalin was shrieking through your body, quite another to be at the controls of a highly technical flying machine.

'Not a problem, Hunter.'

There were beads of perspiration coursing down his forehead but they had nothing to do with the sudden bout of exertion.

'You sure?'

'We won't be in the air long,' Rink said. 'Just long enough to get us the fuck outa here.'

I jerked a nod at him, and swung Petoskey between us as we backed towards the helicopter. From the front of the house, Baron and the others came at a run. Petoskey was a big man, but he wasn't enough for the two of us to hide behind. I angled him so that his body blocked most of Rink's. I hadn't come all this way to let my friend perish now. We continued to back-pedal, but I doubted that we could make it to the chopper intact.

The sound of a rifle snapped from behind us. I didn't glance back because if the bullet had been aimed at me or Rink then already one of us would be dead. I saw Drummond go down, and there was a bloody hole in his chest. Baron dropped to a crouch, his gaze seeking out the shooter. The others had the sense to throw themselves flat.

There was another crack of the rifle and a man on the balustrade dropped out of sight. Permanently.

Harvey, it appeared had come through for us.

'The chopper,' I called to Rink. 'Quickly.'

'Let me go,' Petoskey squawked. 'You don't need me any more.'

'No. You're coming with us.' If I'd let him go then, we'd have been riddled with bullets. Even if we made it into the air, without Petoskey as a hostage, I'd the feeling that Baron wouldn't hesitate in ordering the chopper brought down. There were plenty of assault rifles to get the job done. And who knew what other weapons were in their arsenal? There could be surface-to-air missiles hidden under the topiary for all I could tell.

The pilot who'd flown the helicopter here was conspicuous by his absence. Harvey was prone beneath the chopper, a sniper rifle on a tripod trained towards the front of the house. He was dressed in a drab green jumpsuit, his skin streaked with camouflage grease. The skills he'd possessed from back when he was a Ranger hadn't failed him when entering the compound undetected. He winked up at me, said, 'If I was a betting man, I wouldn't have wagered a cent on us pulling this off.'

'So long as you're not a sore loser.' I winked back. Then I covered for him as he rolled out from under the chopper and climbed inside. Rink clambered into the cockpit next to him while I dragged Petoskey into the rear compartment. I left the door open so that his henchmen were reminded of where blind shooting could get them.

My Special Forces training didn't extend to flying helicopters. I was more used to rappelling from them, or parachuting into bandit country from a high-altitude airplane. The flying was left to those who knew what the hell they were doing, so the routine Harvey went through to get us off the ground was lost on me. All I know is that the blades cut the air, there was a lot of high-pitched engine noise, and we were up and away, drifting on the night breeze like a fleck of lint.

We banked right, then soared up into the sky. Below us in the grounds of the mansion, gunmen aimed useless weapons at us.

'What are you going to do with me?' Petoskey asked.

'Depends.'

'Just tell me what you want. I swear to God, Hunter, I'll give you it.'

I considered his offer for a split second.

'Call Tubal Cain off my brother.'

Petoskey made big eyes at me. 'I would, but . . .'

'But nothing,' I told him. 'Do that and I'll let you go. Call off the contract.'

'I can't,' Petoskey yelped. 'Cain isn't doing this for *me*. He's working for Kurt Hendrickson. *Your argument is with Hendrickson, not me!*'

Shaking my head slowly, I stared into his eyes. I pictured Petoskey lifting his gun to the back of Louise Blake's head. That innocent girl had suffered enough because of Hendrickson. Then, on the bastard's behalf, Petoskey had put a bullet in her head.

'You're right. There's no argument for what you did to Louise,' I said.

Petoskey's face fell. There was resignation there, but it was far outweighed by fear.

My fist connected with his throat. He gagged, bending over, and I grabbed and spun him round. I stamp-kicked his buttocks and Petoskey was propelled out of the open door. He screamed as he fell.

There's this urban legend about a man falling for thousands of feet, landing on his feet and walking away uninjured. We were only five hundred feet up; so maybe Petoskey would get lucky.

CHAPTER 20

As emotionless as driftwood, Baron watched Petoskey plummet from the sky.

The Arkansas mobster screamed all the way down then went deathly silent as he struck the roof of the house. He smashed through tiles, made it through the support beams and ended up in the attic space. The blood pouring down the steepled roof was an indication of what would be found when Petoskey was retrieved from the wreckage.

Setting his mouth in a tight line, Baron reached into his pocket and took out his cellphone. He pressed a speed dial number. The phone rang three times before it was picked up.

'Bad news, I'm afraid, sir,' he said into the phone. 'Hunter and Rington have escaped.'

He tolerated the shouting in his ear, knowing that this was nothing compared to what was coming.

Then he said, 'It's worse than that, Mr Hendrickson. During their escape, your business partner was killed.'

Hundreds of miles away, Kurt Hendrickson screamed blasphemous threats down the phone.

'Yes,' Baron acknowledged. 'I will do everything in my power to stop them.'

He quickly disconnected to avoid a further berating, slipped the phone back in his pocket then turned to the men standing next to him. He indicated the shattered roof. 'Come on. We'd best go and see what's up there.'

'It's not going be pretty,' one man said.

No, Baron thought, and neither is our future if we don't stop Hunter.

The phone chimed again. Sighing at the intrusion, Baron pulled his cellphone out. The screen was blank. He heard the tone once more and slapped at his other pocket in confusion. He dug out a second phone. This one's screen glowed with a cold blue colour. As it rang it vibrated softly in his hand. Baron nodded to himself. It was the phone taken from Hunter when they'd snatched him off the street in Little Rock. On the screen the caller's name was displayed.

IMOGEN BALLARD

Baron pressed the green button. 'Hello?' he asked, deliberately muffling his voice with his free hand.

'Is that you, Joe? I . . . uh . . . I've been thinking. Things shouldn't end like this between us. We need to talk, Joe . . . I was just wondering if you'd come back to Maine when you're finished there.'

Baron breathed into the mouthpiece.

'Joe? Are you there? Can you hear me?'

Baron switched off the phone and dropped it back into his pocket. Maybe his future wouldn't be so grim after all, not now he'd found a new way to control Hunter.

CHAPTER 21

Some might say that my treatment of Sigmund Petoskey was excessive.

That would be a valid point of view, but I didn't look at it that way. Cold-bloodedly shooting an innocent woman in the back of the head *is* murder. The way I saw things, I was totally justified in executing him for his crimes. Pro-lifers would undoubtedly argue otherwise, but I wouldn't lose any sleep over Petoskey's violent death.

My friends didn't know about Louise's murder, so their reaction to me throwing Petoskey out the helicopter was stunned silence until I told them what he had done. Then both lamented that I hadn't saved a piece of his ass for them. With no time for ethical debate, I put the miserable bastard out of my mind and turned to something far more important to me. 'How are you holding up, Rink?'

'Still ticking, brother,' he said.

Rink has the type of mentality that should he lose all his limbs he'd still try to rip an enemy's throat out with his teeth. But he was only human, and despite his desire to go down fighting, he barely had the strength to keep his eyes open.

Leaning into the cockpit, I peeled back the dressing on his shoulder, concerned by what I might find. Luckily it wasn't a bullet wound as I'd first feared but a rip in his flesh. It was raw and angry looking. Someone had slapped on the rudimentary dressing, but it didn't look like the tear had been cleaned or treated. I could feel the heat radiating from Rink's body and knew that he was feverish.

'It's nothing, Hunter,' Rink said, pressing down the bandage to cover the wound. 'I ran into a goddamn tree branch, is all. Goddamn fool's trick, you ask me.'

'How'd they manage to get you?'

'That slimy little punk, Baron. There was a group of 'em that ambushed me, forced my Porsche off the road and into the swamp. Managed to take out some of them, but then Baron came from nowhere, hit me with a goddamn Taser. Before I could recover from that, a couple of others had me down and had my weapons stripped from me. I fought back, got free and ran full tilt into a freakin' tree. Almost impaled myself . . . was hung up there while Baron gave me another blast or two of his Taser. Then I must've been given a shot of somethin' 'cause the next I knew I was in that cellar having my ass kicked all over again.' The heat radiating from him now came from a different source.

'It's nothing to be ashamed of, Rink.'

'You reckon? Time was they wouldn't have taken me.' He swiped the cold sweat from his forehead.

Careful not to touch him anywhere it would hurt, I placed a comforting palm on his good shoulder. 'Not alive anyway. It's better that things turned out the way they did. At least this way you get a chance at payback.'

'He's a sneaky one, that Baron. We gotta keep an eye out for him in future, Hunter.'

Recalling the speed with which he'd shot at me – luckily with a blank cartridge – I knew that Baron could prove to be a deadly foe. But he wasn't my main concern at that moment. Another more potent killer was out there, someone more dangerous than ten of the likes of Baron. Tubal Cain was seeking my brother, but he was also standing between me and a reckoning with Kurt Hendrickson. I'd decided that Petoskey, for all his faults, had been correct about one thing: my argument now was with Hendrickson. He was the current force behind all our other enemies. Stopping him would fracture their alliance, weaken them, and then we could take them all out.

To Harvey, I said, 'Can this thing take us where we need to go?'

Harvey shook his head, indicating a dial on the controls. 'The chopper wasn't refuelled after travelling here. We're only good for a few more minutes, then we'll have to set down. But don't worry guys. I've got things under control.'

He piloted the helicopter towards a distant copse of trees, swooped over it and then set down in a clearing on the far side. At my estimation we were barely ten miles from the house where Rink had been held. Harvey indicated another, smaller helicopter resting in the moonlight. Harvey must have made his way here via this route, so the appearance of his personal craft was no real surprise.

'There could be a tracking device on this bird, so I suggest we don't hang around, guys.' Harvey clambered from the chopper, then went to help Rink out the other side. Grabbing the sniper rifle Harvey had brought with him, I decamped by way of the side door through which Petoskey had exited a few minutes earlier. When my friends were safely out of the way, I shouldered the stock and fired a few rounds into the engine housing. Apart from the clatter of shredding metal and the occasional spark there was nothing as dramatic as an explosion, but this helicopter wouldn't be capable of following us. A waste of a good machine, but anything to slow down Baron and the rest of his gang was a help.

Hendrickson's chopper was a Bell UH-1N Twin Huey, whereas Harvey's was nowhere near as flashy. His was the more familiar Bell Jetranger that was the mainstay of many commercial helicopter companies. It wasn't as big or as intimidating as the modified military aircraft we'd ditched, but it would get us where we were going. Harvey once told me all about his little pleasure craft, stating it could go for three hours and still have fuel in the reserve tank. At over one hundred miles per hour, it would get us to our destination with no need for a refill. Again Harvey took the pilot's seat, but unlike on the first trip I moved Rink into the back with me. As we lifted into the sky, Rink reached across and took my hand. 'Thanks for coming for me, brother.'

'Did you expect anything different?'

'You shoulda told the frog-gigging muthas to go fuck themselves . . . just like I said. You shoulda went after Cain. It's more important that you kill him. He won't stop until he's stripped the rest of John's hide from his back.'

'I couldn't do that without you beside me, Rink. Cain's unfinished business for the two of us, remember?'

He ran a palm down his face, lingering a moment just below his bottom lip. On Rink's chin was a livid white scar, a token of the last time we'd fought Tubal Cain. I had a similar scar but mine was only an inch or so from my heart. Cain had almost finished the two of us before we'd managed to stop him. So I wasn't kidding when I told him I wanted him there when next I faced the killer: it might very well take the two of us to stop him again.

'John's safely out of harm's way,' I said. 'Walter has him surrounded by armed guards. I think we should be proactive, take the fight to Hendrickson.'

From the front, Harvey called back. 'We should get Rink to a hospital is what we should do.'

'Told you,' Rink said. 'I'm fine. Let's just go get the fuckers and have done with it.'

'You need medical help and you need rest.'

'Need a stiff drink is what I need,' Rink grunted.

'Best I can do is this.' Harvey slung a drinking canteen back towards us and I snatched it out of the air. Carefully I dribbled tepid water into Rink's mouth. My big friend didn't have the strength to steady the canteen, didn't even attempt to lift his hands. Harvey was right. First stop was a doctor.

'Where's the nearest hospital?' I asked. It only then occurred to me that I'd no idea where on the Eastern Seaboard we were, let alone the location of a medical facility.

'South-west of here, we have a choice between Raleigh and Greensboro. We go north into Virginia, nearest city I can think of is Richmond.'

We were somewhere in North Carolina? That surprised me as my initial thought on waking earlier was that we were further north: Maryland perhaps.

Rink stirred, leaning forward in his seat so that Harvey could hear him. 'You think you can find Selwin, Gates County?'

'There's a hospital there?' Harvey asked.

'No. But there's a cute veterinarian that can patch me up.'

'That sounds about right.' I smiled. 'I always said you were a bloody hound dog.'

'Nah, Hunter. What you're thinking of is, I've got animal magnetism. That's why that pretty little vet will be over the moon to see me.'

'Where the fuck is Selwin?' Harvey's grumbling was followed by tapping on instruments and I guessed he was accessing a sat-nav system. A moment later the helicopter shifted and we began streaking due east.

'You gotta find somewhere just north of town. Moulder has her practice about a mile out.' Rink smiled at the memory of when he'd last been out at the veterinary centre. He closed his eyes, perhaps savouring the moment, and I waited and waited for them to open again. His soft snores told me I might have a long wait. I studied his fatigue-loosened features and a pang of melancholy went through me. Rink was now in his early forties, but never before had it looked like age was beginning to creep up on him. There were deep lines around his hooded eyes that I'd not noticed before, and even a few errant grey hairs peppered throughout his raven hair. Jesus, I'd always seen Rink as being invincible, so this was a real lesson. There were more than a few grey strands in my own hair now . . . a reason why I kept the damn stuff cut so short these days.

Using a lap-belt I strapped Rink into his seat, before clambering over and into the co-pilot position. Harvey nodded back towards our friend. 'He's OK, just sleeping,' I said.

'He needs more than a shot from a goddamn veterinarian. I think we should head for a hospital while he's out of it, get him some real help.'

'Ordinarily I'd agree, but do you think the big

155

guy would be happy if we did that? Probably he'd kick both our arses.'

'He's a stubborn son of a bitch.' There was only fondness in Harvey's words.

Normally it's me who's accused of being too stubborn, usually by Rink, but Harvey was right. Rink would see it as a personal failure if he was holding up our mission and I wasn't going to be the one to cause him any further shame than he'd already endured these past couple of days. 'Let's just go see Vet Moulder and get her opinion first.'

'That Rink, he seems to have a lady in every town.'

Yeah, but just like me he had never been lucky enough to find someone he could spend his impending old age with. Maybe it was my sigh of regret that swung Harvey's gaze upon me. He said, 'You should call her, you know.'

He wasn't talking about Vet Moulder.

When I didn't immediately respond, Harvey went on, 'She deserves more than a goodbye in the middle of the night, Hunter. That woman, she's been around for you this past year, like you've been for her. Just my opinion, but I don't think you should sever all ties.'

I thought that the best way to let Imogen get on with her life would be to do exactly that. Being around her was always going to be a reminder of how we'd both failed her sister. Phoning her wouldn't help.

Harvey's a handsome man. He has that very

black skin that's as smooth as silk, spread evenly over a finely shaped bone structure and a slightly aquiline nose. Yet, right now, his features were set, his lips stretched taut over his teeth. His face was almost skull-like in its intensity. It wasn't my failure to acquiesce in his opinion that made him angry. We shared a moment that was statically charged before Harvey looked at me. His eyes were twinkling with unshed tears. 'I should've looked out for Louise more than I did. I called her, told her to lay low for a while, but it wasn't enough, Hunter.'

'You couldn't know what was going to happen to her.'

'No. We *both* guessed what the consequences were. That's exactly my point, man. We should've done more, just like we should to keep Imogen out of this. No one around us is safe any more . . . *everyone* we care about is a target to these bastards.'

'They don't know about Imogen,' I said. But my argument was hollow. They'd found Walter's hideaway in the Adirondacks, so finding Imogen would be a piece of cake. Hell, all they had to do was Google her name and it would lead directly to her home: the problem with using it as the registered office of her internet business.

'Are you sure about that, Joe? You want to take that chance?'

OK, I thought, phoning her wouldn't help, but then again, it couldn't hurt either.

157

I touched my pocket before remembering that my phone had been taken from me along with my weapons. Having it with me had been a huge error of judgement, I feared. 'Can you patch me in from here, Harve?'

He was already on it. He passed me a satellite phone, hit a switch and then gestured at a set of headphones. I pulled them on, began tapping numbers. A long way up the coast, Imogen reached for her phone. 'Hello,' she asked, possibly frowning at the UNKNOWN CALLER display on her handset.

There was a momentary hitch in my voice, like I didn't know what to say. Jesus, I thought, this is exactly the type of scenario I didn't want Imogen to have to go through again. Finally I managed to say her name.

'Joe? Is that you?'

'There's a lot of noise here,' I said, adjusting the headset, 'can you hear me now?'

'Whose phone are you using?'

'It's Harvey's,' I said.

'What's wrong with yours? I couldn't hear you talking.'

'Just the sound in the chopper, I adjusted the volume.'

'No, I didn't mean just now. I meant when I rang you earlier.'

'You rang me?'

'Yes. You answered, I could hear you breathing, then you said hello.'

'Shit!'

'What's wrong, Joe?'

'What did you say, Imogen?'

'I can't remember.' She paused, trying to pull the threads of her memory together. 'I said that we should talk, asked you to come up here.'

'You mentioned Maine?'

'Uh, I can't remember. Joe, what's going on? Has this something to do with Walter's murder?'

I didn't have the time to explain. 'Imogen, I need you to get in your car and drive immediately to Machias. Don't stop for anyone. Go directly to the police station there and don't move. I'm going to get someone to come for you.'

'Joe? What the hell's going on?'

'There's no time. Do it. Get in your car now!'

Imogen wasn't the type to miss the subtext of my instructions. She was in extreme danger and knew not to argue. She'd survived being hunted by the Bolan twins, and had also managed to get away from Luke Rickard last year, but perhaps a third time would prove unlucky.

'OK, Joe,' she said.

'Good,' I said. 'Imogen . . .'

'What is it?'

'When this is over with, I'll come and find you.'

I caught an approving glance from Harvey. Knowing that she'd already be heading for her car, I ended the call and jabbed other buttons on the phone.

'You are supposed to be on your own, Hunter.'

That Walter knew without asking that it was me calling didn't surprise me. Maybe he'd been expecting it.

'I need you to send someone to pick up Imogen. I think she's been compromised. Hartlaub and Brigham,' I trusted them to get the job done, Hartlaub especially, 'send them.'

Give Walter his due, he didn't quibble. He merely asked where they should go and I directed them to the rendezvous at Machias. 'Keep her safe, Walter. Same deal for John. I'm still on the case at this end.'

'That was you in Little Rock, the crazy gunman who went after Sigmund Petoskey? That's an outstanding issue that could come back to bite you on your ass, son.'

'Don't know what you're talking about,' I said. 'Anyway, Petoskey's no longer a problem.'

'You killed him?'

'Not me. He took a wrong step out of a helicopter. It was the roof of the house he landed on that killed him.'

Walter chuckled into the phone, bloodthirsty son of a bitch that he was. 'What about Rink?'

'He's with me now.'

'How is he?'

'As ugly as ever.'

Walter chuckled again. I wouldn't be making jokes if there was anything seriously wrong with my friend. I told him about Baron, about Hendrickson, what had happened since our meeting at the lake house. Walter promised to dig up what they had on the ex-spook; on Hendrickson he didn't need to tell me much. 'Son, after what's gone on, we have enough to take Hendrickson down. You can concentrate on Cain.'

'That's not exactly true. You have only our testimonies on Hendrickson's involvement. It was Petoskey and Baron who kidnapped Rink, Petoskey who murdered Louise Blake. Petoskey's dead. You've no evidence to tie Hendrickson to any of it.'

'We could bring him in on a conspiracy charge.'

'Only for him to walk free again as soon as his attorney shows up.' I paused, glanced back at Rink who was still in an exhaustion-induced sleep. 'Look, I've got something to see to, but then I'll bring in Hendrickson myself. But I can't promise he'll be fit for court.'

'Bryce Lang was a good friend.'

Walter was giving me his blessing to do with Kurt Hendrickson what I wanted. Maybe he wanted to save taxpayers' money by negating the need for a lengthy trial.

CHAPTER 22

The Challenger 604 private jet took its single passenger back to Kurt Hendrickson. It landed at a private airstrip and was met by a contingent of armed men. Not that Tubal Cain was concerned about them; these men were here to protect Hendrickson from someone other than him.

Hendrickson was sitting in the rear of a Lincoln town car. As soon as Cain was inside, an instruction was given to drive. The sedan was like a boat on wheels, and it drove like one, albeit a boat gliding on a smooth lake. A bodyguard sat up front alongside the driver. Ushering him inside, Hendrickson had made room for Cain in the back. They sat side by side, but the bench seat was large enough that there was room for two others between them.

Neither man wore a happy face.

'When you are finished with Telfer, I want you to kill Joe Hunter slowly,' Hendrickson said. 'I want you to make the bastard suffer.'

The point was academic; that had always been Cain's intention.

'Problem?' Cain's damaged throat was handling words easier now that he was talking more regularly. Still, the sounds he made were like the rasp of steel on steel.

'Hunter and Rington escaped.'

'It doesn't matter,' said Cain. 'They were never going to give you Telfer's location anyway. It was a stupid plan to use them for that. You should have had both of them drugged and brought here to me.'

'It got my partner killed,' Hendrickson said. His head bowed over his steepled hands. Not that he was praying for his departed business associate. 'Maybe involving Hunter was a bad decision. If we hadn't plotted to get at Telfer through his brother, then perhaps Sigmund would still be alive.'

'Sigmund obviously messed up,' Cain said. Careless of Hendrickson's feelings, he added, 'Maybe it's best he died. He can't ruin things a second time.'

Hendrickson glanced sharply at him. Cain went on.

'If you hadn't taken Jared Rington, Hunter would still be unaware that we were after John. Isn't that what you told me, that he'd gone up north on a trip?'

'That was the info we had from the team we sent to Florida. Hunter wouldn't have had a clue where we'd taken Rington. He'd have still been in the dark if you hadn't slaughtered those CIA agents in the Adirondacks. My sources in law enforcement tell me the murders were immediately tied to you.'

'Yes,' Cain agreed. 'I have a certain recognisable flair. It's just a pity I missed Walter Conrad. Killing him would've compensated for the mess we now have to clean up.'

'Conrad's dead.'

'No. Not Conrad. He gave me the slip and I killed another man instead.' Cain tapped a hand to his jacket pocket. Hendrickson averted his gaze, having no wish to know what was in the madman's possession. 'Conrad must've come clean about my escape from Conchar. He must've been the one to tie my escape to you, and to send Hunter after you. Makes sense that Hunter should go after Petoskey first, does it not?'

'I'd been hoping that Hunter would make a try for him, that's why I dispatched a team to watch Sigmund's back.' Hendrickson shrugged. 'I still believe the plan would've worked. Hunter would've given us Telfer once he witnessed Rington being tortured.'

Cain sniffed. 'You obviously don't understand Joe Hunter.'

'He's an ex-counterterrorism soldier. I know he's good, but he's still only one man.'

'He's better than that.' Cain sat back in the seat, his head lolling on the headrest. His scarred throat punctuated his point. 'You should've had him brought here for me to deal with. By making these ridiculous plans you've over-complicated things. You helped me to escape from prison so that when Telfer is killed it would look like the act of a vengeful murderer. You'd have been above suspicion. Now you've ensured the finger of blame is pointed directly at you. You've messed up, Hendrickson, and I'm concerned that you could mess things up again.'

Cain turned and held Hendrickson's gaze. Hendrickson frowned. 'Don't threaten me, Cain. We're partners, remember?'

'I'm not threatening you . . . partner.' Cain patted Hendrickson on his knee. 'I'm taking charge of things.'

'In what respect?'

'In respect of *the planning*.' Cain smiled. 'We're going to keep things simple. I'm going to kill Telfer. You are going to bring Hunter to me.'

'I can't promise that I'll deliver him alive. Not after what he did to Sigmund.'

'Hunter won't let you kill him.'

'The team took him easily enough last time,' Hendrickson pointed out. 'He's only alive because Baron's orders were to torture Telfer's location out of him.'

'If Baron is that good, how did Hunter and Rington escape? He was one man, unarmed, against a team of your *best* hired killers. It sounds like Hunter allowed himself to be taken in order to find Rington. I'm only surprised he stopped at Sigmund. Baron and the others are lucky to be alive.'

'It sounds like you respect him.'

'Respect?' Cain tasted the word. 'Yes, I do. He stopped *me*, didn't he? What's not to respect?'

'He's an asshole,' Hendrickson snapped. 'He killed Sigmund.'

'Hunter was protecting his loved ones. How does that make him an asshole?' Cain squeezed Hendrickson's knee. 'You, Mr Hendrickson, are merely protecting your liberty and wealth. Your selfishness and greed killed Sigmund. Who does that make the better man?'

Hendrickson snorted. He removed Cain's hand from his knee. 'I take it that you don't respect me?'

'No.'

'But you're still prepared to work with me?'

'Yes.'

'So who does that make the better man?'

Cain's laughter sounded genuine.

'Touché, Hendrickson.'

Hendrickson's cellphone rang. By the look on his face he was pleased at the distraction.

'Baron?'

Cain listened to the one-sided conversation.

'You're on your way here? Good. Have the bitch picked up,' Hendrickson said. 'Then have her brought here as well. And, Baron . . . no mistakes this time.'

He snapped the phone shut. 'We're in business again,' he told Cain.

Cain sucked in his bottom lip.

'Turn the car around, Hendrickson.'

'Why?'

'I need the use of your jet.'

'Where are you going?'

'You're over-complicating things again. Play your games if you must but I'm going to get Telfer. It's just occurred to me how I can draw him out of hiding.'

'How?'

'Leave that to me.'

'Where are you going?'

'Do you have connections in England? I need to get into the country but in a way that bypasses security.'

'We've been smuggling people and contraband in and out of the UK for years.'

'In and out? That's good.' Cain touched the objects secreted in his pocket. 'I might be bringing back another keepsake.'

CHAPTER 23

If there was a way to turn back the clock, so that it was she and not Kate who'd died, Imogen would gladly have done so. Her younger sister had been shot by an assassin's bullet intended for her. But her sister could never be brought back and Imogen didn't want to die needlessly. The men threatening her life now had nothing to do with those who had been chasing her before, but they would be just as ruthless. Joe had warned her to run, and he wasn't one for hysterics. If Joe said run, he meant it.

She bundled a few belongings into her car, locked up her house, and headed for Machias without a look back. Joe's rented Audi was under a layer of snow a hand's-breadth deep and it was an indicator of what the roads would be like between her home and the highway. It would be slow going, but that would prove the same for anyone coming after her.

Taking things at a steady pace, she followed the road off the promontory, watching for tracks in the virgin snow. Those made by the CIA car that had whisked Joe away had been obliterated by the

168

blizzard that had blown unabated since they'd left. The slope was the most hazardous, but being from Maine, she was used to traversing a winter landscape and made the coast road without any drama. The ploughs had been through, but that must have been hours ago because the road was white and her tyres crunched through drifts where gaps in the forest had allowed the storm to dump all of its fury. There were short-cuts to the highway, but not in this weather. Her best bet was to follow the coast road all the way around the northern edge of Little Kennebec Bay and pick up the highway there for the short run into Machias. Joe had told her to go directly to the police. Machias had three different law enforcement offices, but she decided to present herself at the one on Valley View Road. Joe had been specific about that; it was just a pity he hadn't been as clear when he'd said goodbye.

She was confused.

From the way that he'd left with the CIA agents she'd thought he wasn't prepared to give their relationship the chance it deserved. Yet by ringing her he'd proven he did still care for her. He had called because she was in danger. He didn't have to be in love with her to do that. But, then, he had said he'd come find her. Did he want to give their relationship another chance or finish with her for good? Kate was always going to be a weight on both their shoulders, but she wanted Joe to put Kate behind him and love her for herself.

The snowfall was growing heavier. No, the

reason that her vision was becoming obscured was because tears had sprung into her eyes. She dashed them away with the sleeve of her coat, gritted her teeth, aimed for the highway, and only occasionally glanced at the revolver on the seat beside her.

Her brother Jake had been with Delta Force and later Arrowsake; Kate had been a NYPD officer, but, up until the incidents last year, Imogen had never been in a situation where firearms were necessary. She was a web designer and photographer. Christ, all she'd ever shot was pictures on a digital camera. However, following her kidnapping by Luke Rickard, Joe had taught her how to handle the revolver, having her shoot at paper targets he'd strung to the trees in her back yard. He'd told her to keep the gun handy at all times. On the seat beside her was about as handy as it could get.

The highway was mainly cleared of snow, but it was piled at each side in huge mounds. The trees were heavily laden, the lowest boughs hidden in the drifts. There was little traffic, but she tucked into the wake of a truck and followed its lights through the swirling storm. It became apparent that other road users had the same idea because another car tucked in behind hers and one behind that. She made it to Machias in just under an hour, following the road through town and over the Machias River and out towards the police office. Joe had promised that he'd send someone to collect her, but how would they get here in this storm? The same way the bad guys would, she realised, and glanced once more at the reassuring presence of the revolver beside her.

Flakes of snow drifted slowly across the road, caught on the breeze from a cross-street, as she waited for a traffic signal to turn green. On the sidewalks there were few pedestrians, but she watched a father trail two small boys on a sledge. The children were laughing and exhorting their dad to greater speed. They were approaching her car, and from his higher vantage the man would see her gun. She tucked it inside her coat. The man leaned down and grinned at her as he passed, a small-town gesture of friendship.

Imogen flapped him a brief wave of her hand.

She watched in her mirror as the man picked up speed, turning to run backwards as he yelled something at his cheering children. For a moment Imogen forgot about her worries in thoughts of children of her own. Could she imagine Joe Hunter hauling their kids along on a sledge? Then the tears were back. When next she checked in her mirror, the family had gone round a corner, but there was someone else on the sidewalk.

A man was walking quickly towards the rear of her car. He had his head tilted down against the weather, his collar turned up, both hands stuffed in his pockets. She had no idea where he'd come from, but suspected that he had climbed out of the vehicle two back in the line. She wondered if it was one of the two cars that had followed her trail along the highway. His head came up, and there was nothing of a small-town welcome in that glance.

She jerked her gaze up at the lights. Still on red. A bus crossed her path, slowed and angled for a turn past her car. The driver was taking things easy on the slushy surface, but even so the back end of the bus slewed slightly. The driver adjusted his approach, and began to creep around the corner. The lights changed, but Imogen could go nowhere yet. When she glanced in the mirror again, the man was passing the car behind hers. She touched the gas pedal, readying to take off.

Then something unexpected happened.

He yanked open the passenger door of the car behind and leaned in. Over the roar of the bus's engine Imogen didn't hear the bang of a gun, but she saw the flash of flame and the spray of blood that misted the interior of the car.

'Oh my God!' Caught in a panic, Imogen grabbed at the steering wheel, seeking a way around the rear end of the bus.

There was another flash inside the car behind, a second shot. Then the gunman stood up, and this time he was heading for her. The second car back suddenly peeled out, barrelling along the sidewalk and past the walking man. It screeched to a halt to Imogen's side, blocking her with its fender. Boxed in by the bus and the vehicle, she'd nowhere to escape to. Imogen let out a series of frightened cries, struggling to extract the revolver from her coat. The hammer snagged on the lining and she knew she'd never get to it in time. She cast a terrified glance at the car blocking her in, but couldn't make out the face of the driver.

Another prayer escaped her, and she saw the gunman reach for her door. Any second now he'd lean inside and shoot her. She tore at her coat, almost had the gun clear but it slipped from her fingers. The door began to swing open and Imogen screwed her eyes up in anticipation of a bullet in her head.

'Imogen,' a voice snapped.

She made a mewling sound, but reaction forced her eyes open.

A man with a scar on his lip and missing a chunk of eyebrow held an empty hand to her.

'Come with us now.'

Imogen was too terrified to recognise the face.

'It's me, Brigham. Joe sent us for you.'

The name Brigham meant nothing to her. But he'd spoken the magic word: Joe. She looked at him now with a mix of hope and revulsion for what he'd just done to the people in the other car. He read the horror in her face. 'If I hadn't stopped them, they'd have killed you. Now, come on, we're sure there'll be others.'

Afterwards, Imogen didn't recall being hauled out of her car, or being hustled into the government vehicle. Once she was down on the back seat, with Brigham covering her with his body, she sucked in a deep gulp of air, realising that she'd been holding her breath since she'd been grabbed.

Her heart thundered in her chest and she felt woozy, on the verge of passing out.

The government car bumped down off the sidewalk, weaving around Imogen's stalled vehicle and the back of the bus. There were faint shouts of consternation from within the bus as its passengers realised what they'd just witnessed. Imogen tried to sit up.

'Stay down,' Brigham hissed. 'I told you there might be others.'

'Those people . . .'

'Punks sent after you.' It was the man in the front who'd spoken. Now that she'd had a few seconds to think, Imogen recognised both men as the two who had taken Joe away from her. 'Looks like we made it here just in time.'

'How can you be sure?'

'We're good at our jobs. They're local scum, but they'd been sent orders to capture you by someone called Baron. Joe Hunter warned us that was going to happen.'

'Local scum! What if they—'

Brigham cut her off. 'We were listening in with a directional microphone. They were armed and they were following you, plotting how to take you down. We had to take them down first.'

Imogen was too confused to make any sense of it or the implication of their deaths. Was she complicit in murder? Should she bail out of this car at her first opportunity and run to the police for help? Or should she be thankful that the two

CIA agents had risked their own lives on her behalf? After all, it was Joe who had sent them. She shut up.

When Brigham finally allowed her to straighten up in the seat, they were beyond the town limits and heading for Machias Valley Airport. Imogen blinked at the snow-laden trees flashing by. Hartlaub glanced in his mirror at her. 'You OK?'

'I . . . I think so.'

'Good. Now sit back and relax. I think we're out of the fire for now.'

'For now?'

'Who knows when they might try again?'

Imogen ran trembling fingers over her face. 'Why are people always trying to kill me?' Even to her own ears she seemed on the verge of hysterics.

'That's what comes of having friends like Joe Hunter, I guess.'

CHAPTER 24

Selwin, North Carolina, was about a mile to the south of Rene Moulder's veterinary practice. Between her tiny clapperboard house with its purpose-built annexe and the small town, the countryside was dominated by thick woodland, interspersed with the occasional cattle-dotted meadow. It was into one such meadow that Harvey put down the Bell Jetranger and from there we transferred Rink to the rear of the vet's flat-bed truck. I guessed that in the past Rene had utilised it to cart away sick or dead livestock, so it was big enough to accommodate an ox like Rink. I crouched in the back with him while Harvey clambered into the cab with the woman. Rene set off for her practice, taking it easy over the rutted dirt trails.

Rink had come round from his deep slumber, but he wasn't looking much better for the rest. His usually tawny skin had a grey tinge that made him look a decade older. That said, he was his usual self in other ways. 'What do you make of Rene? Told you she was a pretty little thing, didn't I?'

We'd found her telephone number en route and a quick call was all it took to arrange the pick-up. Rene Moulder hadn't even questioned why we were in her neighbourhood or why Rink required immediate attention. She came across as being a no-nonsense type, a professional who just got down to business. Rink was right about something else: she was a pretty little thing. She stood only a fraction of an inch over five feet – albeit in flat work shoes – but was curvy without looking frumpy in her tie-dye skirt and gaudy alpaca-wool cardigan and knitted hat pulled low to her ears. She'd big brown eyes and apple cheeks, ruddy without the application of make-up. It was dark and cool out, and someone rousted from their bed would be feeling the chill, so her attire made sense.

Because I'd explained over the phone that Rink was in a state of undress, she'd brought with her a couple of heavy duvets that she'd wrapped round him. She was brusque, but cajoling as she'd made him comfortable.

'I barely know her yet,' I said, 'but already I like her.'

'Yeah,' Rink murmured into the folds of the duvets. 'Would've liked to have gotten to know her better myself. Shit happens, though.'

I didn't know how Rink and Rene had met; there seemed to be many women in Rink's past, and it never failed to amaze me how they all were happy to see him when he turned up again.

'She's an old girlfriend?'

'Old commanding officer,' he corrected.

I knew that Rene Moulder had been no part of Arrowsake while we were there, and before that Rink had been an Army Ranger, so it was unlikely he knew her from those days either. He must have read my confusion because he expounded, 'She was a medic attached to our troop. She was a major . . . out of bounds to a lowly grunt like me.'

'So she went from humans to animals after she got out?'

'Animals complain less,' Rink pointed out. 'And their gratitude is unconditional.'

'So you won't be expecting a belly rub after-wards?'

He chuckled. But the act seemed to send a flare of pain through him and he shut up.

'They were kind of rough on you, I suppose.'

'Fuckin' Baron,' Rink growled. 'I'm looking forward to a little *me* time with him.'

Rink told me how Baron had got the drop on him with a Taser. Having been taken to the mansion, Baron had reintroduced the Taser to him to force him into recording the message that was subsequently played back to me in the warehouse at Little Rock. Baron, it seemed, enjoyed causing pain.

'You know something, brother? I was pleased when that little punk left to go over to Arkansas. I've never known a man who could hurt you so bad without killing you. But at the same time, I knew it meant the bastards had got you.'

178

'Well, you know different now. We planned for them to take me. It was the only way I could think of to find you before it was too late. Harvey wasn't sure it'd work, but, well, here we are.'

'Some plan. Left a hell of a lot to chance, brother.'

'Worked though, didn't it?'

He laughed again and this time fought through the pain. 'Fuckin' Baron, I think he broke my ribs.'

It was obvious from the multiple bruises on his torso that Rink had been subjected to more than just a stun gun. There were burns, a number of them, but they were outnumbered tenfold by the grazes and haematomas.

'I'll save a piece of his arse for you.'

'No need for saving anything,' Rink said. 'I'm coming with you.'

'Rink, you're not in any state for it, man.'

'Frog-giggin' motherfuckers won't be enough to stop me.'

'Rink,' I said, trying to make him see reason. 'You need to rest. You need to get well again. If me and Harvey get ourselves killed, we're going to need someone who can finish the bastards for us. That isn't going to happen if you get injured again.'

'I'm good, Hunter.'

'Sure you are,' I agreed, 'but you need to be better.'

Rink scowled at me, but then he adjusted the duvet round his chin. He touched that white scar. 'Yeah,' he rumbled.

We pulled into the front yard outside Rene Moulder's house. It was quaint, and despite her professional brusqueness, I could see that she'd lavished much care on her home. There was nothing brusque about the paint job that had decorated the house. It reminded me of the house in that Calamity Jane movie, when she tried to get in touch with her feminine side. It should have looked twee with the flowers painted over the door lintels, but it didn't. It looked, well, homely. In contrast the annexe was a utilitarian building: white, with a shingled roof, large blacked-out window in front and a door on which the venetian blind had been lowered. Rene led us to the latter building while Harvey and I supported Rink between us. Sweat was pouring off him before we could get him laid on top of an examination table.

'Smells like dogs in here,' Rink muttered.

'Then you should feel right at home,' Rene said. She ushered Harvey and me through a connecting door and into her house. 'I've enough to be getting on with. You know how to boil a kettle, gentlemen?'

'You want us to bring clean towels?' Harvey asked.

'He isn't pregnant.' She waved us towards a kitchen. 'Go make yourselves coffee and something to eat. I've enough with one patient, I don't want you two fainting out of hunger, as well.'

There was no hint of a Mr Moulder in residence. The interior of the house was as girly as the outside. Maybe Rene enjoyed the contrast after working in the stark confines of an examination room all day. Harvey and I moved about the kitchen, taking things easy, feeling like a couple of lunks as we fixed a sandwich and a pot of coffee. Sorted with food and drink, we finally sat on chairs padded with gingham-covered cushions, and tried not to make a mess on the pale lemon tablecloth decorated at the edges with blue forget-me-nots. Talk about a clash: I'd never felt so out of place.

When we'd done eating, we cleaned up and put the dishes away, but I refilled my coffee mug. I stuck my head through the connecting door and checked on Rene's progress. She had Rink's jeans and boots off, but there was nothing intimate about the way she ran her hands over his body. It was brisk and professional, checking him for breakages and internal damage. Rink's eyes were open, but he was staring into middle space and wasn't even aware I'd popped in. Rene had already dressed the ragged cut on his shoulder and cleaned up many of his other grazes. Empty syringes lay in a kidney dish on a counter; antibiotics, I presumed, that had already been administered.

'Does that hurt?' I heard her ask him.

'It does when you jab me with your knuckles, goddamnit!'

'Aw, quit complaining. Some soldier you are, whining like a little girl.'

I grinned, crept back out of the room and closed the door silently. Harvey was watching me.

'Sounds like Rink's going to be fine.'

'I'm sure he is. You made the right call, though, Harve. He needed looking after and Rene's the right person for the job.'

'She's a tough one, I'll give you that. She'll need to be to keep Rink flat on his back for a day or two.'

'Rink will thank us once we get back.'

Harvey rumbled out a laugh. 'You good to go?'

'I think it's best that we leave while Rink's otherwise engaged, huh?'

We slipped out of the front door, and rather than take Rene's pick-up, we jogged back to where we'd left the Jetranger.

Dawn was breaking.

We took off with the first rays of daylight refracted on the windshield, turned north for Virginia and headed for our date with Kurt Hendrickson.

CHAPTER 25

Tubal Cain was also high in the sky.

The Challenger 604 jet had taken him as far as Newark, New Jersey, where, posing as a crew member, he'd boarded a second airplane for the international flight over the Atlantic. For the last twenty minutes or so, the plane had been in descent, huge billowing clouds obscuring the approach to Manchester International Airport in the north of England. In his previous life as a member of the US Secret Service Cain had had occasion to visit the British Isles, but this was his first time this far north. The plane circled for its final descent. When the aircraft touched down, Cain was waiting by the cargo hold doors until the baggage handlers arrived to offload the passengers' suitcases, then blended with them as they transported the bags to the waiting carousels. With that done, it was a simple task for Cain to make himself scarce. Within twenty-five minutes of touching down, he was in the back of a car driven by one of Hendrickson's UK contacts.

It had always been a possibility that he'd be approached by security, and although his papers would have passed scrutiny, his weapons would not. Therefore, he opened the case on the back seat of the car and studied its contents. The replacement weapons were exactly as he'd requested.

There were three knives – the main tools of his trade.

Each was a different size and weight. The first was similar to a box-cutter but with a fixed blade. The next was a Recon Tanto like the one he'd employed against the marshal's back in Montana when his wild goose chase had led him to Jeffrey Taylor. The final one, the most unwieldy, but terror-invoking, was a Bowie knife with a blade more than a foot long and as broad as his palm.

He smiled in satisfaction, then turned his attention to the gun. It was a Walther P99, with polymer frame and steel slide, and internal striker as opposed to a hammer. The gun was the modified model designed to take a box magazine of 15 × .40 Smith and Wesson rounds. There were four magazines in total. Sixty bullets: enough to start a small war if need be. He slapped one of the magazines into the gun, racked the slide, noted the *chamber loaded* indicator on the side registering that the gun was good to go. As was he.

The driver knew enough to keep his eyes forward, happy to have as little to do with Cain as possible. Cain only conversed with the man enough to get to where he wanted to go; everything else he needed was in a folding leather wallet he found beneath the spare ammunition. While he'd been flying over the Atlantic, Hendrickson's people had been busy gathering the necessary information. He could have done it himself, but anything that speeded up the process was good by him.

The driver took the car out along the M60 northern ring road, past the Trafford Centre shopping mall, before picking up the M602 through the Greater Manchester city limits, past Eccles and Salford and into the town centre. Joining the A6, the driver passed through the district of Ardwick towards Longsight. Taking a left, he nosed into a housing estate, a mix of council houses and private rented flats. At the end of the road was waste ground and beyond that the main railway line into Piccadilly Station.

The driver brought the car to a halt. 'There's a left turn up there, takes you back into the estate. You want me to drive in, mate?'

'Here will do nicely, driver,' Cain said, distributing his newly acquired weapons about his body. He checked the wallet, saw some sterling cash inside, but didn't deem it appropriate to tip the man. He shoved the wallet into an inside pocket of his jacket.

'Take this.' The driver handed back a mobile phone. 'It's pre-programmed. Give me a call when you need to arrange collection.'

Cain dropped the phone in an outer pocket.

'Take it easy,' said the driver. 'Rough neighbourhood, this.'

Cain didn't know if the man was being sarcastic or not. English wit was lost on him sometimes. He got out of the car and closed the door behind him. He stood on the pavement – it wasn't called a sidewalk over here – and watched as the driver spun the car in the road and headed off. Cain wore a waterproof jacket and pulled on a cap: not so much as a disguise, but more against the damp chill that swept down the street. He couldn't remember being in the UK when it wasn't damp and chilly.

It was a school day, he was sure, but there were still a couple of kids hanging about on old bicycles, dressed in a uniform of tracksuit bottoms and hooded sweatshirts. They couldn't have been older than ten or eleven years old, yet they stared at him with eyes as hard as those of the patrons of Fort Conchar. They'd made him as a stranger within seconds. Cain didn't bother about that: as long as the local police weren't as perceptive.

Ignoring the young hoods, he strode along the street and took the left Hendrickson's man had indicated. Here he found old-style tenement flats. Alleyways ran between the buildings. He checked numbers on plaques on the walls; saw the building he was looking for. Good enough, he thought, and angled over to an alleyway on the opposite side. This one dead-ended at a corrugated sheet metal wall to dissuade pedestrians from crossing the rail tracks. It was the home of discarded junk, broken bottles and human waste judging by the smell.

186

Standing in the mouth of the alley, he surveyed the tenement opposite him, allowed his gaze to climb a couple of storeys and saw a window with the drapes closed. Didn't look like anyone was home. Good enough again. He would come back later, as he'd always planned.

CHAPTER 26

Rink was in good hands. Rene Moulder would return him to full health within a day or two, and we'd made the right decision to get him help. On the other hand, it felt weird heading off on a mission without my friend watching my back. Harvey Lucas was no one's second best, and I was thankful that I had a soldier of his calibre along with me. But, for all that Harvey was strong, fit and highly capable in a fight, we didn't share the same symbiosis as I did with Rink. It came from years of working closely together in the field, where we could second-guess each other's intention without having to verbalise our thoughts. Harvey was one for questions. Me, I was more the type to allow action to speak for itself.

I had to be blunt why I wasn't calling in CIA assistance from Walter, or any other of the agencies.

'I don't intend arresting the bastard, Harve. I'm going to put a bullet in his face.'

'For what happened to Louise, I'm with you. But do you really think you're doing the right thing. I mean . . .'

188

'It will make me a murderer? OK, I have to admit, it doesn't sit well with me. But when I think of the alternative, I'll accept it. Hendrickson has already tortured Rink, murdered Louise, and is trying to kill my brother. It's better that I stop the prick than allow him to go through with his plans. If I pass on my responsibility, that makes me a coward.'

Harvey rolled his head at that.

'I'll understand if you don't want anything to do with it, Harve.'

'Yeah,' he said. 'But then that would make *me* the coward. I'm coming with you, man.'

We were in a suburb of Richmond, Virginia, on the northern shores of the James River, looking at an anomalous structure. In keeping with his love for mansion-style houses, Kurt Hendrickson lived in a Tudor hall originally built in Lancashire, England, in the late fifteenth century, but bought at auction in the early 1920s and transported here and reconstructed by someone with more money than altruism. There were other buildings of this nature in the vicinity, but whereas they'd been given to the state as museum pieces, Hendrickson's home was strictly a private residence. The onus was on *private*. The Tudor hall sat at the heart of its own estate, within a walled enclosure. Dotted along the stone walls, alongside plaques relating the history of the house, were signs that warned against trespass, and advised that security guards patrolled the grounds. Good of Hendrickson to forewarn us.

We were in a rental car, parked on a rise just under a mile to the west of the building, using binoculars to study the black and white façade. Nearby the James River rumbled over rapids.

'Hendrickson's security is one thing,' Harvey pointed out. 'What about the cops?'

Kurt Hendrickson was almost certainly under the scrutiny of the law enforcement community. There would be FBI, ATF, DEA and other agencies all with an interest in what he was up to. His home would be under twenty-four-hour surveillance. That could cause more of a problem than any of the hired guns Hendrickson had at his beck and call. The last thing I wanted was for them to hear the gunfire and storm the compound before I was finished.

'We'll have to make sure that we aren't seen or heard.' For emphasis I tapped the hilt of my Kabar knife.

'Shit,' Harvey said. 'I never did take that mail order Ninja course.'

We shared a grim smile.

Many surveillance teams have an ingrained weakness. They're alert to anything out of the ordinary, and usually expect any nefarious activity to be conducted under the concealment of night. So we would go in now, calm and controlled, while the sun blazed in the heavens.

Hendrickson was home. We'd already made sure of that on an earlier drive-by. We'd been lucky in that we'd been passing the front gate just as his limousine had been sweeping up the drive towards the house. Parking alongside the road, we'd wandered back, as if interested in the signs depicting the hall's history, and spied Hendrickson getting out of the limo and jogging inside. In the meantime his limousine hadn't moved again.

Harvey was driving and he sent the rental towards Hendrickson's estate. We passed other wealthy residences, traversing streets named after English towns and hamlets. Big money area, but I'd expect to find someone like Hendrickson nowhere else. Some of the other houses had gates and walls, like they were the domains of robber barons, but none were as well protected as Hendrickson's. On reaching the boundary wall it hadn't shrunk from the eight feet tall it had been first time we drove by. There were ingress points dotted around the estate, but all had been locked tight apart from the front gate. It was electronically controlled and covered by CCTV cameras. Easiest way in, I decided, would be over the wall.

We did a half-circuit of the estate, turned round and headed back again, watching for anything that would indicate a surveillance point. Where the geography allowed for hidden observers we found none. There was always the possibility that remotely controlled cameras had been erected, but that also meant that the response time of those watching would be slower than if they'd been parked nearby and ready to descend on Hendrickson en masse. I had no intention of spending any unnecessary time inside, so thought I could be out again before a response team arrived. I indicated that Harvey park the rental in the mouth of a tree-lined side road.

Harvey would be my spotter, and my guardian. We clipped on the Bluetooth microphone/earpieces and switched on the mobile phones we'd purchased earlier in the day. Harvey readied the sniper rifle he'd used when covering Rink and me in our escape from Baron and his men. I had my SIG primed, but unless it was absolutely necessary I wouldn't be using it. Like I said, calm and controlled was the order of the day; I had to get in and out again without raising too much fuss.

Making a ladder of his bent knee and cupped palms, Harvey boosted me up and on to the wall. I caught his rifle and placed it on the wall next to me, before reaching for Harvey's arms and hauling him up and over. He landed cat-footed and I passed down the rifle. In the next instant, I was in the grounds, Harvey had set up behind the base of a tree and I was racing across the sculptured garden towards the house.

We were taking a hell of a chance, but I'd learned that sometimes the best approach was the least expected. A team of Navy Seals or SAS troopers would have approached in a totally different – read cautious – manner, but when an assault was down to only one or two men, fast and fearless was best. Unlike the charade I'd played in Little Rock, there'd be no shooting blanks into the sky this time.

The lawn was springy underfoot, and I could smell the loamy aroma of turned earth. Something else too: diesel fumes. From some distant side of the grounds came the competing put-put-put and high-pitched whine of a sit-on-and-ride mower. I'd been hoping for this, because when there were groundskeepers on site the likelihood that anyone was paying attention to any of the security measures was lessened. In keeping with the Tudor hall, the grounds had been designed to evoke a formal English garden. I utilised each tree, bush and flowered arch as I came nearer to the house. Behind me, Harvey too would be moving closer, keeping me in sight.

Besides the 'murder' question, there was another moral conflict to contend with here. I'd read files on Kurt Hendrickson, knew he was a piece of shit that I'd no qualms about killing, but what of others inside that house? He had no family listed, but there would be staff members innocent of his criminal dealings. Maids, cleaners, cooks, gardeners: I could come across any of them at any time, and whereas I wouldn't pause to take out anyone with a weapon who even looked at me cockeyed, I'd have to be careful. I didn't want to hurt any of them, but neither could I allow them to raise the alarm.

I made it to the western corner of the house. There I paused, pressing my back to the wall, hidden from the view of anyone coming out the front door by the black beams that interspersed the whitewashed panels. I freed my Ka-bar and readied myself. Then I sneaked a look through one of the windows. I could see a dining room. Chandeliers, wooden floor, large round table like something King Arthur would preside at. No Hendrickson, though. I moved on. The dining room was large enough to encompass this entire wing of the house, so I didn't bother peering inside again. I went round the side of the building, passing a small fleet of vehicles arranged on a space laid to gravel.

At the back of the house I found that another gravel path snaked away into the gardens, while a right-angle spur led unerringly to a back porch. The sound of the lawn mower was much louder here. Crouching below the window ledges, I headed for the porch. Above the sound of the mowing machine I detected another buzz; this one made by two men engaged in chatter. Cigarette smoke puffed from the porch. Some of Hendrickson's guards had sneaked off for a quick drag while he was engaged elsewhere in the house. At least I hoped that they were guards, considering what I planned to do.

'I've lost you, Hunter.' Harvey's voice was a whisper through the Bluetooth set.

'Hold your position. I'm going in.'

'I'll be waiting.'

I continued towards the porch, taking it slowly.

Another torpedo of blue smoke shot into the air, followed a moment later by the butt-end of a cigarette that arched towards the garden.

'Better not leave that there. The boss is particular. He sees that and you'll be wearing your balls in a sling.'

'Jesus Christ,' a second voice moaned. 'It's not like I've emptied a goddamn trashcan on the lawn.'

I no sooner heard the exchange than a man followed the direction of the cigarette butt. I flattened myself to the wall, watching as he retrieved the stub. He searched around for some loose earth, dug a hole with his fingertip and then inserted the tab into its grave. He scuffed earth over the evidence with the sole of his boot. There was a click and a thump as the second man made his way back inside. I glanced around: no one else in sight. I stepped out from my hiding place.

The smoker had his back to me. He was tall and square shouldered, dressed in a polyester suit and scuffed rubber-soled shoes. Didn't look like either a maid or cook to me. He wasn't finished concealing the cigarette. I saw him duck down and brush more dirt over the incriminating hole, probably stalling before returning to his duties. As he crouched, his jacket rode up on his hip. There was a gun clipped to his belt. That made up my mind.

As the man stood, brushing soil from his fingertips, I moved on him. I slipped my Ka-bar into my belt so both hands were free. Moving low so

195

that he didn't catch me in his peripheral vision, I raced towards him. I caught him just as he was turning back to the house, looped one hand under his jaw and grabbed at his opposite shoulder. My other hand I latched on to his hair, yanking him backwards as I stamped into the soft flesh at the back of his right knee. Twisting him as he fell, I jammed him face first into the lawn, stifling his shout of alarm. Then dropping to my knees, straddling his lower back, I hauled up and back and heard the resulting crack of his spine. I allowed him to flop down, inert. His nose was inches from where he'd concealed the cigarette butt in the earth, and I wondered if his final living sensation would to be to smell the tobacco he'd planted.

Rolling the man on his back, I saw his face for the first time, and was surprised to find that I knew him. He was one of the men who'd survived the breakout when I'd liberated Rink from the house in North Carolina. He'd stood alongside Baron, ineffectively aiming a gun at us as we'd taken off in the Bell UH-1N helicopter. If he was here, then it stood to reason that Baron might be here too. Better and better: the opportunity to finish two of my enemies at the same time.

Of course, the stakes had just risen tenfold. Despite downplaying Baron's abilities earlier, I knew he wasn't going to be easy to kill. Indeed, he might take me out first. His presence made me wonder about Imogen. Had she made it safely to Machias as I'd hoped, and had Hartlaub and

Brigham successfully picked her up? Surely Baron couldn't have got to Maine, snatched her and then travelled back here in the time we'd been over at Rene Moulder's place? No, I decided, it wasn't possible. I tried to put Imogen out of my head, but it wasn't easy. Since rescuing Rink I'd been pretty single-minded, but now that she'd intruded on my thoughts, Imogen wasn't going away.

I gave myself a mental shake. I remembered thinking once that I couldn't allow a pretty face to distract me from my mission. On that occasion the face had belonged to Imogen's sister, Kate. The reminder was equally valid now. I bent and grabbed the dead man's ankles, dragged him across the lawn and shoved him between two large bushes. Then I set to my main agenda. Kill Hendrickson and Baron. Then kill Cain. Otherwise no one I cared for was ever going to be safe.

CHAPTER 27

Jennifer Telfer was a pretty woman. A little thicker around the waist and thighs than Tubal Cain preferred in the female form, but she had an excuse. Bearing two kids had left its mark on her body as it did for many mothers. He watched as she walked from the black taxi to the front doors of her tenement building. She was laden down with six plastic carrier bags full of frozen food. Cheap brand name on the bags. The weight of the bags made her stoop and he could detect the strain in her face and the cords of her neck. Her hair was swept up and knotted at the back, a mother-of-pearl clip holding it in place. Beneath her lightly tanned skin he could see the fine line of her mandible, the high cheekbones, and the curves of her orbital sockets. He looked beyond the flesh, judging the bone structure, knew that her cranium would be a fine trophy.

Jennifer entered through a glass door smudged by thousands of handprints. The interior of the building was deep in shadow, but within seconds a spill of light fell across her as the doors of an elevator swept open. Jennifer stood aside, making way for an old man. They exchanged a nod and a couple of words then Jennifer stepped inside, placing the bags down gratefully. She looked out as the doors began to close. She seemed to have straightened, looking even prettier now that the effort had disappeared from her features.

From his hiding place, Cain watched as the old man came out on to the street. He didn't even look Cain's way, just bent at the waist and set off with a determined stride, as though conscious of stepping on cracks and inviting bad luck to fall upon him. When the old man was out of sight, Cain moved out of the alleyway and across the road. He shouldered his way through the palm-smudged glass door and into the foyer of Jennifer's building. The gloom wasn't so bad once he was inside, most of it down to the effect of the leaden sky on the glass doors. Opposite him the elevator doors had closed but the mechanism still groaned as it delivered its passenger to the upper floor. He made instead for a stairwell. The stairs were filthy, mud-stained and streaked with other things Cain shuddered to imagine. He went up as quickly as he could, pushed through on to a landing and saw the door to Jennifer's flat closing. There followed a rattle of deadbolts and chains.

Cain shrugged, went back down the stairs.

The children weren't home yet, so it was too soon at any rate. He left the building, made his way back across the road and took up position again. Then he thought, To hell with this! Jennifer wasn't going anywhere. She'd be busy unloading her budget-priced shopping into her freezer. She'd be preparing a meal for when the children got in from school. Maybe she'd tidy up the house a little, or read a novel or watch some daytime TV. He didn't have to stand in this crappy alley all day long.

He walked back out through the estate.

Manchester was a city with many faces. After a bomb was detonated by the IRA, it led to a revamp of the city centre, but here where the normal people lived things still looked a bit like the Bronx did in the 1970s. The only thing that shattered the time-slip illusion was the profusion of satellite TV dishes bolted to the sides of the buildings. Some of the poorer households, where he guessed it was a struggle to put food on the table, weren't without the dishes either. That told him a lot about the people here.

Out on the main road things looked better. There were semi-detached Edwardian and Victorian-era houses with tiny gardens at the front. Parking was a problem; these roads had never been designed with such a number of vehicles in mind. It made him yearn for the wide open spaces of the roads he was familiar with back home. Most of the cars belonged to mothers waiting to go collect their brats from school. Soon enough the rush would be on. He crossed the road – jaywalking wasn't an issue here – and approached a café. More accurately it was a tea shop, as the sign proclaimed.

He pushed inside, a bell announcing his arrival, and caught a young woman picking off a hangnail. She perked up at sight of him, offered a gap-toothed smile.

'Hi,' he said. 'Do you serve coffee on your menu?'

'Yeah, of course. Come and sit down, over here by the heater. Mug of milky or water?'

Milky or water?

'Uh, is a "milky" the same as a latte?'

'Same thing but about two pounds cheaper,' the woman said.

'Sounds good to me.' Cain walked to the table she'd indicated. Beside it was a convection heater that was welcoming after his stroll in the damp air. He held his hands over it while the woman wiped down the table. Judging by the state of the cloth, it would have been better to leave it as it was. The woman bustled off to make his drink, straightening the ties on her apron. He studied the menu that had quite obviously been designed and printed on a home computer. He was bewildered by the food on offer. What the hell was a *barm cake*?

He gazed around the tea shop: six tables, mismatched chairs, floral wallpaper, old black and white prints on the walls. There were no other customers so he studied the prints. The neighbourhood didn't look that different now than it had ninety years ago: just the satellite dishes and more cars. As he looked to where the woman worked, he saw her heading over with his mug of milky coffee.

'Have you had a chance?'

We both speak English, but it isn't the same language at all, he thought.

At his blank look, she said, 'The menu. Did you get a chance to read it?'

'Uh, yeah,' he said, tapping the menu. 'I'll have one of these.'

'Sausage bap? OK, coming right up. Will there be anything else?'

Cain hadn't realised he'd been staring at the woman's hand. Where she'd pulled the hangnail loose, he could see a bright strip of red was showing through. He was picturing how much further he'd have to dig to find the bone. Yes, there was something else he wanted but he had to fight the urge to take it. He shook his head, lifted his milky coffee and tried not to grimace against the sickly sweet taste. As much as he'd have liked to take a bone from this woman he couldn't afford the problems it might incur. He was here for Jennifer Telfer and must not allow his urges to control him. He concentrated on getting the coffee down.

His sausage bap arrived. Links of sausage, sliced and placed in a bun. Some sort of brown sauce had been smeared on them. It was actually delicious and he wolfed it down.

Through the windows he saw that the traffic flow had picked up. He glanced at his watch. Three thirty p.m. 'Are the schools due to get out?'

The woman squinted at her own watch. 'Yes.'

He approached the counter. Coming out to face him, the woman said, 'We don't get many Americans round here. What brings you to Longsight?'

'The delicious sausage baps,' he said, and smiled. He handed over a ten-pound note and got change direct from the pocket in her apron. A jar on the counter said 'tips'. He rattled the coins into the jar. 'Maybe they'll bring me back another day and I can sample some *other* local delights.'

The woman laughed. She thought he was flirting. Let her think what she likes, Cain reflected. If she knew what he was really hinting at she would have run away screaming.

'Well . . . if you need a guide, you know where to come.'

Cain winked at her. 'Bet on it.'

'I'll hold you to that.' The woman pulled her cloth from her apron, sashayed so that they bumped hips. Her laughter was throaty, but more from too many cigarettes than anything sexy. Cain allowed his hand to trail across her hip and down her lower back, as if guiding her around him. She never felt the swish of the box-cutter as he moved past her.

Later she'd note that one of the ties of her apron was much shorter than the other, and perhaps she'd reappraise her meeting with the handsome Yank, but for now Cain smiled as he pocketed his trophy. At the door he turned back. The woman was bending over his table, cocking her hip provocatively and peering doe-eyed over her shoulder. To Cain she resembled a five-buck whore. Jeez, he thought, all bets are off. Still, he offered a smile and a wave, and she grinned back, showing him the gaps in her teeth.

He left the tea shop, wondering if she could eat an apple through a birdcage without opening the door. He chuckled at the image, then let it go. There were more important things to consider. Along the roadside, the parking spaces had freed up and further down the street came the first drift of children in school uniforms. He wondered if he'd recognise John Telfer's children when he saw them.

CHAPTER 28

'**I**'m in.'

Harvey confirmed my whispered message. I stood just inside the back door of the Tudor hall, peering along a narrow vestibule. Inside, the walls were white. Ancient wood along the skirting and picture rails was as dark as ebony. The floor was wood, but a runner of carpet had been laid down the middle, deadening any footfalls. I could almost smell the history embedded in the fabric of the old building. Fleetingly I wondered if this house had known bloodshed in its time in Lancashire. Had it been used as a base during the Wars of the Roses, or witnessed conflict between Roundheads and Cavaliers? Or would this be the first time it had known violent death in its six hundred years?

I took out my knife as I set off along the vestibule, timing my breathing with my steps. On my right I saw a double door that led into the large dining room. I ignored it, continued, and found myself in an entry hall near the front of the house. On my left was a stairway that switched back on itself twice where it met the landings of the upper storeys. There was a man dressed not unlike the one I'd killed outside. His suit was grey, and his shoes buffed to a bright gleam. His hair was so short that his scalp showed through at the crown. He was cleanly shaven. The hands that fiddled at the edges of a newspaper were well manicured. He was the meet-and-greet guy, but also the one who halted any unwanted visitors who made it through the gates. The Galil machine gun hanging from the arm of his chair told me so.

Before moving on him, I listened. There were the sounds of activity further to my left, floorboards creaked overhead, somewhere deeper in the house I heard a buzz of conversation but I couldn't make out what was being said. One voice momentarily rose in volume, and I guessed that would be Kurt Hendrickson making his position known. No one other than the door guard was in close proximity. I strode across the floor. The man wasn't hard-wired to expect an attack from within. In fact, he glanced at me, and my unfamiliar face didn't at first register. By the time he did a double take, I was in position. I clamped my left hand over his mouth, stuck my Ka-bar under his ear and rammed upwards. I lifted him bodily out of the chair, resting his weight against my chest to stop his heels drumming on the hardwood planks. The newspaper fluttered to the floor. He died within seconds and not a sound announced my presence. I dragged the man across the hall and pushed him deep inside a closet, wiped my knife on his suit. Next I backtracked, straightening the rucked carpet and settling his chair, I slung the Galil over my shoulder; maybe I'd need it if things went to shit.

The sounds of conversation drifted to me again. The voice I'd assumed belonged to Hendrickson had grown louder, like he wasn't a happy man. If I had my way, his day would go even further downhill. I followed the voice. The house was best described as rambling. Beyond the entrance hall was another staircase. A second vestibule – this one with low ceilings and doors barely taller than I was – led into the central portion of the house, where I guessed there'd be a kitchen: that was where the raised voice originated. I scanned the other end of the house. Someone walked along a corridor and into a room, closing the door behind them. In the brief moment I'd seen the figure, I noted that it was a woman. Ignoring her, I turned quickly down the narrow vestibule towards the source of the voice.

In my earpiece Harvey whispered, 'Status?'

'Two down. I'm heading to the back of the house. You think you can set up out there and cover for me if needs be?'

'On my way,' he said.

OK, so he wasn't Rink, but Harvey was proving himself just fine.

I recalled the cars outside, tried to estimate the number of men inside the house. It wasn't easy because I didn't know how many of those cars belonged to Hendrickson and which belonged to his visitors. Basically, I had to err on the side of caution. Expect more enemies to come at me and any fewer would be a help. The corridor was like something from *Through the Looking Glass*, seemingly growing progressively narrower and lower of ceiling as I traversed it. It took me a moment to understand that the floor was a steady ramp towards the door at the far end; a quirk of the architecture. Doors on my right were locked. I gripped my knife loosely and went on, conscious that should anyone enter the corridor behind me then I was a sitting duck.

I allowed the door to swing open under its own weight, and found a kitchen area beyond. From a side room sounded a soft clink of pots and pans. I moved quickly, swerved around a food preparation counter, and approached the annexe room. Standing with her back to me was an elderly woman in a dull grey uniform of skirt and jacket, black stockings and black shoes. She sported a pudding basin haircut. As long as it wasn't Rosa Klebb I didn't deem her a threat, so silently closed the door behind her and bolted it to keep her out of harm's way. I went back across the kitchen, bypassing the large island in the middle, and approached a different door from the one I'd entered by. It was shut, but from beyond it came the voices I'd been following, too indistinct to make out words. I eased the door open.

208

There's an old saying: don't take a knife to a gunfight. Good advice. I pulled out my SIG and transferred the Ka-bar to my belt. Taking one last glance at the door I'd recently shut, checking that Rosa Klebb wasn't standing behind me ready to reveal a stiletto blade in the toe of her shoe, I was happy that I was unobserved. This was about the most foolhardy thing I'd done in a long time. Even crazier than the risk I'd taken to release Rink from his captors. I was about to descend into a basement below a house full of armed men. For all I knew the space beneath could become my tomb. But I didn't let that put me off.

Maybe when the Tudor hall was reconstructed here it had been erected upon the foundations of an older structure, because I found myself descending into what once might have been a root cellar. The Galil was cumbersome, so I propped it against the wall so that it didn't knock on the stone and give me away. The stones that supported the floors above were age-worn, grimy with smoke from old kerosene lamps and candles. Still, the steps had been replaced with new ones of preformed concrete, smooth underfoot. I went down them with barely a whisper of my soles on the treads. At the bottom was a sturdy door, more like something you'd find in a bank vault than in an ordinary cellar. Luckily it had already been unlocked. The door stood ajar, little more than a hand's span, but it was enough for me now to hear three distinct voices. The one I assumed belonged to Hendrickson had calmed since earlier, but it still held a dominating edge.

'The point,' Hendrickson said, 'is that you came highly recommended. I'm paying you a fortune, but you're still no further ahead than you were three fucking days ago!'

There was the scuff of a shoe, someone moving uncomfortably as they jostled to reinstate their importance. I heard Baron's insipid drawl. 'We were too late in Maine. Hunter must have figured out that we were going to make a try at his girl-friend. When the team I sent for her arrived, they were ambushed. Two of them were killed and Imogen was whisked away in an airplane. I hardly think that it's a failing on my part if she gave us the slip.'

A wash of relief went through me. It sounded like Hartlaub and Brigham had come through for me, and for Imogen. The relief was only momentary, replaced by cold fury as I realised how close to danger Imogen had been placed again. It made me more determined to end things.

I wasn't the only one who was furious. Hendrickson shouted. 'A fucking failing on your part? Considering he'd no way of knowing you were going after her, I can't see how Hunter could have guessed. You must have fucked up. Simple as that!'

'Sir, with due respect, I hardly think that Baron's to blame.' The third voice struck me. A tiny part of me had hoped that it would be Tubal Cain himself. To take them all out in one swirl of violence would have suited me. Yet, another part – one I can only describe as fear – warned that if Cain was inside that room, then I'd taken on more than I could handle. I was pleasantly surprised to hear the voice of Charters, the arsehole whose arm I'd broken.

'Did I ask for your opinion? No. So shut the fuck up!' Hendrickson turned his ire back on Baron. 'You made a fucking mess of everything, Baron. Sigmund's death is going to cause me real problems in the days ahead. I'm beginning to think that I should've left everything well alone, trusted in the courts to sort things as usual. My attorneys would have ripped Telfer to shreds and I'd have walked free. With Sigmund's sudden disappearance, though, my fall-back plan will fail.'

Reading between the lines, he meant he'd have ensured that Petoskey carried all the shit for him. In real terms, John had worked for Petoskey, not Hendrickson, so I didn't doubt he'd already made plans to disassociate himself from any connections to my brother. He had been behind the hit men who had chased John, but I made myself a silent wager that Petoskey would have carried the can for that too.

Baron said, 'It was a totally unforeseen incident. Who could've guessed that Hunter would've achieved what he did?'

'Broke my fucking arm . . .' Charters began, but his words petered out and I assumed he'd received a filthy look from his bosses.

211

'You deserve more than a broken arm,' Hendrickson spat. 'From what I hear, it was your knife that Hunter got his hands on. Maybe I'm blaming the wrong person for the entire fuck-up?'

'No, sir,' Baron interjected on Charters' behalf. 'I accept responsibility for that. And, yes, as you've pointed out, you are paying me a fortune for a thoroughly professional service. I'm sorry for what has gone before, but I promise you: I will not fail again.'

I pictured Hendrickson's face, dark with anger. Metaphorically, he would be like a pot simmering on a stove, but the flames had just been turned down. I heard him exhale loudly, then there was a metallic clunk. 'See that you don't.'

It was as good a point as any to pour more water on him.

I pushed into the room, lifting my SIG.

'The first man to move dies.'

My face was the last any of them expected. They stood there, dumbstruck. My command had been designed to achieve this. The last thing I wanted was for them to start shouting and bring re-inforcements running from above.

Hendrickson was a bigger man than I had imag-ined. He had strong features, pale blue eyes, and skin dark by heredity rather than holidays in the sun. His chest, shoulders and biceps stretched his suit jacket, and in his day he would have been quite a scrapper. Right now it looked like any fight had gone out of him. Charters shot me a look to

212

curdle milk, while Baron appraised me with that supercilious smile he'd used when last we met. All three men were standing at the far end of the room, Hendrickson facing the other two. Between us were rack upon rack of guns; a good ol' boy's dream world, and a potential nightmare for me. I didn't doubt that any of them were armed already, but just the sight of upward of a hundred weapons gave me pause. It must have shown in my stance because Hendrickson straightened a little.

'Face me,' I said. 'Hands where I can see them.'

They all turned, hands out by their sides. I made a quick scan of the room. None of the rifles or machine guns appeared to be loaded, nor any of the semi-auto handguns, but I couldn't tell with the revolvers.

Ideally I would have liked for them to drop their weapons, but while they were at it one of them could try to be a hero. I was sure that I could drop any of them first, but the sound of my gun would bring reinforcements and I'd be penned inside this room. Something crossed Baron's face: realisation that I required silence to get the job done. He opened his mouth to shout, then realised that even if I did get boxed inside, I wouldn't be the only man to die. I arched an eyebrow at him as he got the point.

'We've a stalemate going on,' he said.

'Nah, Baron. I've got a gun in my hand.'

Baron was quick on the draw, but nowhere near

fast enough when I already had my SIG trained between his eyes. He kept his hands spread.

Charters hurriedly glanced back and forth, seeking direction from his superiors. His right arm was cocooned in bandages, but his left hand was still able to grab the gun tucked in his belt. I eyed him steadily. 'Don't try it, Charters. Even with two good hands you were out of your league.'

Hendrickson had taken stock and didn't like his chances. He held up his palms. 'Tubal Cain warned me that you were a remarkable enemy.'

'Flattery will get you nowhere,' I quipped.

'How about money?'

'How about you call Cain off my brother?'

I'd made Petoskey the same deal. Hendrickson couldn't have known that at the time, but he'd have been fully aware of the outcome.

'I was never in command of that maniac's actions.' Hendrickson glanced at Baron as if seeking support. Baron lowered his face.

'Call him off,' I said again.

'I don't know how to contact him. He calls me, refuses to be on a leash.'

'I don't believe you.'

'It's the truth.'

Actually, I did believe part of what he said: the bit about Cain refusing to be on Hendrickson's leash. But I also believed that Hendrickson knew exactly where he was.

'Where is he?'

'Where is your brother?' Hendrickson sneaked

up the corner of his mouth. At my snort, he went on, 'What I meant was, he's probably where your brother is.'

I gave him a slow headshake. 'This is going nowhere. Unless you start talking the truth, I'm going to start shooting.'

'You may as well,' Hendrickson said. 'Do you think I relish the thought of spending the rest of my life in prison? Death would be a better prospect.'

'I'd be very happy to oblige. Then again, I might just kneecap you and make you easier game in the showers. Try fighting off a gang rape when you're on all fours.'

Baron slowly lifted his head again. 'Hunter, if you kill Hendrickson I won't be paid.'

'Your point being?'

'I'm a hired hand. I have no personal stake in this other than the money. Let me go, I'll walk away.'

I considered his offer for all of a second. 'You're forgetting.' Other than the obvious – that he would try to kill me at his first opportunity. 'You sent men to capture my girlfriend. You had Petoskey murder Louise Blake. You tortured my best friend. For any of those, you deserve to die. My friend, Rink . . . do you know what I promised him? I swore I'd save him a piece of your arse, but I don't think that's a promise I can keep.'

Baron shrugged. 'Worth a try.'

Hendrickson was looking at him open-mouthed. 'That had better have been a bluff, Baron.'

Baron merely smiled. Charters was more animated, his eyes flicking between his bosses like he was watching a tennis match. Suddenly his gaze fell on me, and stuck there. He lifted his bandaged arm. 'Don't you think I've suffered enough? I've got nothing to do with this! I'm just some poor sap who took a fucking protection job! I didn't know I was gonna get involved in anything like this!'

Hendrickson laughed. 'Kill him if you want, Hunter. He's a fucking coward.'

The man, so tough when he had me at his mercy, wasn't so tough now. Tears rolled from his eyes and he shook like a wet puppy. Under the circumstances perhaps he didn't deserve to die. Maybe I would have spared him, but his fate was taken out of my hands. Baron moved, lightning fast, but not for his gun. He grabbed Charters by the back of his neck and propelled him towards me.

Charters wasn't a major threat. Terrified, he didn't even try to get me. But he was blocking my view of both Hendrickson and Baron and there was no way that they were standing still. If I attempted to manoeuvre around Charters, he would definitely grab at me, halt me long enough for Baron or Hendrickson to finish me. That made up my mind. I shot him in the throat. The force of the bullet took him off his feet and I now had a clear view of the others.

Hendrickson had swung away from me, but Baron's hand was going for his gun. At the same time he went into a crouch, making him a smaller target. I fired and knew immediately that I'd missed. Baron's hand was coming up again. I dipped on one hip, swerving my upper torso to one side, and I felt the air buffet my cheek as Baron's return fire cut through the space I'd just vacated. Motherfucker was *fast*.

Trying to keep an eye on both of them, I deemed Baron the most immediate threat. Hendrickson still had his back to me and seemed to be leaning on a counter. Baron had taken two steps further to my right, his arm swinging towards me. I shot at him. My bullet struck his side and threw him against a wall. But he wasn't dead, and I saw his finger pull on the trigger of his gun. There was no way to avoid his shot but go down. His bullet cracked the wall above my head. I'd saved my life, but given up my stability. Down on one knee, off balance, I tried to track Baron but he had already danced a few steps and was parallel to my position. To kill him I'd have to bring my arm fully around. He was as quick on his feet as he was with a gun: he leaped past me and was now almost at the door. I turned, trying to get a bead on him, but it was hopeless.

Baron fired a final round, but he was too busy fleeing to care where it struck. It missed me and hit the inert form of Charters where he lay on the floor. I started to rise. But Hendrickson was also moving, swinging round, and in his hand was a large Colt revolver that glinted silver in the overhead lights. The old-fashioned gun must have been the source of the clunk I'd heard earlier. It had been behind Hendrickson all the time, concealed from my view by his sturdy body.

Shit. I'd wanted to force Tubal Cain's whereabouts from him before he died. But given the choice of letting him get the drop on me and shooting him there was only ever going to be one outcome. Even a disabling round through his body wouldn't be enough, because while I dealt with him, Baron might return. As I told Harvey I would, I shot Hendrickson in the face.

The Colt slipped from his fingers and clattered on the floor between his feet. For a second or two Hendrickson defied gravity, then his knees gave out and he toppled forward. The splash of blood reached all the way over Charters to my boots. For all that he was the source of my woes, I gained no satisfaction from his death. Possibly because the way he went was too easy on the bastard. Justice would have been better served if I'd hobbled him as I'd threatened and left him to rot in jail.

Hendrickson couldn't help me find Cain now, and I barely glanced at him as I moved to the edge of the door. Baron was still up there and the last thing I desired was to start up the stairs and have him fill me full of holes while confined between the two stone walls. Yet I couldn't stay there. The brief gunfight was bringing Hendrickson's men running from all corners of the house.

CHAPTER 29

Deadened by the walls of the basement, the racket caused by our shoot-out wouldn't have carried beyond the house, so there was no fear that the police would come with blue lights blazing. However, Baron must have found where I'd dropped the Galil because suddenly the house rattled to the clamour of machine gun rounds. I was trapped in the cellar, and even if Baron or the others didn't have the bottle to come down and finish me off, the cops would be here soon. That'd be me done for: without the backing of Walter I'd be seen as the aggressor and dealt with accordingly. Either I'd be put down or carted off to prison for the remainder of my life.

The cops would have to be a concern for later, I decided.

Some of Baron's rounds made it all the way down the stairwell and into the basement. They cut chunks out of the floor, throwing shards of concrete and red-hot metal everywhere. Something scored my left shin, and I jumped, slapping down on an oozing wound. I hobbled a few steps away, shoving bodily into a corner nearest the door. The rebounding bullets were still a concern but less likely to hit me now. The last time I'd been in a similar situation my enemy had lobbed a hand grenade at me: this time there was no steel hospital bed and mattress to save me. However, I did still hold an ace card.

'Harvey, I need your help now!'

'Wondered what all that hullaballoo was about,' Harvey said in my ear.

From above there came the retort of a rifle. Someone screamed and I hoped it was Baron. It wasn't very likely, but at least the machine gun fire stopped as the flow of battle surged to a new front. I didn't wait to make sure, just bolted up the stairs and into the kitchen. A man was dead on the floor but he was too big to be Baron. The window was smashed. From outside I heard the repeated crack of Harvey's rifle as he tracked fleeing men through the windows of the house. Someone fired back, but their bullets came nowhere near to him. He continued laying down cover and I went through the kitchen. Didn't bother with the door, just hurdled out through the broken window and on to the gravel path.

'I'm out,' I said.

'See you, brother.'

I looked for targets but saw none.

'OK, start falling back.'

We pepper-potted out of there, taking turns to

cover and run as we retreated through the garden. The lawn mower had fallen silent, but a new sound carried through the air: sirens from responding police cruisers. From further back in the grounds there was the roar of an engine, and the squeal of a vehicle making a harsh turn. I assumed that, like us, Baron wanted no part of the police investigation that would follow. I would have liked to take him out there and then, but at least this way Rink might get his wish.

We went over the wall with little finesse, just ran at it and leaped, caught the upper edge and swung over. Our rental had gone undiscovered and we clambered inside. Harvey drove, I sat in the front passenger seat, and we talked calmly. We kept to the speed limit; just two guys on a drive. Cop cars screamed past us heading for the front gates of the Hendrickson estate. By the time they arrived, gained entry and discovered what had happened we were well out of range of the cordon they set up around the crime scene.

Apart from Baron, nobody had any idea who was responsible for the slaughter, and it was reasonable to expect that he'd keep his mouth shut. That he'd made his escape was a given, so the chances of the police searching for Harvey and me were very slim. We headed out of town and pulled in at a hotel that was more upper-class than anything normally favoured by those fleeing justice. Cops tended to target the seedier flophouses first; they didn't expect felons to lie low in five-star comfort. Forward planning meant that Harvey had pre-booked – under false details – so we weren't like a couple of desperadoes when we turned up and locked ourselves in our room. Harvey even set up a charge account on a credit card, further enhancing our hide-in-plain-sight ethos. He requested a wake-up call and newspaper for the morning.

Our room was on the ground floor and we could come and go without having to bypass the checking-in counter. From the window we could see where we'd parked our rental. There was also a second vehicle that Harvey had ordered via a different rental company: just in case our first car had been noticed near to the shooting we'd planned to leave here in the second.

When the investigation got underway, it was probable that any mobile phone usage in the area would be scrutinised, so the mobiles we had would have to be dumped. Nevertheless I knew how the gears of bureaucracy could grind an investigation to a snail's crawl so thought my phone was good for a while yet. Phoning Walter directly from it was foolish, because the numbers would show on the call log, but not when I went through the relay stations that filtered and encrypted the route. Ensconced in our rooms, I rang the CIA man.

'You can strike Kurt Hendrickson off the list,' I said when Walter picked up.

'He's dead? Hell, son! The Justice Department

isn't going to be happy when they find his trial won't be going ahead. They were looking at a real media coup with this one.'

'Don't worry. Right now a higher power is judging his crimes. Where he's heading, it'll be worse than any hell-hole that the courts could send him to.'

'I never took you for the religious type,' Walter said.

'You know what they say: there's no atheists in trenches, Walt.' Though I didn't pray that regularly, I'd often taken the Lord's name in vain. Maybe I should've got down on my knees and begged for forgiveness otherwise, when it was my time, I might be heading to the same hell-hole as Hendrickson and all the other evil men I'd killed. I told Walter what had gone down at Hendrickson's house.

'So you've no idea where Cain is,' he summed up.

'Drawn a blank,' I said. 'So it's even more important that both John and Imogen are out of harm's way.'

Anticipating my next question, Walter confirmed, 'Imogen was collected by Hartlaub and Brigham. She's out of Cain's reach. There's no one left who he can use to get to John, so you needn't worry.'

'I'm not sure about that. Walt, I need to speak to my brother.'

Walter's silence gave me a sense of foreboding. 'Walt?'

'Uh, I'm just figuring on how best to arrange that, son.'

'What's the problem, Walt, and please . . . none of your usual bullshit.'

Walter coughed into the handset, then must have twisted away because I didn't catch his next mumbled words.

'Walter.'

'I'm here, OK. Look, this won't be easy to set up. We have him in deep hiding. It's going to be a bitch getting you to see him without your involvement throwing problems our way.'

'Seeing as I'm just a fucking crazy vigilante and all?'

'There is that.' He tried to temper his words so they sounded like a joke, but he meant them. 'I'll see what I can do. In the meantime I suggest you get some rest, recharge your batteries, you've been on the go for . . . what? Two days now?'

'I'm fine,' I lied. The truth was, now that the thrill of battle had subsided, I could have slept for a month. 'Just arrange things for me, Walt. I want to speak to John.'

'Get some sleep. Give me a call back in a few hours, OK.'

Walter hung up and I must have looked at the phone strangely. Harvey, currently sprawled on one of the beds, was watching me. His usually bright eyes were rheumy, like I wasn't the only one in need of a nap. 'There a problem, Hunter?'

'I'm not sure . . .'

Placing the phone on the floor, I crushed it under my heel. Then I disassembled it further, separating the battery, the guts and the SIM card and tossing them into a waste basket.

'Destroy your phone,' I told Harvey. 'Then we're getting out of here.'

'I need to sleep, man.'

'Trust me, Harve, we need to get going.'

While he dismantled his handset, I went to the window that overlooked where our cars were parked. There was nothing unusual out there. So maybe the nasty feeling I'd just felt was wrong; but the niggling thought persisted that Walt was up to something. I crossed the room and opened the door. A narrow corridor led back into the hotel one way and to the car park the other. Going to a window, I peered out across the hotel lot on to the main road. Traffic regulations meant that stopping on the highway wasn't allowed, but there were plenty of places where they could pull off the road and into one of the hotel courtyards across the way. A hundred yards up, its front end peeking out from behind a stand of trees, I spotted a navy-blue sedan with tinted windows.

Returning to the room, I said, 'Harvey, we have to go now!'

We fast-walked out of the room, along the corridor and out through a revolving door into the car park. The rifle was still inside the first rental car but we had no time to fetch it. We hurried over to the second car and Harvey bleeped it open. He drove again, with me riding shotgun. We only made it as far as the exit ramp when the first police cruiser screeched up the ramp towards us, its lights flashing balefully.

CHAPTER 30

Tubal Cain watched a young girl leading a smaller boy by the hand. The boy couldn't have been much more than five years old, the girl a little older. She had the reddish hair and slightly upturned nose inherited from her mother, but the boy was definitely his father's son. Cain could even detect a little of his Uncle Joe in the boy. Those bluish-green eyes with a hint of brown at the outer edge of the irises must have been a trait from his grandmother's side of the family, as Tubal Cain knew that John Telfer and Joe Hunter had different fathers. The boy even had that same straight-backed shoulders-held-high walk as the brothers; maybe that was inherited as well and not a stick-up-the-ass attitude they carried with them.

They were too young to be walking these streets alone, so it was no surprise to find that Jennifer was a few paces behind them, deep in conversation with another young mother whose brats trailed in their wake. Jennifer puffed on a cigarette between sentences. Every so often she glanced up, checking the progress of her offspring. She must have gone out to collect the kids while he was sampling the delights of the tea shop.

Cain watched Jennifer say her goodbyes to her friend, then she hurried the few steps to catch up to her children and ushered them through the entrance to their building. She wasn't laden down by grocery bags this time, and Cain noticed that she used the stairs, sending the kids off at a gallop ahead of her. In no major hurry to follow, Cain hung back in the alley that had become his surveillance point. While he waited for the Telfer family to settle in he studied the graffiti. Why do all ignorant people have a fascination with genitalia? he wondered. Someone had daubed the legend MANU FOR THE CUP in bright red paint. A different artist, but equally industrious, had scored through the final word and written the word CHOP. Under it in even larger letters they'd added CITY RULES! Cain was unfamiliar with soccer, but even he knew that there was a rivalry in this city where wearing the wrong-coloured jersey could get you a whupping.

The floor of the alley was littered with a filthy collection of debris, including broken glass, crushed drinks cans, cardboard and other things he didn't care to imagine. The carcass of a rat had rotted down to the skeletal bones, but they held no interest for him. Cain looked up to the window of Jennifer's flat. He could detect movement there. Good. Hands in his coat pockets, he walked out of the alley and on to the road. From his left three figures emerged.

They were dressed like the bicycle-riding kids he'd seen this morning, their hoods pulled up, and their sneakers whitened to a gleam. It didn't matter what colour jersey you wore, these were the kind of youths who were going to kick your ass just for being different. Already he'd noted their posture had changed. There was a lot of hand-flicking going on, gruff expletives exchanged that he couldn't understand. Cain didn't have the inclination to waste time with these punks.

They moved close, enclosing him in a three-sided box.

Ordinarily it would have been a fatal error to allow them to shut down his options like that, but Cain didn't fear them. In fact, if it weren't for the fact that it might draw unwanted attention he would quite happily butcher them.

'Hey, mate, you got the time?' The elected leader postured in front of Cain, bouncing loosely on the balls of his feet. Another of the boys fiddled with a cellphone, as though engrossed, but really readying himself to sucker punch Cain from the side. All he was waiting for was the nod from the leader. The third youth was standing at the leader's shoulder, ready to leap on board as soon as Cain was hurt.

'No, but I've got some of these.' Cain drew the Recon Tanto from one pocket, then the box-cutter from the other. The youths took a step back, but they were used to dealing with sharp-edged weapons. Nevertheless some of the cockiness had

229

gone. Now they were trying to decide if this was such a good idea. Cain gave them even more to think about. He slipped the box-cutter away, snaked his hand under the tail of his coat and pulled out his Bowie. 'Then there's this mother-fucking brute!'

Subtly the distance between them had widened again.

'And if that's not enough . . .' Cain put away the Tanto and pulled out the Walther P99. 'There's always this.'

'Fuck me,' the leader said.

'I haven't *the time*.' Cain lifted the barrel of the gun so it was aiming directly at the youth's groin. 'So I suggest you just get the fuck out of here. All of you.'

'Fuckin' psycho!'

'Yes.' Cain gave them a death's-head grin. 'I am.'

The three spun away and headed off the same way that they'd come. There was little swagger in their mincing steps now. He glanced around himself, checking that the small drama hadn't earned him any unnecessary attention. The incident had gone unobserved. He slipped the gun away. The trio had made it to the far corner of the street. Feeling brave they offered him the finger, plus the two-fingered salute particular to the UK. Cain mimed an oral sex act, then mouthed, 'Blow me.' The youths decided there were less dangerous victims to be had elsewhere and headed off out of sight.

Cain scowled, his anger directed internally. He loathed degrading himself, lowering himself to their base level, but 'when in Rome'. These young thugs understood only one language. They were sufficiently cowed to stay out of his way, so that was one bonus. He looked up at Jennifer's flat. It was time to get on with something more productive.

Settling his clothes over his weapons, he walked through the glass doors and into the foyer. Having experienced the foul-smelling stairwell once today, he elected to call the elevator. A dull groan announced it was on its way down. Under his heels Cain could feel the grime adhering to the tiles. Unmoved as he was by gore, the thought of germs gave him the creeps, made him feel unclean. He shivered.

The doors shuddered open and Cain stepped aboard. The doors juddered to, then the lift set off for the designated floor. It was a short ride and he found himself in the hallway along from Jennifer's flat.

He recalled a conversation with John Telfer in which the thieving asshole had bemoaned the fact he'd let down his wife and children. It was clear from the way in which he'd delivered his words that Jennifer and the kids still meant an awful lot to him: not so much as to stop him going on the lam to the USA, but enough. John was the type who'd come running if he knew they were in danger, and if not John, then Uncle Joe certainly would.

Cain opened his wallet and slipped out a plastic card.

He shook out the last feelings of revulsion, and knocked on the door.

Voices chimed from within; the kids announcing to their mom that they had a visitor. He waited, heard Jennifer tell the kids to go to some other room, then the sound of footsteps. A chain rattled and the door swung inward a couple of inches. Jennifer peered through the gap at him. She didn't say anything, just stared at him with suspicion.

Cain held up the plastic card identifying him as Special Agent Kenneth Myers of SOCA. The Serious and Organised Crime Agency was something that most Brits were still unfamiliar with, as it had only been in existence a few years. Joe Public knew that it was akin to the FBI in the US, but then they rarely had any idea what the FBI's remit was. Cain was relying on the fact that the acronym would hold enough authority to get him inside without resistance.

'What do you want?' Jennifer wasn't the type to fold at the first suggestion of officialdom.

Cain feigned a glance back over his shoulder. 'I'm here on official business, Ms Telfer. It's not something I'd care to share with your neighbours.'

Jennifer craned her neck, listening. 'There's no one else around.'

'Ms Telfer,' Cain said in a hushed voice, 'I'm here with news about John.'

'What trouble is he in this time?' Jennifer's tone

was exasperated, but she couldn't prevent the sudden widening of her pupils at the mention of John's name. 'I have no idea where he is.'

'Like I said, it's official . . .' Cain glanced around once more. 'But also very personal. To you.'

Jennifer turned her attention away from him, possibly checking where the children were, or if they were listening. While she was distracted he could have easily kicked the door in, but that wasn't his purpose. He waited patiently for her to come back to him. When she did, she was frowning, 'What's this all about? You're an American, aren't you?'

Cain didn't flinch. 'I'm an American, yes. I'm a liaison officer, seconded to SOCA to combat international crime that affects both our countries. Look,' he turned the card over, indicating a telephone number, 'if you'd like to confirm my identification, you can call this number. They will verify that I'm who I say I am.'

Jennifer took the card from him, studied it for a few seconds, turning it over again to the photo ID and official governmental seal. It was a gamble: if she should deem it necessary to call the number it would only go to a dead line. But it appeared that his bluff worked, because she handed back the card.

'Thank you, Ms Telfer,' Cain said.

'Mrs. John and I were never divorced.'

Cain nodded, accepting her correction, the way an official would under the circumstances. He waited while she closed the door, heard her unlatching the security chain. She opened the door and waved him inside. Cain entered, politely wiping his feet on the welcome mat.

'Don't bother,' Jennifer said. 'I haven't had a chance to clean up yet.'

He continued to scrub his feet. The door opened directly into a living room. Jennifer's words weren't completely accurate, as the carpet looked freshly vacuumed. Perhaps she was just embarrassed at the shabby appearance of her home. The furniture looked well worn, and possibly handed down from previous families. There were a number of DVDs scattered on the floor in front of the TV, some toys left where they'd fallen. Smoke hung in the air, and an ashtray on a dining table was in need of emptying. Jennifer walked past him, heading for an open packet of cigarettes. She sparked a lighter and held it to the end of a cigarette, inhaled.

'Well?'

Cain indicated the toys. 'Your children are home?'

Jennifer pinched her lips around the cigarette. After considering his question, she asked, 'Why do you need to know where my children are?'

'I have to arrange transportation for the three of you.'

'Hold on a minute! What do you mean? We're going nowhere.'

Jennifer was as tense as an alley cat ready to spring at his throat.

Cain sat down on a couch, defusing the moment. 'You will no doubt have heard that your husband was involved in a serious incident in America? Since then, he has been under the protection of a federal witness protection scheme, seeing as he is *the* key witness in the impending trial of a suspected underworld figure. Well, Ms . . . uh, Mrs Telfer, certain complications have arisen whereby you and your children could be in danger. We don't wish for that to happen, nor, I suspect, do you. I am here to place you into protective custody while we negate the threat to you and your children.'

There was fear in her face, but not a little resistance. 'Protective custody? That sounds like prison to me!'

Cain chuckled. 'Nothing so dramatic, I assure you. I'm just going to transport you to a safe house that is unconnected to you. We have rooms organised in a five-star hotel, Mrs Telfer. See it as a few days' luxury on the government's tab.'

Cain stood up, took out the cellphone supplied by Hendrickson's man and jabbed the hot key. 'Can I organise a pick-up for four passengers?'

'Just hold it!' Jennifer stubbed her cigarette in the ashtray. 'I haven't agreed to anything yet.'

Cain ignored her, gave the address of her flat and agreed that twenty minutes would be fine.

'What are you doing? You can forget it. I'm not going anywhere with you until I've checked things out. Give me your ID card again; I want to phone your bosses!'

'Sure,' Cain said, closing the phone. He slipped it into his pocket and brought out the SOCA card.

As Jennifer reached for it, he snapped hold of her wrist and pulled her on to his lowered forehead. His skull connected with her jaw and Jennifer folded at the knees.

'You've had things tough these last couple years, Mrs Telfer. For that reason I did try to do this the easy way,' Cain whispered in her ear. 'But I'm afraid you've left me little option.'

From the wallet he took a small syringe.

He jabbed it into the flesh of Jennifer's throat.

Then he looked over at the door to the kids' bedroom.

CHAPTER 31

'What do we do now?'

'We get the hell outa here, or we go to prison. Which do you prefer, Harve?' My ill-directed sarcasm demanded only one answer.

Harvey floored the pedal, aiming the rental at the police cruiser.

Seeing us barrelling towards him, the cop swung the heavier squad car across our path, trying to block us so that his colleagues could arrive and take us down. Harvey didn't stop. There's a knack to pushing your way through a roadblock. You drive at no more than fifteen miles per hour, aim for their front wheel hub with the near corner of your vehicle, and shunt the offending vehicle aside. Of course, what's good in theory isn't always so in reality. Harvey pushed our car just a little too fast and the fender struck nearer to the front passenger door. The result was that the cop car was pushed along with us, its tyres juddering and bouncing on the asphalt. The noise was horrendous; the whooping of the siren competed with the scream of metal on metal, the repeated bang as the cop car lifted and fell. Finally, Harvey pulled hard right, caught the front end of the cruiser and shoved it aside. We tore round it, taking off the back bumper of our car in the process.

'There goes my deposit!' Harvey said.

The exit ramp twisted to the left, following the line of the hotel wall down to street level. At the bottom another police vehicle screeched to a halt. This time Harvey hit it just right, spinning the back end of the cruiser out of our way. Momentum carried us across the highway and into the oncoming lanes. A large furniture removals van howled like a wild beast as the driver hit the brakes. The van skidded, turned sideways in the road, then flipped on to its side. Grit pounded our car as the van tore up the road surface. Harvey just hauled on the steering so we went up on the pavement at the far side, then around the bulky vehicle. As we passed I saw that the driver, his face an open shout of alarm, looked unharmed. Thank God for that.

'What I said earlier,' I said, 'I didn't mean at the expense of innocent lives.'

'I'll try not to do anything stupid,' Harvey replied straight-faced.

He whipped the car off the kerb, through a gap between a tan Land Rover and a green Toyota. Back on the correct side of the road he hit the throttle and sped along the highway. Behind us, other cop cars took up the chase, sirens whooping.

'If they get an eye in the sky on to us we're fucked.'

'Best we lose them before they can arrange one, then.'

Ahead of us a police cruiser shot from a side street. From the passenger seat a cop aimed a shotgun at us. Harvey bit down on his bottom lip, at the same time popping a handbrake skid, taking us into a ninety-degree turn. Side on we caromed into the cruiser, and the cop had to throw himself inside to avoid being crushed. Harvey pressed the throttle, hit another skid and punched our way around the obstacle. The pursuing cars braked to avoid hitting their colleagues, giving us a couple seconds' respite. Harvey made the most of the time. He pushed the car up to around seventy miles an hour. It felt much faster when weaving between the slower-moving city traffic.

On our left was a strip mall, and behind it a huge Wal-Mart superstore. Harvey sped past the mall, swung a left and into the superstore parking lot. We streaked between rows of parked vehicles, customers leaping out of our way, abandoning their shopping carts. Our pursuers were too close for us to ditch this car and steal another, but that had never been Harvey's intention. He went out the other side of the lot and on to a service road that connected to another store, this one an electrical giant. Harvey sent the rental over a grassy strip and we joined another highway, this one heading back towards Richmond.

We'd given the cops the slip, but that wouldn't last long. Harvey floored the pedal, while I clung tight to the dashboard. There was a junction ahead. We could take the correct route around the sweeping ramp, or we could be more direct. Harvey chose the latter, pulled into oncoming traffic and across to the hard shoulder. Streaking past the horrified faces of commuters heading out of the city, we tore along the shoulder and on to Route 76. Here the two carriageways were separated by a median, but thankfully there was no crash barrier like on the motorways in the UK. Harvey sent the rental across the lanes, whipping between a Kenworth truck hauling cattle and a fuel tanker. I closed my eyes, expecting an impromptu beef barbecue, but there was no accident this time. When I opened my eyes again, we were on the median and spitting divots of grass and soil in the air.

Medians are designed to halt out-of-control vehicles, the soft earth catching and holding the tyres firm, but Harvey continued to hammer down on the throttle and the median finally gave up its hold and spat us on to the carriageway on the far side. Thankfully we were now heading in the same direction as the traffic flow. There was no sign of the cops: no way were they going to attempt the insane manoeuvres that Harvey had. They would be trying to catch us, but they were far enough behind for us to have won a minute or so of respite.

Then unfamiliarity with our terrain struck us a cruel blow.

'Shit. We're on a goddamn toll road.'

I looked ahead and saw that the traffic was slowing, moving into lanes to crawl through between the toll booths. Every lane had a red light flashing overhead: the cops had called ahead and had the road closed.

'There,' I said, pointing at a small housing estate on our right. There wasn't a road into the residential area – possibly to foil any plans to avoid the toll charge – but all that separated us from escape was a chain link fence and a drainage gully. Harvey didn't even slow, just aimed the car at the fence and blasted through. We ramped over the gully, then hit the ground hard. The car didn't make it in one piece, the suspension was shot, but I was relieved to hear the engine continue unhindered. We swept between two rows of houses, trailing wire mesh behind us. At the end of the street, Harvey slowed, took a right and went at a moderate pace along another residential road. A left took us to another junction and across the way we saw another strip mall, this one catering to the discerning diner. There was an Italian restaurant, a Chinese restaurant, a rib shack and something called the Food Lion. Jammed between them was a chemist store: could have been where diners picked up a bottle of Pepto Bismol after their dinner.

We abandoned the rental in the mall parking lot,

then jogged back to the intersection towards a petrol station on the far side. While we caught our breath, we watched until an old model station wagon pulled up at the fuel pumps. A skinny kid climbed out and headed for the store. Like many at service stations, he hadn't bothered to lock his car or even remove the keys from the ignition. While he was inside, picking up a newspaper or bar of chocolate or whatever, Harvey and I were in his car and heading out of town.

The cops arrived, but they were looking for the bashed-up rental car, and we slipped by them, unnoticeable in our equally bashed-up but thoroughly anonymous station wagon. The kid would report his vehicle stolen, but by the time two and two were put together we would be well beyond the cordon.

A short time later we dumped the station wagon.

We caught a bus that took us back into town, where we hopped a cab and headed off to where Harvey's Bell Jetranger waited for us at a small private heliport on the northern fringe of Richmond. The last place a police helicopter would be looking for us, we decided, was in the sky.

I didn't know how I felt. The hit on Kurt Hendrickson hadn't exactly gone as planned. That he was dead and gone was a bonus, but it hadn't brought me any nearer to finding or stopping Tubal Cain. In fact, if anything, it had made matters worse. Not only was I now a hunted man, probably by every cop in the USA, but it was also likely that the police were being helped along their way by the very person who'd set me on this task.

Walter Hayes Conrad IV.

It couldn't have been a coincidence that the cops just happened to turn up when they did, could it? No one knew where we were, or even who. The fact that I'd telephoned Walter, he'd played a stalling game and then a government car had turned up to scope us out hadn't escaped me. But: why?

What purpose did it serve for Walter to betray me?

Was he disassociating himself, ensuring that his part in our scheme to finish Tubal Cain was never discovered? Or had his role already been revealed and forced him to hand me over?

I didn't know; that was the truth of it. Thinking about the possible betrayal made my head hurt. More likely that was down to lack of sleep, and a dump of noradrenalin into my system after the sustained action of the last couple of hours. It was a good job that Harvey was at the controls of the chopper, because I was seeing double. I inhaled, shuddered out some of my tiredness. When I looked across at Harvey I could focus again. Harvey had his earphones and microphone in place. I pulled mine on.

'That was some fancy-arsed driving you did back there.'

Harvey gave me a short, derisive laugh. 'Fancy-assed? I was crapping my pants, man!'

'Well, you did OK. Did you study defensive driving when you were with the Rangers?'

He shook his head. 'I was just winging it. Sheer adrenalin got me through.'

His comments had shut down my line of conversation, and I sat there ruminating for a moment. It got me thinking on how earlier I'd have preferred if Rink had been the one covering my back, and now I felt a little ashamed of myself. 'Harve.'

He glanced over at me, inclined his chin.

'I'm sorry I got you into this.'

'Anything for a friend.'

That made me feel worse. 'You do realise that we're probably going to go to prison for a long time.'

Harvey bit down on his bottom lip. 'There's always the possibility we'll get away with it. I've taken precautions. The rifle can't be traced to me. I had my gloves on when driving the car we dumped.'

These days the science of forensic investigation was more sophisticated than looking for fingerprints. And even if that's all they went by, the police wouldn't go with the obvious. Harvey hadn't been wearing gloves when we were in the hotel room, so they could find plenty of evidence there. Identifying Harvey would be a piece of cake for any investigator. Christ, all they had to do was look at my known associates and the first black man to jump out at them would be Harvey. Not only that, but if Walter had been responsible for betraying us, the police had arrived at the scene with prior knowledge of who was assisting me. Of course, if I was to be captured, they wouldn't get his name from me.

'I think it's time I finished this alone.'

Shaking his head adamantly, Harvey said, 'I started this with you, I'm gonna finish it with you.'

'Not a good idea, Harve.'

'Has anything we've done been a good idea?' He considered his words, then added, 'With the exception of saving Rink and killing the bad guys, that is?'

'There are still two bad guys out there. Baron I'm not worried about, but this won't end until Tubal Cain's finally in his grave. No, scratch that. A grave couldn't hold him last time. This time I'm going to have to make sure there isn't enough of him left to put in a coffin.'

'That's the big problem. How do we find him?'

'We set a trap.' I dropped the subject of going it alone. Jesus, if I suggested as much, Rink would likely hand me my arse on a platter. 'That's why I wanted to speak to John. To see if he was prepared to help us.'

'You'd use your brother as bait?'

'I'd have made sure that he was never in any physical danger. But that's moot now. I don't know how to contact him.'

'I thought Walter was setting that up for you?'

I hadn't yet shared my suspicions with Harvey,

but it looked like it was time. 'Who do you think sent the cops after us, Harve?'

'I don't know Walter the way you guys do, but I find it hard to believe that he'd turn you in.'

'Walter plays a constant game; one where he's only interested in being the winner.'

'Could have been someone else,' Harvey pointed out. 'Baron escaped. Could have been him who directed the police to us.'

It was plausible, I supposed. When I thought about the slimy bastard, Baron had made his escape in a vehicle. It was possible that he'd followed us as we got away from Hendrickson's estate, and had tried to have us captured by the police. I thought that Walter had been stalling in order to triangulate my mobile phone, and had then sent a car to keep an eye on us. But, the omnipotent eye of the CIA wasn't as all-powerful as made out in movies: what were the chances that he could have located us and dispatched a car to our location in such a short time? Pretty slim.

I tried to picture the scene outside the Tudor hall. I have trained myself to take snapshot images that I compartmentalise for future use. But it's one thing when consciously deciding to save an image for later, quite another when concentrating on something else. I couldn't bring to mind the makes and models of the vehicles in the small fleet arranged on the gravel parking space. One of them could have been a dark sedan with tinted windows.

Perhaps the blame had been wrongly targeted at my old friend. I felt a trickle of relief, but then it was pushed aside by a different concern. If Walter hadn't set us up, then why had he stalled over John's unavailability?

I used the satellite phone to call Walter.

'Walt, it's me, Joe.'

'Hunter, I'm glad you called.'

'Really?'

'Yes, really. I told you to leave phoning me for a few hours. Big mistake! I've been frantic to get a hold of you since.'

'You didn't hear about Richmond yet?'

'Richmond? No, I've been too busy dealing with what else has happened.'

'What *has* happened? Is it John? Does Cain have him?'

'It's worse than that, son.'

'What could be worse than Cain capturing my brother?'

When he told me, he was right. It was much worse.

CHAPTER 32

Over in Manchester, my old home town, three boys had *innocently* enquired of the time from a stranger. Mistaking them for thugs, he'd threatened them with a collection of knives and a gun. Upset by the incident they'd debated whether to telephone the police, but it seemed that the one mobile phone between them had a flat battery, and public telephone kiosks – those that hadn't been vandalised – were as rare as chicken's teeth in their neighbourhood. Instead they'd decided to spy on the stranger and see what he was up to. He'd allegedly gone into a block of flats, where shortly afterwards a Ford Transit van had arrived. The youths then swore that the stranger and driver had carried the body of a woman to the van and placed it inside. The van drove away and they'd come out of hiding and immediately ran to a friend's house where they'd alerted the local police. The police officer dispatched to investigate their claim soon discovered my niece and nephew, Beatrice and Jack, unharmed and safely locked inside their bedroom. But of Jenny there was no sign. My parents had gone to the kids' rescue, taking them home out of the hands of the social workers. The street on which the Telfer family had lived was now a major crime scene while the police tried to determine what had happened.

That Jenny's abductor was Tubal Cain was obvious. I didn't need the boys' description of the fair-haired Yank with a scar on his throat for confirmation. The knives did it for me.

If it wouldn't have sent Harvey and me plummeting to our deaths, I'd have turned the cockpit of the Jetranger inside out. That was the level of my rage. No, it was worse than that: it was the measure of my sense of *futility*. I was thousands of miles away, and Jenny was in danger.

I lost track of things after that, and rode the chopper with intense dread gnawing at my insides. I tried not to conjure the nightmare scenario of Jenny eviscerated, her skeletal remains displayed as an insane trophy, but it was there. Closing my eyes made it worse, so I stared straight ahead, trying to bury the horrific image behind the clouds.

Things were totally out of control.

For years now, I realised, I'd been very lucky in that the events I'd chosen – or been manipulated – to involve myself in had been resolved with the back-up and resources of a certain friend. But this time, trying to fix things without the benefit of Walter's sanction made me understand how ineffective it was for one man to try to combat the evil of the world. It was always a demanding mission I'd set myself, but it was one thing punishing a low-life criminal, quite another to take on an entire network of world-class villains. Petoskey was dead, and so was Hendrickson. So what? What exactly had I achieved if it meant that Jennifer might also be slaughtered? There was no balance in that. I could kill a hundred, a thousand gangsters, and their lives would be nothing compared to that of one innocent woman.

I'd been a soldier most of my adult life. I'd been trained by the best and had served with the best. But I was no Superman. I was a human being and I suffered the same weaknesses and frailties as any man when faced by a situation beyond my control. I wanted to scream and shout and rail at the world. And God – though at that moment I couldn't believe that a benign all-powerful being could allow such an injustice to occur – I wanted to wring His fucking neck!

Despite all that, I kept my peace. Violence, rage, anger pointlessly directed wouldn't help anyone. Luckily Harvey could still think clearly enough to have a destination in mind. He'd had the chopper refuelled while at the heliport in Richmond, so we were good for the trip to the north. Somewhere along the way I fell asleep. Mentally exhausted, I didn't wake again until Harvey shook me gently and I unglued my eyes and peered over at Walter Conrad's fishing retreat.

My first sight of the cabin brought everything

crashing down on me again. The last time I'd been here was to witness the deranged work of Tubal Cain. I didn't want to be reminded of it, when in place of Bryce Lang and the bodyguards I super-imposed the face of Jenny. It took me a few seconds to get a grip of myself, and yet when I did it was with a new resolve. The cabin horrified me, but I'd always been one for facing my fears. There's an old adage I subscribe to: *If you are afraid of what lies within the cave, walk in.* No matter what kind of monster lurked in the darkness, running away didn't diminish your fear of it. You have to face it and – if needs be – rip the fucker's throat out with your teeth.

I hitched up my jeans as I stepped down from the chopper and led the way to Walter's front door. Now that it appeared that Tubal Cain was out of the country and Hendrickson no longer a threat, Walter had chosen to return to his cabin. We found him in the living area, supervising a clean-up crew. The air was redolent with the sharp smell of disinfectant, but it couldn't hide the sickly undertone of the depravity that had gone on here so recently. Walter was chewing on a fat cigar, but had not as yet lit it. He'd been trying to give up the vice of tobacco for years, and had only recently been able to ditch the panacea of the unlit stogie. Still, I couldn't blame him for grasping at his old habit. He needed the comfort of it, I guessed. The truth be told, I could have smoked a cigarette myself.

Sometimes I forgot how old Walter was. He was now in his late sixties, but looking at his haunted features, I'd have put him at twenty years older again. His normally rotund body was deflated and his jowls, usually plump and full around the stub of cigar, looked like those of a bloodhound. The whites of his eyes were reddened with broken capillaries. His bald pate seemed to be expanding daily. He made me feel my own mortality like a leaden weight.

I touched the old man on the shoulder and watched as he hung his head. He'd lost a dear friend in Bryce Lang, and most likely in his regular bodyguards as well. I felt for him. But more than that, I felt for Jenny.

'We need to end this fast.'

He nodded silently.

'I'm a wanted man,' I went on. 'There's no way that I can do things by the regular channels. Even with false documents, I can't beat the security measures now that they're watching for me.'

'I'll see to it that you're given immunity,' he said.

I'd been expecting him to deny me help this time. I was supposed to be on my own. He had to be kept out of the entire fuck-up. But he came across as being more intent on stopping the monster than concerned about protecting his own arse. Maybe he too was feeling his mortality.

'You know why Cain has done this.' I wasn't referring to the splotches of gore the clean-up crew were tackling.

Walter chewed furiously at his stogie, but didn't answer.

'He intends using Jenny to bring John out of hiding. He has only one way of making his demands, and that's through you, Walt. I want to be there, ready for the bastard when he makes the call.'

'What if he has already killed her?'

'I'll make him pay.' Never in my life had I made a more powerful resolution. 'I don't think he will, though. He'll keep her alive as bait. I need you to play your part in this, Walt. I need you to have John ready to make the exchange. When that happens, I promise you, Cain won't live a second longer.'

Walter stood there, wouldn't even look at me. Finally he nodded and said, 'Best prepare yourself then, son. I think he'll make contact soon.'

I'd forgotten that Harvey was standing by my shoulder until he stirred uncomfortably. 'What about me?'

Walter looked up at him like he was a stranger. I turned to Harvey and gave him his answer. 'I'm doing this part on my own.'

'Now hold on a minute!'

'Look, Harvey,' I said, 'I've already dragged you and Rink through a huge pile of shit, but it ends here. You're both great friends, and it has to stop. I've fucked your lives. It's about time I let you get back to some sort of normality.' Before he could argue, I turned to Walter again and I wasn't going to take no for an answer. 'Harvey and Rink's involvement has to be covered, Walter. I don't care how you do it, how many strings you have to pull or how many favours you have to call in, they weren't involved. Got it?'

'I'll do what I can.'

'That's not good enough. I want your word on it. Their inclusion is buried. Full stop.'

'My power isn't infinite, son.'

'I know. Blame everything on me if you have to, but my friends are kept out of this.'

I grew aware of a hush in the room. The cleaning crew had all paused at our raised voices. I shot them each a dark look and they went back to what they were doing. Quieter, I said; 'You owe them as much as I do, Walt. Make sure that they're exonerated. And,' I leaned in close to his ear, 'make sure that John is ready for when he's needed.'

'OK.' Walter walked away without further comment. He went through to the back rooms where I'd entered when Hartlaub and Brigham first brought me here. I trusted that he was already on to it. Harvey clutched my shoulder. 'Let's go outside, Hunter. We need to speak.'

I followed him outside and I could tell from the way his shoulders had bunched tight that I was in for more raised voices. Yet he surprised me. 'Thanks for what you just did for me and Rink, Joe.'

'It's not right that either of you should suffer for my mess.'

'It's not your mess. You didn't start this.'

'Maybe I did, Harve. Maybe I did.'

I'd turned my back on my brother when he was at his lowest. Christ, I'd been close to punching his lights out, but had walked away instead. I've often asked myself whether, if I'd just handed over the money he needed then, everything would have been different. Because I hadn't helped him, John had sought to solve his problems by running away. That had led him to cross paths with Petoskey and then Hendrickson. In turn, that had brought him into the crosshairs of Tubal Cain. It was the butterfly effect, my inaction reverberating down through the years to this point where all those I held dear were in more danger than ever. Shit, it had even made me the man I'd become. Some legend: a fucking vigilante guilty of murder. Well, enough was enough. It was time to send the bad karma back at the person who truly deserved it.

'Do something for me, will you?'

'Anything,' Harvey said.

'Go back and check on Rink. Tell him I'm sorry for taking off without saying goodbye.'

'Tell him yourself when you get back.'

'*If* I come back,' I corrected.

I wasn't talking about running away from the law; I seriously doubted that I'd return in one piece. If it meant the difference between John and Jenny's safety, and me dying under Tubal Cain's blade, then I chose the blade. No question.

CHAPTER 33

Getting into the UK had been relatively simple for Cain; not so getting out again with a hostage added to the equation. Nevertheless he was resourceful, and using Hendrickson's contacts he arranged flights for himself and Jennifer Telfer on a private jet employed to shuttle a TV mogul back and forth across the Atlantic. Said mogul was known to travel with a contingent of staff and 'guests', some of the latter often a little the worse for wear when arriving at their destination, so Jennifer blended in nicely.

Cain found the flight interminable. Not because he was surrounded by starlets stoned out of their heads, but because he had no way of satisfying his urge to take a memento or three from their skinny bodies. The TV guy was an insufferable ass, someone whose ego was larger than his fat head, and was sarcastic without wit. He sat in his plush leather seat, liquor flowing freely, and a couple lines of white powder offered to him on a tray. He used a glass tube to snort the cocaine, and Cain considered going and giving him a pat on the head for all he was doing for the TV ratings. He wondered if one pat would be enough to ram the glass tube all the way into the unctuous bastard's brain. The two minders wouldn't be able to stop him; in fact, they were an embarrassment, engaging in the party the way they did. Cain had once worked as a bodyguard to US dignitaries, and these scumbags brought shame to his trade. The only thing that stopped him from slaughtering them was that he'd have to go through the entire retinue, and the cabin crew, and Cain did not have the ability to safely land the plane.

As a consolation prize, Cain lifted a steak knife from the silver service galley and went to thank the TV guy for his hospitality. Up close his eyes were a little crossed, and he had accepted Cain's hand without listening to a goddamn word, but when Cain walked away again he was palming a strip of cloth snagged from the asshole's necktie. Neither the mogul nor his inept guards realised how close Cain had got to slipping the knife under the man's sternum and into his heart. Cain returned to his seat, and showed Jennifer his prize. She was decisively underwhelmed, as the TV guy was wont to say. Cain spent the flight rubbing the fabric between his index finger and thumb like it was an executive stress ball.

On arrival at Baltimore/Washington International, Cain had mingled with the noisy group, swaying along with the rest of them, even cackling with everyone else at a girl who went down on her hands and knees on the tarmac. As the giggling TV mogul lent his arm to the stoned girl, Cain supported Jennifer on his elbow and handed over both their passports. Used to dealing with celebrities and dignitaries, the security was lax and the couple were waved through as readily as all others in the entourage. Their fake passports would have passed muster even if Homeland Security had studied them, but the young guard manning the booth at the private entrance had eyes only for the beauties that flanked the haughty celebrity star-maker. The leggy blonde who'd recently taken the tumble was a minor celebrity in her own right, having been a stand-out on a countrywide talent show. Her mediocre singing voice might have ensured she was voted through each week, but the way she was nibbling on the TV boss's earlobe indicated a more likely explanation.

Cain was pleased to be leaving them all behind and quickly veered away once they were through the first-class arrivals lounge.

Cain had a van waiting outside and helped Jennifer in and strapped her into her seat. For good measure he gave her another shot of anaesthetic to ensure she remained drowsy. Regretfully, he'd dumped his weapons back in the UK, but there was another set waiting for him on the passenger seat. He had been mildly surprised to find that everything was in order for his return, but it seemed that Kurt Hendrickson's name carried weight even after his death.

News of Hendrickson's demise had filtered through to him via the gangster's contacts back in England. Cain hadn't been upset at the news. Neither was he surprised. He had cautioned Hendrickson that Joe Hunter was remorseless, but his warning hadn't been taken seriously. He was only amazed that Hunter had allowed Baron to escape when he had him in his sights. That was a big mistake, because the man had taken the loose reins of Hendrickson's empire and was even now plotting vengeance. That he had organised the pick-up and supply of weapons for Cain meant that Baron intended using him to finish Hunter once and for all. Well, Cain thought, let Baron think he was in command, but he would be used by no one. Especially by someone who'd made so many mistakes that he was becoming a liability.

Following a foolhardy attempt at having Hunter captured by the police, Baron had fled back to the house where Jared Rington had been tortured, and where Sigmund Petoskey subsequently died. Cain had no intention of taking Jennifer there, because it was already on Hunter's radar. Instead he'd have her held somewhere neutral, a place that he could control. If only Jubal's Hollow had gone undiscovered . . . but his ossuary had been dynamited, the ground levelled, and it was now a featureless destination for ghoulish tourists following the serial killer trail.

Climbing in the van, he studied the man who was at his disposal. He liked that choice of word:

disposal. He'd been so well behaved on his jaunt to England, maybe he could try out his new knives when the driver was no longer needed. He'd taken bones from Jeffrey Taylor and his bodyguards in Montana, as well as from the CIA man in the Adirondacks, plus a couple treasures from Michael Birch, the cowardly DA's assistant, but since then his collection of trophies hadn't grown. From his trip to England he'd only gleaned the tail-end of a waitress's apron and a strip of a multi-millionaire's necktie – though they were still valuable trophies. No, wait. He did have one other trophy and it was worth more than any he'd taken since his escape from Fort Conchar. He looked into the back of the van to where Jennifer Telfer slumped in her seat.

Jennifer would bring John Telfer to him.

He wondered if the woman was enough to bait his trap, or if he should have brought the two children along as well. The problem with that scenario was that getting all three of them into the country undetected would have been nigh-on impossible. No, he decided. He recalled his conversation with Ol' Johnny Boy, and how the man had wished only to do right by his family. He would not want the mother of his children to die: Jennifer still meant an awful lot to him, Cain was sure, and would bring John running to save her.

Of course there'd be one other coming to rescue her, too.

Bring it on!

Almost as much as he wanted his final reckoning with John Telfer, Cain looked forward to reacquainting himself with Joe Hunter.

'I've a bone to pick with you,' he said.

'Say what?'

'Private thoughts,' he told the driver. 'Just do what you're supposed to and drive.'

'Would if I knew where you wanted to go.'

Cain studied the man, giving him more attention this time. He was a hard-faced punk, fair-haired, with a wispy beard, and spectacles perched on a crooked nose that looked like it had been broken more than once. He had the look of a street fighter, and from the tattoos on his forearms Cain deduced that he'd had a tough upbringing. The coded tats were *de rigueur* in prison yards for someone who had killed another man. If Cain had followed that practice he'd need a body the size of a house.

'You don't know?'

'I didn't ask.'

Cain nodded. The driver was to be trusted. By omitting knowledge of a destination, he was showing that he wasn't leading Cain into a trap. Thoughtful, Cain decided, but unnecessary. The driver was still at his disposal, whether or not he was trustworthy.

'Take us to the harbour at Baltimore,' Cain said.

'You have someone meeting you there?'

'No. I'm hungry and I hear they have great crab cakes.'

The driver adjusted his spectacles before setting the van rolling. Along the way, he cast sidelong glances at his passenger, generally followed by frowns that marred his rugged complexion with even deeper folds. He had no concept of a man like Cain, but then again, not too many people did. Cain ignored him, choosing instead to lean over the seat and keep an eye on Jennifer. She was sleeping, her head drooping over her chest. She'd have a hell of a stiff neck when she woke up, but Cain could help loosen it with a few expert probes of his knife. He smiled at the thought, and in his mind's eye began stripping back the outer dermis to display the spine hidden beneath.

Taxis rocketed by, but the driver held the van at a couple miles below the speed limit. He had no intention of giving the local cops a reason to pull them over. The distance to Baltimore was short, and within half an hour they were moving through traffic that had slowed to a crawl as it navigated the routes into the centre of Charm City. Jennifer's eyelids began to flicker: she was lost in a dream, but as long as it wasn't a nightmare and she started screaming, she was of no concern for now.

Cain eyed a Gothic building standing alongside more recent skyscrapers. The look of the building conjured years gone by, an anachronistic monument to older, simpler times. Cain grunted when he saw that it was an original Bank of America tower; nothing simplistic about that. Now the tower was a symbol of control and order, the antithesis of everything he stood for. He turned his eyes from it and towards the Inner Harbor directly ahead of them. From their slightly elevated vantage he could see across to the headland where Fort McHenry squatted, but he'd had quite enough of forts in the last year or so. Instead he directed the driver to the left, passing the *Spirit of Baltimore* that was moored at the wharf, and a twin-level collection of restaurants and boutique shops. Towering over it all was the World Trade Center, an odd construction with five sides, and beyond it a massive indoor aquarium complete with a cascading waterfall tumbling through a faux rainforest. A Hard Rock Café, a book store and sports bar dominated a reclaimed power plant and offered lively entertainment. None of those sights held any attraction for him.

'You want crab cakes still?'

Cain frowned at the driver.

'Crab cakes?'

'You said you were hungry.'

'Not for crustaceans, my friend. I prefer my bones on the inside.'

The driver adjusted his glasses again.

Another one that his wit was wasted upon, Cain thought. Maybe if the driver knew his passenger was the famous Harvestman he'd have chosen to be less trustworthy. That was a point worth redressing before they parted company. 'Just take me to Fells Point, willya?'

'Good restaurants there,' the driver acknowledged with a wry smile. He knew exactly where Cain was heading to.

Baltimore Inner Harbor was the tourist destination of sightseers, Fells Point the place those same tourists flocked to of an evening, but beyond the spit of land were the shipping wharfs and one in particular owned by associates of Kurt Hendrickson. Baron had suggested it as an appropriate place for Cain to hold Jennifer.

Fells Point passed without attention from Cain, who was too intent on studying Jennifer again. When first he'd laid eyes on her he'd thought she was beautiful, and he didn't give much credence to the old adage that beauty was skin deep; quite the opposite in fact. He couldn't wait to discover Jennifer's hidden treasures. He must keep her alive to bait his trap, but that didn't mean he couldn't make a start on her. Truth be told, it was a struggle not to clamber into the back of the van there and then and try out his new blades.

The van edged along an industrial area, warehouses alternating with freight yards stacked high with containers destined for locations throughout the world. It passed through a gate electronically controlled, but also under the baleful gaze of an elderly black man. The old guy had suffered an accident at some point and the lower half of his right leg had been amputated. Cain idly wondered what had become of the limb. The gate closed behind them and the driver directed the van along smooth concrete paving towards a loading dock and a decrepit container ship. The ship was circa 1950s vintage and carried each of its six decades etched in the corrosion of its metal work. The *Queen Sofia* now had the look of an aging dowager, and was about as appealing. In this case, Cain thought, ugly is also more than skin deep, and definitely runs to the bone. But to him the ship was a real sight for sore eyes.

Leaning into the rear compartment, Cain shook Jennifer's shoulder. 'Hey, Sleeping Beauty! Wakey wakey!'

Jennifer stirred, her mouth opening wordlessly, a string of sticky saliva glistening on her chin. The anaesthetic was still doing its work, and her vision went unfocused. Cain leaned deeper into the compartment, took her chin between his fingers and directed her gaze to the front.

'Didn't I tell you that you'd get treated to five-star accommodation?' he said. 'Jeez, first you get to hobnob with TV stars on an executive jet, now you get an all-expenses paid cruise. Hell, I keep treating you like this you won't want anything to do with your husband any more.' Cain pushed his thumb against the tip of her nose and Jennifer's head rolled away from the pressure. 'But, we can't have that, can we? We can't keep all this to ourselves, Jennifer. John has just got to come join us.'

CHAPTER 34

I was in no doubt that Cain would contact Walter soon. He hadn't gone to all the trouble of snatching Jennifer to now sit on his thumbs. Pretty soon the demands would start, and I could be in motion again. I hated the feeling of futility while waiting for the deranged bastard to call, but had no choice. Waiting I'm not good at. My need to get going was like an itch I couldn't scratch and the longer it went on, the more agitated I became. I considered taking Harvey's advice and heading back to Rene Moulder's place to check in with Rink, but that meant putting myself out of the loop for the best part of the day. I wanted to be on hand the moment that Walter gave mc the nod. That meant staying close to his retreat, and the transportation I'd require.

Harvey left reluctantly, and I knew he wasn't happy leaving me to deal with Cain alone. Just before setting off he appraised me with his molten chocolate gaze and I knew he was considering the alternatives and didn't like what he was coming up with. Finally he'd just shaken his head slowly, clambered into his chopper and lifted off. I watched until the helicopter was lost in the cloud haze to the south. I was sorry to see my friend go, but at the same time happy that no one else I cared for was involved in the danger that constantly dogged me.

I tried sleeping; bunking in a back room as far away from where Bryce and the others had died as I could find, but sleep eluded me. Instead, I got up, showered, ate a sandwich and drank some coffee. Then I set to prepping my weapons. The SIG gleamed by the time I was done, and I turned my attention to the shells supplied to me by Walter. Contrary to popular belief, guns don't jam, ammunition does. I checked each bullet individually before feeding them into three clips. Choosing .40 S&W or .357 SIG ammo would have given me more stopping power, but the clips held less capacity than the fifteen rounds that 9 mm Parabellums allowed. I had the feeling that I'd need plenty of bullets before I was done and the forty-five I had to hand wouldn't necessary be overkill. Next I honed my Ka-bar.

My weapons prepared, I turned to honing my natural weapons.

I ran, following the river through the wooded valley, one ear always on my cellphone should Walter call me back in a hurry. When my breathing had settled into a rhythm, and my body was sufficiently warmed and lubricated, I incorporated strengthening exercises into my workout. On a large boulder that jutted over white water, I went through a sequence of attack and defensive movements taken from various martial arts forms. I finished my workout by stretching, then sat on the rock, listening to the sound of the rapids below me. Rink could have lost himself in the hypnotic lull of the rushing water, but I was too edgy for that. I got up and ran back, forcing myself to even greater effort. By the time I arrived at Walter's cabin I'd killed a couple of hours, but there was still some waiting time ahead of me. But maybe it wouldn't seem as interminable.

Imogen was standing on the stoop, her chin tucked low into her collar as she watched me jog across the field towards the house. She had her hair under a hat that was as much a disguise as it was to keep off the cold. She looked much as she had when we'd stood over her sister's headstone back in Maine, only her tears were for something different this time.

Slowing, I walked the last twenty yards or so. Imogen kept her face dipped, but her gaze on mine. When I was still ten paces away, she came to meet me. Maybe I didn't have the right, but I opened my arms and she entered their circle and snaked her hands around my waist.

We just held each other and I could feel her heartbeat against my chest. When we finally stepped apart, Imogen held on, her right hand clasping a handful of my sweatshirt like she'd never let go.

I'd thought that the best thing for her would be

if I walked away, but I could see that I'd been wrong. Walking away didn't change a damn thing. Imogen was inexorably tied to me and she always would be. I could be on the other side of the planet and she'd still be within the sphere of influence that surrounded me, and therefore in peril from those who would do me harm. Better then that I keep her close and that way she'd be much safer. I pulled her into my embrace and she tilted her mouth to mine in silent acknowledgement.

When she stepped back she did let go, but the bond between us was stronger than before.

'I'm sorry, Imogen . . .'

Really I had no way of explaining myself, feeling awkward as I attempted to order an apology in my mind.

Imogen placed a finger to my lips.

'It's behind us. Let's leave it there, Joe. Let's leave everything there.'

Everything.

She wasn't talking about the recent attempt on her life, or any of the other times she'd been in danger because of her attachment to me. Neither was she talking about the fact I'd walked out on her leaving Hartlaub and Brigham to pull her out of the fire. She was talking about Kate. If I'd thought about it too long, then maybe my answer would have been different, but right then, right there, I had only one way of showing her everything would be OK between us. I took her in my arms and kissed her again.

The cabin was no place to take a lady, so we strolled down by the river, out from under the prying eyes of the CIA men. My clothing was damp from my exertions, but I didn't feel the cold. Neither of us did as we took up where we'd left off that night in Maine before our rude interruption. Afterwards we sat side by side and watched the water flow by. I found the soothing pull of the river easier to lose myself in that time.

'Hartlaub and Brigham are going to stay with me until you're through.'

'They're good men,' I said.

'They're killers.'

Yes, they were, but that's the type of men I needed watching over her. I looked at her studying me. Maybe she was reassessing exactly what I was.

'Once I'd have found that abhorrent,' she said. 'But now . . .'

Hers was a moral dilemma I'd often struggled with: in a civilised world there should be no need for men like me, or her CIA minders, but civilisation was just a veneer. Despite four thousand years of supposed development we were no more than a rung above our savage forebears. Actually, I'd often thought that we'd taken a step back down the ladder and were worse than the beasts that only killed to survive. There was nothing in nature like Tubal Cain, I was certain. And, as long as something like him lived, it vindicated my existence.

Changing the subject, I asked, 'Whose idea was it to come here?'

'Whose do you think?'

I rolled my neck. 'I thought Walter was behind it.'

'Walter tried to put me off. He said it wasn't appropriate. He was wrong. It's shown me exactly the kind of life you have to . . . endure.' She laid a hand on my forearm and her expression was earnest. 'But I wanted to see. It has helped make my mind up. It doesn't matter to me where you go . . . what you have to do . . . I want to be there for you, Joe.'

'They showed you what happened inside?' Even after a clean-up crew had sanitised the room, I hoped that Imogen hadn't been exposed to the pall of violence that still hung over it.

'No. But I didn't need to see that. It's enough that I can imagine it. You shouldn't have to deal with things like that alone.'

'I'm not alone. I have Rink and—'

Imogen cut me off. She put her hand against the side of my head. 'I'm talking about up here, Joe. I'm talking about you carrying the burden inside your mind. I want to help take some of the pain away.'

I held my palm on the back of her hand. It was soothing, but I doubted anything could take away the guilt I carried. Her offer was generous, though, and not one I wanted to turn down. Finally, I twined my fingers with hers and brought down our clasped hands on to my thigh. 'Thank you. I want that too. But . . . well, there's still things I have to do alone.'

271

'I understand. I just want you to know that I'll be waiting for you when you come back. OK?'

'OK.'

We leaned in and kissed, gently this time, as if sealing a pact. Then we stood, straightening our clothes. Imogen jammed her hat down over her mussed hair. Now it was no kind of disguise. Anyone who looked at us would guess exactly what had gone on. We smiled like abashed teenagers.

'Come on,' I said, leading her by the hand. 'I don't know about you, but I think I need a shower.'

Just like last time, it seemed that our lovemaking heralded future dramatic events and that my shower would have to go on the back burner. No sooner had I made the suggestion than my cellphone bleeped. I dug it out of my sweats and looked at the screen. It was Walter. He knew I was out there making amends with Imogen and there could be only one reason for disturbing me. Cain had made contact.

CHAPTER 35

Tubal Cain studied Jennifer Telfer with detachment. He did not see her as human but as a tool to cut the heart out of her husband's chest. To him, she was as important as the Recon Tanto or the Bowie knife he carried on his belt.

Because his plan relied on Jennifer being alive and relatively healthy, he couldn't allow this ill-treatment to go on. Leaving her in squalor, unfed and without proper sanitation, was akin to allowing his blades to tarnish. Cain regularly oiled and sharpened his knives, and this woman should be afforded the same treatment.

He peered through the letterbox-sized slot in the door, noting how Jennifer huddled in the corner for warmth. She was done with crying for now, probably from dehydration, because Cain knew she hadn't been given water since her arrival. Or maybe she'd finally realised the futility of weeping; it engendered little response from pitiless men. There was a bucket in the corner of her cell, and judging by the smell wafting through the opening she had availed herself of it. It needed emptying. Jennifer required nourishment.

The fat man sitting at the end of the narrow corridor seemed less inclined to leave his porn magazine than see to either task. Cain paced along the corridor, taking a single step in time with each measured exhalation. It was a process to calm himself, so that he could communicate with the dirt-ball without allowing his urges to overwhelm him: he so wanted to slash the pervert's sweaty face to ribbons. It also helped calm Cain's stomach, as the floor lifted and fell with each swell that the container ship rode.

Coming to a halt he waited for the fat man to thumb over another page. He was an 'ass man' by all accounts, because the big-breasted woman spread over two pages didn't hold his attention long. He flicked a glance up at Cain, then turned back to another page where a svelte young thing was hiking up the hem of her dress.

'What would you like to do to her, huh?' asked the fat man, smoothing his fingers over the woman's backside.

Exactly what I'd like to do to you, Cain thought. There was nothing erotic in the idea, but he had to concur that hacking away the flesh to find what lay within was very sensual.

'Feed the woman and give her water.'

'What the fuck am I? A fuckin' nursemaid?' The man went back to his skin mag.

Cain exhaled, and this time it had nothing to do with the nauseating movement of the ship.

The man sneered at another young woman, this one in an even more revealing pose. 'Fuck, you can see what the bitch had for breakfast!'

'I told you to feed and water the woman.'

'You ain't my boss. Fuck off and leave me in peace.'

Cain stood impassively. 'You do know who I am?'

'Do I look like I give a flying fuck?'

'No, you look like a piece of crap with a cesspit for a mind. It would explain the bile that flows from your mouth.'

The man pushed up out of his chair. Sitting down, his fat had been bagged around his middle. Standing, he tightened himself, spreading his shoulders so that he loomed over Cain like a grizzly bear. He had twice the girth and at least three inches on Cain. He pressed a thick finger smeared with printer's ink to Cain's chest. 'Just who the fuck do you think *you're* talking to?'

Cain shook his head sadly. 'Like I said . . . cesspit, crap, bile. Take your pick. If you don't understand any of those words, I'll gladly explain them in simpler terms.'

The fat man mulled Cain's reply over in his mind. 'You're making a joke, right? Only I'm just not getting it.'

'So do something useful; go and feed and water the woman.'

'I'm busy.' The man reached down to his magazine. He shook the pages under Cain's nose. 'I'm making plans for what I'm gonna do to her. Getting what you call *inspiration*.'

'You will not touch her.'

'Says who?'

'Says me.'

The fat man laughed. He rolled the magazine between his hands, squeezing it into a solid tube, and waved the impromptu phallic symbol towards Jennifer's cell. 'I think I'll start by softening her up with this. Otherwise she will be no good to a man of my size.'

Cain closed his eyes. His lids flickered.

The fat man jabbed the rolled paper into Cain's chest. 'You coming in your pants at the thought of that, you sick fuck?'

Cain's left hand snapped on to the exposed wrist. He pulled, snaring the man's thumb so that it was held tightly to the rolled paper. His other hand merely caressed the bulging flesh where wrist became hand. The movement was so subtle that at first the fat man did not realise what had happened. Only when he saw the blood pouring along his forearm did he try to snatch his hand away. Cain let it go, and watched as the man's goggle-eyed incredulity centred on the lifeless thumb hanging alongside his palm.

'Jesus Christ! What the fuck have you done to me?'

Cain said, 'Severed both the abductor pollicis

brevis and longus tendons. You'll find you can still wiggle your thumb, but you'll never make a fist again. It will, I'm afraid, impede the manner in which you seek "inspiration" in future.'

The man looked again at the pinkish ends of the tendons poking from his opened flesh, then up at Cain. His mouth was open, and Cain realised he'd lost him. Just too many long words. To clarify, he mimed the sex act of manual self-gratification.

The fat man's hand was limp, and to prove the point the magazine fluttered from his grasp. He watched it hit the floor, then followed the lines of Cain's body all the way up to where he held the Tanto. Cain waved the knife. 'You still have one working hand. Are you going to put it to good use and go fetch the woman something to eat and drink?'

The fat man suddenly shrieked: his voice high like a little girl's. Lurching around the chair, he grabbed at the exit door he'd been guarding. His instinct was to go for the handle with his right hand, but it had become a hindrance. Wide-eyed he cast frantic glances at Cain, then tore open the door with his left and fled up a second corridor. Cain doubted he'd be coming back. He snorted at the man's fleeing back, then went to peer through the hatch at Jennifer.

'I'm having something to eat and drink brought for you,' he said.

Jennifer didn't reply, but he saw her eyes flashing in the dim light. She finally sat up. Her gaze had never left his. 'Where are my children? If you've harmed them . . .'

'They're safe,' Cain said. 'I didn't touch them.'

'You left them all alone?'

'I did. But I trust that they'll have been collected by now. As soon as John arrives, you will be released and you can see them again.'

'John won't come.' Her words were like a mantra.

'Oh, I'm sure he will.'

'No.' Jennifer struggled up from the floor, still unsteady from the residual effects of the drugs he'd administered. She approached the door, her hands fisted at her sides. She thrust out her jaw and said again, 'John won't come. But his brother Joe will.'

Cain stared into the woman's eyes and believed her. 'Won't that be great? A nice little family reunion?'

'Joe will make you sorry you ever came near me. He'll tear your throat out.'

Cain touched the scar tissue on his neck. 'He already tried that, but failed. This time I'll show him how it's really done.'

'Joe will kill you, and I'll spit on your body when he's finished.'

'Steady on, there,' Cain laughed at her. 'Don't forget that I'm your only hope of getting out of here alive. I'm here to protect you. The fat guard . . . do you know what he'd do to you if I wasn't here?'

Jennifer was no fool; she recognised the implications of the fat man coming into her cell unchaperoned. Her features slipped into open shock.

'He comes to the door and . . . says things.' Jennifer's voice had lost its vitriol towards him.

'I've punished him for that, Jennifer. He won't bother you again.'

She nodded silently, wrapping her arms around her body.

'Now, you should remember that when next you make threats,' Cain went on. 'I'm your only friend and protector. I'm the only one who's having food and water brought to you.'

'It won't mean a thing when Joe gets here.'

'Then I'll just have to show him how misguided he is.' He jiggled the point of his knife in the air, grinning as he mimed cutting a throat. Cain halted the charade on hearing the clatter of feet in the outer gangway. He slid the blade out of sight. 'I'm just going to close this flap for a little while, OK? There are some others who may need putting in their place.'

He closed the steel flap over the slot and slipped a bolt across. Walking back along the short corridor, he timed it so that he met the group of men just as they were about to storm through the bulwark door at the end. There were three of them, two of whom he already knew. One was the driver who'd helped him transport Jennifer here from the airport, the other a tall Russian with steel-coloured hair and eyes the shade of a Siberian winter sky. Cain had been introduced to Grodek as the captain of this ship when he'd boarded. He did not at first know the third man.

'Cain,' the stranger said, eyeing him up and down. 'It looks like I got here just in time.'

Cain recognised the voice from having conversed regularly with him in the past day or so. 'You did?'

'The name's Baron.'

'I know who you are. You're the one that allowed Joe Hunter and Jared Rington to escape.' Cain appraised the man. He was shorter, and slighter of build, than the others but there was a detachment about him that appealed to Cain. Not much, though.

'That was Sigmund Petoskey's fault. He allowed his defences to drop and Hunter managed to take him hostage.'

'And Kurt Hendrickson's death?'

'Nothing I could do about that.'

'Joe Hunter outsmarted you again, huh?'

Baron smiled whimsically, and Cain could feel the man's gaze caress the scar on his throat. 'The way I've heard the story told, you weren't so successful against Joe Hunter either.'

Cain returned the smile. The two men were like a viper studying its reflection in a mirror, ready to sink in its fangs the second it found an opening.

'Looks like we have something in common, then.'

'Not to mention a common enemy.'

Grodek stepped forward, and Cain noted the gun in the man's big fist. His own hand, concealed by his hip, still held the Tanto. Yet neither man made a play with their weapons. Grodek merely used his to point out the splashes of blood on the floor. 'I made a deal with Hendrickson. I agreed to extend my hospitality and resources to you, Baron. But that did not include allowing this *maniac* to injure my men. Brady's hand has been crippled.'

'Didn't Hendrickson warn you? He should have. Cain slaughtered one of his men at their first meeting.'

'Aah, yes, my old pal Getz,' Cain said, recalling the incident. 'Maybe killing him was a little extreme, but I had a point to prove. I am happy to go on proving myself if necessary.'

Grodek made a noise that sounded like *Paaah!*

'That fat pig – Grady, was it? – is arranging food and drink for our guest?' Cain asked.

'Our guest? We should kill her now before things get even further out of control,' Grodek snapped.

Baron laid a hand on the Russian's wrist, making the bigger man lower his weapon. 'You promised that you would help.'

'I promised Kurt Hendrickson, but he is dead. So is my promise.'

Cain merely tilted his head, as though listening to distant music.

Baron lifted the tails of his jacket and shirt, showing a large dressing bandaged to his right

281

side. 'I took a bullet for Hendrickson. Alive or dead, I think he owes me. I think you do also, Captain.'

'I owe you?'

'Yes. Your allegiance. I have taken charge of our boss's interests, one of which is the smuggling operation you are involved in.'

Cain listened to the exchange as though unconcerned. He'd changed his mind: Baron was an asshole. But there was still something about him that Cain could work with.

Baron's watery gaze shifted from Grodek to Cain. 'We all owe each other our allegiance. It's the only way we can finish what was started.'

Cain sheathed his knife. 'Then we'd best get on with it. Grodek, take me to the comms room. It's time I contacted the man protecting John Telfer.'

Grodek shook his head. 'No, Cain. I am finished with this. My deal was with Kurt Hendrickson, not either of you. There's no way I'll be paid for my trouble, so I'll have to recoup my losses another way. The woman,' he gesticulated along the corridor, 'she belongs to me now. If I cannot get a good price for her, I'll give her to Brady as compensation for his hand.'

'Your fat friend would enjoy that,' Cain said. 'But I'm afraid it's not going to happen.'

'Don't forget who is in charge here,' Grodek snapped as he lifted the gun. 'I say what happens on *my* ship.'

'I can see that might be a problem,' Cain said.

'No problem for me. I will have my crew remove you. Do you think yourself strong enough to swim all the way to port?'

'How far from port are we?'

'A couple miles,' Baron offered.

'Then no,' Cain said. 'But it's far enough out to offload some unnecessary cargo.'

Grodek sneered. 'You mean the woman? I told you I have new plans for her.'

'No, not Jennifer,' Cain said. 'I meant you.'

He struck lightning fast, his Bowie knife whipping up and under the Russian's chin before the man could think about aiming his gun. The tip of the knife sank through flesh without a whisper, but the hilt jamming against his jaw produced a thud that echoed the length of the corridor. Cain held the ship's captain on the end of his blade until all life had fled. It took only seconds, then he allowed the blade to dip and the man to slide off.

Baron took a half-step backwards, his fingers edging towards a gun on his belt. The driver swore gutturally, but his hands stayed in plain sight. Cain brought up his other hand, showed the Tanto. A simple lunge would put it through Baron's chest. Baron lifted his hands and showed whose side he was on with a less than puissant smile. 'I meant what I said about working together.'

'Looks like a mutiny is in order, eh, gentlemen?' Cain said. 'Some of the crew might not be pleased about their sudden change of captain. Shall we go together and show them how to walk the plank?'

Baron touched his injured side. 'I owe Joe Hunter for this, and I guess if I'm ever going to get revenge, it will mean sticking with you.'

The driver was one of Hendrickson's men, not Grodek's. Still, witnessing the Russian's death had thrown him into flux over where his loyalties lay. He was sinking fast. 'Can you cook?' Cain asked.

The driver blinked his incredulity. Then, realising he'd just been offered a lifeline, he nodded.

'Good.' Cain bent and wiped his Bowie clean on Captain Grodek's trousers. 'You can feed the woman. I don't think that fat-assed Brady will be coming back.'

CHAPTER 36

'I thought I was doing this on my own.'

I was wrong about that, and I was wrong about why Walter had rung me.

Cain hadn't yet been in touch to organise an exchange of hostages. Walter had summoned me to his cabin because he wanted to set the terms of another deal, this one with me. I wasn't entirely happy about it, but neither could I see how I could refuse him.

We were in the room where Bryce Lang died, and it was a less than subtle manipulation I could have done without. However, Walter was in charge and there was nothing I could do about it except walk out and force the others to follow. It still felt like an abattoir in there, despite having been thoroughly cleaned, disinfected and the stained upholstery shrouded in plastic sheets. But I stayed. At least Imogen had been spared the reek of chemicals that failed to mask the undercurrent of slaughter. She'd been whisked away to a safe location, carrying with her a promise that I'd join her as soon as I was finished. It had struck me when Brigham and another younger agent had been her chaperones this time, that there was more to Hartlaub staying behind than met the eye.

'It's still a deniable operation, but Hartlaub is going to accompany you. We feel there should be certain controls in place.' Walter was sitting in a shrouded plastic chair but I couldn't bring myself to join him; I just stood at the centre of the room with my hands jammed in my pockets. The plastic crinkled as he lifted a hand. 'Hartlaub is going to accompany you. It's the only way we could see to stop all the shit from falling on your shoulders. If Hartlaub is along for the ride, and you're just a civilian who helps him in pursuit of his duty, then where's the blame going to finally stop?'

'That's about the stupidest thing I've ever heard,' I said.

'On the surface it sounds pretty lame, I'll give you that, but buried in a classified report, it'll suffice to keep your goddamn ass out of prison. Why are you being so ungrateful?'

'I'm not ungrateful, Walter. I'm trying to figure out your real motive. The last time I was sent after Cain, the bastard's life was saved. Is Hartlaub coming along to make sure he's saved this time too?'

Walter stood up surprisingly fast for a man of his bulk, and the plastic was sucked up by the vacuum. It settled slowly as Walter took three solid steps towards me. 'What are you saying, Hunter? That I'd protect Cain over you?'

I just met his purpling face with a cool expression, and that incited him all the more.

'Son of a bitch! Did you *see* what that murderous piece of shit did here? He dismembered my oldest friend, took parts of his skeleton as trophies. Jesus fucking Christ! Do you think I want to see that bastard sent back to prison? I'd love to come along and watch you tear his fucking heart out! I'd tear it out myself if I was able!' His language, not to mention the force with which it was delivered, surprised me. It took him off-guard too. Walter staggered and by the way he grasped at his chest I feared that his rage had brought on a heart attack. I reached out to steady him, but he threw my hands aside. He stood, gulping air, trying to calm himself. 'You have a job to do, Hunter. But you're there to save Jennifer first and kill Cain second. No . . . don't deny it. That's your priority, and I can understand that. I'm sending Hartlaub to make sure that Cain *does not* survive this time.'

Hartlaub and I shared a glance. I looked back at my old mentor and found him digging in his shirt pocket. He plucked out a cigar, and without preamble jammed it between his teeth. He'd said what he was going to say on the subject, and I'd have to like it or lump it. I was still going after Cain, and if that meant that Hartlaub accompanied me then so be it. I lifted my hands to signify surrender.

Walter was right. My priority was to get Jennifer away from Cain and if Cain escaped while I was otherwise engaged then that's the way it would be. I'd prefer to kill the son of a bitch myself, but if Hartlaub got to him first then I could live with that. My only regret was that I'd sent Harvey away. I'd rather it was him or Rink accompanying me. Still, I recalled when I first met Hartlaub and had judged him as a warrior to be admired. Maybe things wouldn't be so bad with him watching my back.

I offered him my hand. 'Nothing personal, mate.'

He unfolded his arms, stuck out his hand and we shook. 'I know.'

'Thanks for saving Imogen, as well. I owe you one.'

Hartlaub shrugged. 'I was just the driver. Brigham did all the wet work.'

Walter had transferred the cigar to his fingers. 'Are you two all made up now, because we've more important things to be getting on with?'

'We're good,' I confirmed.

He returned to his seat and the plastic crackled as he sat. He frowned at the other furniture in the room, likely thinking he'd have to replace everything. However clean it appeared on the surface it was still drenched with the blood of his murdered friend. Personally I'd have dumped it all in a huge pile outside and set it on fire. No, scratch that. I'd have torched the building.

Walter stuffed his cigar between his teeth, speaking out of the corner of his mouth. 'You asked me to bring John in. Well, I'm finding that difficult. He's under the protection of the US Marshals and I haven't been able to find a good enough reason for them to release him into my custody.' Walter sneaked a glance at Hartlaub, but I didn't miss it. When I glanced the CIA agent's way, he was studying his feet. Without missing a beat, Walter continued. 'So, your plan to use him to draw out Cain must be put on the back burner. If it comes to it, I'll pull rank and demand John's attendance but for now we will concentrate on freeing Jennifer without him.'

'I never intended placing him in harm's way. I just wanted Cain to hear his voice,' I said. 'Surely you can have him brought to the other end of a phone?'

'Yes, yes, if it becomes necessary. But let's concentrate on what we can do without him.'

'What's going on, Walt?'

'We're planning on taking down Tubal Cain, that's what's going on.'

'You act edgy every time I mention John.'

'Because we've more urgent business to contend with, that's why. Now . . . can we plan on how we intend to kill this bastard or not?'

'Make all the plans you want, Walter. You can come get me when you're done.'

'Where are you going?'

'I'm going to take a shower. It stinks in here.'

The room wasn't the only thing that stank. So did Walter's lies, and the more I tried to make sense of them, the more they made me feel sick to the core.

Trying to expunge the nausea, I spent some time

under a hot shower in the stall at the back of the cabin. Soap and shampoo didn't help, so I turned the dial to its lowest setting and cleansed myself with its icy chill. When I was done, I found the roughest towel I could get my hands on and practically flagellated myself with it, like I was paying penance. I dumped my sweats and dressed in my spares, settling my weapons about my body. For a moment I considered walking away. If what I suspected was true then I wondered why I was still involved. But the thought was fleeting. Jennifer was in peril, and therefore I was going to do everything I could to save her.

When I got back to the living room their anticipation hit me like an electrical charge. Walter and Hartlaub were bent over a laptop and when they looked up I knew that the waiting was over. Hartlaub was as steady as usual but Walter looked pale, a sheen of perspiration on his forehead. He licked his lips, tongue flicking rapidly as he moistened his dry mouth. 'We're on.'

CHAPTER 37

C ain considered his new domain and hated it. The *Queen Sofia* was a rusting hulk, an ugly, sprawling container ship that carried with it a memory of all the nefarious activity it had been involved in over the years. Most recently it had been used to transport girls snatched from the Balkans and destined for the sex trade in the US. It was no better below decks; the interior of the ship was as unsavoury as the crewmen who worked there. He hated the stench of unwashed bodies, the grease that got everywhere and the ever-present acidic undertones of corrosion. He felt itchy, unclean, as if bugs crawled under his clothing and burrowed into his skin. He couldn't wait to be off the vessel, back in the good clean air again.

He walked down the corridor – he couldn't be bothered with all those fancy nautical terms – towards the rooms that Captain Grodek had made into temporary holding cells. At his shoulder walked Baron, seemingly as unconcerned with the filth and stench as he was with the blood now decorating the front of his jacket. Baron, to prove his allegiance to Cain, had shot fat Brady point-blank in his gut despite the blow-back from the wound. He'd stood there impassively while Cain had bent over the dying man and finished the job he'd started on his thumb. Cain nicked it off with the Recon Tanto and tossed it to Baron.

'Hold that for me will ya, I'm all fingers and thumbs these days,' Cain had quipped.

Baron hadn't acknowledged the joke, just slipped the severed digit into a pocket for safe keeping.

Now Cain ignored the man's presence; his wit seemed to be wasted on everyone these days.

They'd only had to kill another two of Grodek's men. The others had grumbled at the sudden shift in command, but only until Cain had slaughtered the ringleaders. After that they acquiesced in his way of thinking. As long as they were paid for their efforts, they didn't care who their masters were. Cain promised them a good pay day once this trip was over, and they bought it. The fact he'd no intention of being aboard the ship within the next couple hours didn't matter. He was no fool. He'd used various means to cover his tracks while making contact with the black-ops controller, but it didn't matter how many firewalls he directed the calls through, they'd have been tracked back to this ship. Chances were that Walter Hayes Conrad would consider having the ship torpedoed rather than allow him to escape a second time, which was why Cain had organised a second boat to take him and Jennifer elsewhere.

Cain fancied himself as a Prince of Chaos. He didn't care if plans went to crap, for that was the nature of the universe he inhabited. Let Conrad nuke the ship if he wanted to, let him send an assault team of Navy Seals; all they'd find was a *Mary Celeste* when they got here. Cain's plan was always adaptable, to take into account the whim of chaotic influence, and it didn't matter that his original plan to lure John Telfer wasn't as easy as he'd assumed. He was confident that Telfer would be delivered to him sooner or later.

He unlocked the letterbox hatch and peered through the slot, nodding in satisfaction at the empty room. Jennifer had been moved to somewhere less odious, as he'd commanded Pete Eckhart, the driver. By doing his bidding, Eckhart had proven his loyalty. He was one of the few who would be allowed to live when they disembarked the ship. Cain and Baron would have their hands full with Jennifer and whoever showed up to save her, someone had to steer the launch to land. Eckhart could always be disposed of later.

He glanced over his shoulder at Baron. The man was standing calmly, staring into space. Weirdo, Cain thought. He walked on and heard Baron falling into step behind him.

They took a turn in the passage, and approached another room. This one had a similar door to that of the first cell, with a hinged flap cut into the metal. Cain unlocked the hatch and let it drop with a clang. Inside, Jennifer didn't respond. She was sitting in a chair, her wrists and ankles bound with leather straps. Her head hung down, her hair masking her features. Eckhart had reported that she'd refused to eat and had spat the mouthful he'd forked into her mouth back at him.

'Wait here,' Cain said. Baron pursed his lips, but stayed exactly where he was. Though he'd taken hold of the loose threads of Hendrickson's organisation, Baron knew that he'd never control Cain. He'd offered his loyalty, though Cain suspected it was tenuous. It did the man good to be put in his place.

Opening the door fully, Cain stepped inside the room. It had been decorated to offer some comfort, but was still disgusting: the off-white walls, stained by who knew what, and smelly threadbare carpet reminded Cain of times he'd holed up in the cheapest of motels. Even his cell at Fort Conchar had been more stylish than some of those.

'Do you remember when I brought you here?' Cain stood with his hands clasped behind his back, rocking on his heels like a Gestapo interrogator. Jennifer made no move to reply or to even lift her head. 'That time I had you drugged and carried here. I can have you drugged again, or you can walk. Which will it be?'

'Where are my children?' Jennifer's voice was hoarse, not unlike Cain's.

'We've been over this before.'

'If you've hurt them . . .'

'What? What will you do? Kill me?'

'Yes.' Jennifer's head finally came up and the look on her face was like that of a wild beast. Her lips peeled back from her teeth, and she stated the point more forcefully. 'I will tear you apart.'

'I love your spirit, Jennifer. If you weren't already spoken for I'd ask for your hand in marriage.' He looked at where her left hand was strapped to the chair, traced the lines of her metacarpals beneath the skin. 'Actually, your hand would be all I'd take.'

'I want to see my children.'

'Didn't you hear me?' Cain wondered if she had surfaced enough from the drugs to have taken in anything when last he'd spoken to her. 'They're waiting for you back home in England. If you want to see them again you will have to do as I say. Now . . . are you going to answer my question?'

'I'll walk.'

'Good. It's so much easier if you do that.'

'Did John come?'

Cain didn't answer.

'I told you he wouldn't.'

'He's on his way now.'

'Don't bet on it.'

'I think you should stop being so negative about John. It's only because he's agreed to come that you're still alive. Why don't you cut him some slack?'

'Like he did for me you mean?'

'Actually, he probably did you a big favour when he left. How did you manage to live with such an insufferable man for so long?'

'You don't know him.'

'You're wrong. John and I shared some quality time. I know what kind of person he is. He will come, you can be sure of that.'

'He won't, but Joe will.' Jennifer peered at the scar tissue marking Cain's throat. 'Did Joe do that to you?'

Cain stretched his neck, fancying that he could hear the cartilage pop in his windpipe. 'This is just a scratch.'

'Next time he'll finish the job. He'll cut your head off to make sure you're dead.'

Cain clapped his hands rapidly, bouncing on the balls of his feet. 'You make it all sound so *very exciting*,' he said gleefully. 'I can't wait.'

'You should let me go now while you still have the chance.'

Cain went very still. 'Oh, no, no, no. I think that you're placing too much faith in Joe Hunter. Right now he's a wanted felon, running around like a headless chicken. Does that sound like the kind of man who's going to race in on a white charger and whisk you out of harm's way?'

It was Jennifer's turn to go still, but her jaw was set and she held his gaze. 'You're afraid of him.'

Cain knew that Hunter was a skilled and resourceful enemy. Though it pained him to admit it, he respected Hunter's dogged approach to the chase, but fear him? No. He feared no man.

'I'm only afraid he's going to arrive late and miss what I'm going to do to John,' he said.

A shiver ran its icy finger up Jennifer's spine and he took that moment to step forward and place the tip of his Tanto beneath her left eye. 'Now, Jennifer, *this* is the situation. You can walk out of here and do exactly as I say, and at the end of it I will release you. The alternative is that I cut off your face and leave you here for the rats. I do not need you. I can always find your children again. They would be sufficient to bait my trap.'

'I'll do what you say.'

'Good. Get moving.'

'I can't walk anywhere strapped to this bloody chair.'

Cain withdrew the knife, smiled down on the woman. She had more spunk than he'd have given her credit for: it was something he could admire.

'OK. No trouble from you, and we'll get along fine.' Cain turned and saw that his new partner was still standing motionless in the corridor. 'Baron, come and loosen Mrs Telfer.'

Baron walked in as Cain stepped aside.

Cain nodded at the contraption on Baron's hip. 'Be careful, we've a live one here. First chance she gets she might go for your eyes. Maybe you should zap her first.'

Baron's unclipped his Taser.

Despite what he'd just said, Cain did prefer it

that Jennifer stayed alive. But her dig concerning Joe Hunter had stung. He couldn't cut off her face – yet – but he could still punish her. That'll teach her for insinuating I'm a coward, he thought as the room filled with an electrical crackle and corresponding scream.

CHAPTER 38

A fast flight took us to Langley Air Force
Base, just north of the city of Hampton,
Virginia. One reason for heading there was
to drop off Walter so he could continue to co-
ordinate things from the headquarters of the Air
Force's 480th Intelligence Surveillance and
Reconnaissance Wing. The other was that it was
a short hop for Hartlaub and me to the nearby
naval base at Hampton Roads, the harbour at the
mouth of the Elizabeth and James Rivers where
they spilled into Chesapeake Bay. From there it
would only be a short chase to catch the freighter
currently cruising south past the Barrier Islands
off the coast of North Carolina.

My original plan was to steal a boat and chase
Cain by sea, but that held a couple of major flaws.
For a start, an underpowered craft would never
catch a ship going at full steam, so I would have
to take something big and powerful. Something
like a launch or speedboat would have been ideal
for my purposes, but easily missed. The Coast
Guard would be alerted and we'd be captured in
no time. There was no way I wanted to hurt anyone

in pursuit of their duties, so a fight with the Coast Guard wouldn't happen. I could approach a civilian crew, tell them of my problem and throw Jennifer's life on their mercy. But any sane person would tell me to sling my hook and immediately alert the authorities. As much as I hated to do it, I had no other recourse left to me. I had to work with a naval crew.

The sun was casting its last fingers of day over the harbour as we stood on the dock, studying the boat that sat below us. It was akin to the lifeboats I was familiar with from back home in the UK, a metal shell with inflatable cushions and a small cabin towards the front. The boat bore no insignia, which was good, because Cain had warned he'd kill Jennifer immediately he saw a naval vessel approaching.

'We're going to have to take the crew with us,' I told Hartlaub as we made our way down to the boat. 'But there's no way they can be involved.'

'They won't be. They have their orders to drop us and then pull back.'

'That suits me fine. If we do this the way I intend, I don't want any witnesses.'

He showed me an eye tooth. 'Don't worry, that also suits me fine.'

I took the lead, moved down and on to a gang-plank out to the boat. Smaller craft bobbed on the dark water of the dock. Across from us was a rusting hulk that looked like it hadn't put to sea in the last decade or two, but the backdrop was dominated by massive aircraft carriers and warships. If we failed to stop Cain, I wouldn't put it past Walter to order one of them after him instead.

There were only two crew members on board, one of them a fit young guy with corn-coloured hair and freckles, and another man, of stockier build, maybe ten years older with the ruddy complexion of a seafarer. Neither was in uniform, but they still struck me as military men. The younger one had a flashlight in his hand and was crouching down at the motor, going through maintenance chores. The other was in the cabin, nose deep in paperwork. I took it that he was the commanding officer.

Maritime protocol usually requires permission for you to come aboard, but I didn't rest on etiquette. With Hartlaub at my heels I stepped over the thick rubber and on to the deck. My boots thudding on planks brought the older man's head out of his papers. Dumping my backpack on one of the benches, I walked towards him, extending my hand. 'You were expecting us?'

'So you guys are my mysterious passengers, huh? Am I allowed to know your names?' The older man's eyes twinkled. He had received his orders and understood that this trip was off the record. Reading the humour behind his gaze I decided he could be trusted.

'Hunter,' I said shaking his hand. 'My friend's Hartlaub.'

'Call me Lassiter.' He winked.

'Which of you is the pilot?'

'I am,' said the young man, as he approached with Hartlaub.

'What's your name?'

'Terrence. Terrence Fletcher, sir. US Navy.'

'Terry?' The young man nodded back at me. 'Drop the formalities, OK? Forget that you're with the Navy for the next few hours.'

'I'm not sure I can do that, sir. I'm—'

'Getting off the boat if you don't do as I ask,' I finished for him.

He squinted, glanced sharply at the other man and Lassiter shot him a grin. Finally he nodded, 'You've got it, sir.'

'Right, Terry, work your magic and take us out of here.'

Terry looked at the older man again. Terry was the pilot, but the other was in charge. Lassiter had final say on whether the boat sailed or not.

'Forget rank, Terry. Just take the fucking boat out before I decide to do it myself.'

Behind me Hartlaub chuckled. 'I like your style, Hunter. How to win friends and influence people.'

'If no one else has noticed, we're in a hurry here,' I said.

Terry took us out of the dock and into Chesapeake Bay at a steady clip. Above us rose the bridge connecting Norfolk to Northampton, crossed by a steady flow of traffic, lights sharp against the darkening sky. Beyond the bridge the bay widened as it greeted the open water of the Atlantic, and I urged Terry to speed up. He gave the boat all it had; the nose lifted and we shot across the waves at what I guessed was a steady forty knots.

Terry was a good man and my surliness had possibly ruined his day. It didn't sit well with me, but needs must. When weighed against the fate Jenny faced, a harsh word or two was a necessary evil. Still, I couldn't let it go on. Once we were a couple miles offshore, I clapped the guy on the shoulder and made my apology. Leaving Terry at the controls, I moved to his friend. Lassiter had sat on a folding chair bolted to the cabin wall so he could watch an instrument panel. There was a chair opposite him and I perched myself on it.

'Sorry for being an ass back there,' I said.

'We're service men. We're used to taking orders from asses. As, I'm damn sure, are you.'

He had that right.

'Look, I guess you got your orders, but apart from that you're most likely in the dark.'

'What's new, huh? But you're right, I think we do deserve an explanation,' Lassiter said. Terry turned from the controls, nodding in agreement.

Where did I start? There was far too much back story to give them all the details, so I elected to go directly to the finish. 'Put it this way, unless we get there in time an innocent woman is going to die horribly.'

Then I told them about Cain and what he would

do to his hostage if we didn't stop him. They wanted to know why a full response team wasn't dealing with things. It was a good point, but I explained that Cain would slaughter Jenny if a response team showed up. By the time I'd finished Terry was shivering with the flow of adrenalin through his body and Lassiter had gone a funny green colour that had nothing to do with either the play of light in the cabin or with the rise and fall of the waves. I noticed that Terry had leaned heavily on the throttle again. I'd won a couple of new allies.

Lassiter tapped the instrument panel. Back at Langley Air Force Base someone under Walter's guidance was feeding through coordinates for the suspect freighter. 'She's off the Barrier Islands, east of Roanoke,' he said. 'She's come to a stand-still.'

'How long until we get there?'

Looking at other displays, he said, 'There's a storm heading in. It's going to slow us down.'

I nodded at the dials, unable to decipher them. 'What's your best guess?'

'We could throttle back, conserve fuel and still be there within a couple hours. Or we can go full out and do it in half the time.'

'Full throttle then.'

'We won't have enough fuel for a return trip.'

'Doesn't matter,' I said. 'As soon as we're on board I want you to call the Coast Guard, the police, the rest of your Navy buddies if you have to. If we manage to get Jenny off the ship, I'll only need you to take her a safe distance away. We can always have the boat towed back to port after.'

'And what if you don't manage to get her off?'

'Don't, whatever you do, try anything heroic,' I cautioned. 'Back off to a safe distance and do like I said. Call in reinforcements.'

'You said this lunatic will kill the woman if he sees a naval vessel.'

'Yes, that's true. But if we get on board and fail to save her, she was already dead. Most likely me and Hartlaub won't be coming back either. If that's the case the Navy's welcome to Cain and anyone else still alive.'

'Jesus,' Lassiter said. 'To think this morning I was complaining that I was sick of routine duties.'

Taking the man's comment as a sign of approval, I relaxed back on to the chair. Hartlaub had been watching us all and his amused demeanour hadn't changed. He couldn't have heard much of our conversation over the noise of the engine and the slap of the boat on the waves. He indicated a solid wedge of steel-grey clouds piling in the night sky. 'Looks like there's a storm brewing, guys,' he called. His words would prove prophetic in more ways than one.

CHAPTER 39

Hartlaub nudged me awake.

'Shake a leg, Hunter, we're on.'

I hadn't meant to sleep, but the last few days had been an eventful journey where I'd managed only a few hours here and there and fatigue must have finally caught up with me. Even the silencing of the engine hadn't roused me, or the sudden cessation of forward movement. I blinked out of the fog of my dreams and looked up at Hartlaub's angular face. One of the crewmen had switched off the lights and Hartlaub was a dark blur against the night sky. His eyes and teeth glistened against the backdrop of billowing clouds.

'We've found the ship?'

'We've found it,' Hartlaub confirmed. 'Maybe you want to take a look?'

I'd fallen asleep on one of the benches, my head propped on my backpack. Over the space of my nap, I'd managed to slide all the way across to one side and now had my head pillowed on one of the rubber floats. Hartlaub stretched out his left hand to help me up. My neck felt stiff.

'Here.' Hartlaub handed me some night vision binoculars. They must have belonged to the boat.

I was surprised to find that we were so close to a large ship. It was about two hundred yards away, a freighter with cargo containers stacked on the deck, cranes and winches bristling along its sides, and a tower containing the bridge perched towards the front. Ambient light pulsed from within the bridge, but all other lights had been extinguished. It was no pleasure cruiser, but an ugly rusting hulk that had been patched and painted over many times. There was little decipherable of the name that was etched on the ship's hull, and some of that was in Cyrillic that I couldn't read fluently, but I was certain that it was the *Queen Sofia*. There was no other reason why it sat out here in the middle of the sea, seemingly drifting under the power of the tides, than that something major had happened on board, or was under way.

'Have you noticed any movement on deck?'

'None,' Hartlaub said. 'We haven't heard any voices either. Sitting there in the dark like that, it looks like a goddamn ghost ship. Maybe we're already too late.'

I hoped that his words weren't a bad omen. My stepfather, Bob Telfer, used to warn that mockery was catching: whenever anyone made a dire prediction of things to come he'd offer his own brand of psychobabble, as if by the simple act of voicing something it would come true. I prayed that Bob had been full of crap and that Hartlaub's comment hadn't invited bad luck. If Cain had already left the ship there'd be no way to find him in time, and that meant that I'd never save Jenny.

'I'm going aboard,' I said.

Hartlaub slung me my backpack. 'So am I, buddy, I'm just not sure it'll do much good.'

Mockery is catching.

I couldn't think that way. I had to approach this mission hopeful of a successful outcome. If I went aboard fearing the worst, my response to finding Cain might be driven by anger and that would likely prove the death of me. No, Jenny was still alive; I was determined I'd continue to think that way.

'Priority is Jenny, Hartlaub. We get her off first. We deal with Cain and anyone else afterwards, OK?'

'Unless we find them together,' Hartlaub said. He opened his own backpack and pulled out a midnight-black jumpsuit. I had a similar suit in my pack, along with greasepaint to smear on my face, and a wool cap to disguise my hair.

Lassiter approached from the cabin, riding the pitch of the boat like a seasoned pro. He slid on to the bench beside me. 'When you first told me your mission I thought you were crazy.'

That was about as candid as it came.

'And now?'

'I still think you're crazy.'

I laughed softly. Lassiter gripped my wrist and

gave it a reassuring squeeze. 'You don't have to worry about me or Terry. You're a good man doing the right thing for his family. We're not going to take off, we'll wait right here for you and come as soon as you call.'

Their original instructions were to leave the scene the second Hartlaub and I went overboard, but I trusted both Lassiter and Terry to help. He didn't need to confirm that; maybe it was his way of offering to come aboard the ship if I'd asked him to. They were brave men; all the more so because they were risking their lives when they had no personal investment in what was about to happen. I'd been dealing with bad men for so long I sometimes forgot that there were plenty of good people left in the world.

'Thanks, Lassiter.'

He got up, walked back to the cabin and nodded at Terry. It seemed like Lassiter had been voted the spokesperson. I waved to Terry and got a rapid salute of respect from him. Then I set about preparing myself.

It didn't take long before I was standing by Hartlaub, our weapons in ziplock bags to keep them dry. Greasepaint made our features unidentifiable below our caps, and our clothing blended with the night. Two shadows ready to slip undetected through the darkness. I took one look back at the crewmen, nodded silently then slipped over the side of the boat. The tide had brought us close to the ship, but we still had a swim ahead of us, one that must be conducted in silence. Though all was quiet on the deck overhead, that meant nothing. Cain could be up there, watching us, practising his shark's smile as we approached. He could open up on us at any second with a gun, but I didn't believe that would happen. Cain was all about his ego: he liked to talk, to taunt, and he'd want me to come on to the ship. There was a gantry-cum-platform lowered midway down the side, from which dangled ropes, and it wouldn't have surprised me to find that he'd left them there for me to climb aboard.

The water sucked all warmth from my body in an instant and I was tempted to stroke hard for the dangling ropes, but I disciplined myself to a gentle breaststroke, riding the swell of the waves towards the ship with my ziplock bag bobbing in my wake. Beside me Hartlaub spat out a mouthful of salty ocean.

Over us the freighter creaked ominously, something metallic clanked and machinery groaned from somewhere within the hull. Pausing, treading water, I searched the decks for movement but there was still no sign of life. Hartlaub was right: it was like a ghost ship.

Every second we spent in the water was a second nearer death. The temperature was somewhere between deathly and painfully cold, and it was like my entire frame was sheathed in crushed ice. Conversely my flesh began to sting as though I'd been doused in acid. Hypothermia was a very real threat, so I moved for the nearest trailing rope. It was out of reach.

I'm not one to panic. Not normally. But for the briefest of moments I felt that I'd made a ridiculous error of judgement and that Cain wouldn't need to kill me when he could allow the sea to do that for him. I blinked water from my eyes, looked for Hartlaub. He'd slipped a few yards to my right and was reaching for another rope. When he couldn't reach it, he dived beneath the surface, then erupted back upwards like a cork from a bottle. He snatched at the rope, snared it around his wrist and hung on, looking for me. I had a better idea. I struck out for Hartlaub, grabbed hold of his jumpsuit and then clambered up him so that I got a two-handed grip on the rope. Once my feet cleared the water, I placed my soles against the hull and walked up the nigh-on sheer wall to the platform. Gratefully I swung on to the gantry and lay there for a moment, staring at the wall of steel overhead as I pulled in a deep breath. I could only afford to give myself a moment's rest, before I rolled over and helped haul Hartlaub upwards as he used the rope to steady himself in his climb. As soon as he was kneeling alongside me I pulled my gun out of the waterproof bag and checked that it hadn't been compromised. It was bone dry, but my fingers were so cold the metal felt slick. I shook blood into my fingers, watching as Hartlaub aped my movements. We stood up together, and I went to the steps that led upwards. Glancing out

311

over the water, I could see no sign of the inflatable boat, although I knew that Lassiter and Terry
were still out there somewhere. That confidence
made me think about Rink and Harvey. I missed
them at my side, but I couldn't dwell on that, so
I pushed up the stairs thankful now for Hartlaub's
presence. A twinge of guilt speared me. I'd given
Hartlaub short shrift at first, and he deserved
nothing but respect. Coming along like this,
Hartlaub had put his career, his liberty and quite
possibly his life at risk for me. I placed my hand
on his chest, stopped him in his tracks.

'What's up?'

'Just wanted to say thanks.'

'You already did.'

'I mean for this.'

'All part of the service, Hunter.'

We shared a grin of comradeship, then continued
up the stairs. The jumpsuits sluiced water on to
the steps, and by the time we'd reached the top,
apart from our hats, boots and exposed flesh, we
were almost dry. Nevertheless we were still wet
enough that leaving a trail was unavoidable. We
could only hope that no one came across the
watery tracks and raised the alarm. A gate was
open in the rail and we stepped through it, easing
down on the deck. Like the rest of the old
freighter, the deck was metal and corroded. On
our left the cargo containers were stacked high,
huge towers of multiple hues all bound for far
destinations. I'd no idea what was inside them,

but decided that none of them would be an appropriate prison for Jenny. The *Queen Sofia* was suspected of being a carrier of illegal immigrants – or sex slaves depending on your outlook – but the metal containers were too obvious a hiding place for human trafficking and would be the first things checked by the authorities. I believed that there'd be another place in the bowels of the ship where Jenny would be held. The problem was I didn't know where to begin looking.

'Feels like a trap.' Hartlaub had leaned very close to my ear to whisper, but even so his voice was too loud. I raised a finger to my lips, indicating silence. I pointed to the nearby stacks of containers and to a deep ribbon of darkness between two towers. Hartlaub followed me into the narrow space.

In a low whisper, I said, 'You're right. This could be a trap, but there's nothing we can do about that now.'

'We should split up. That way if one of us gets captured at least the other still has a chance to save Jennifer.'

Splitting up would normally be a very bad idea: alone we were more vulnerable to ambush. Even so, Hartlaub was correct, because there was nothing normal about this mission. 'I'm going to go below deck. You check out things up here, then go towards the bridge and check that out. Engage the enemy only if you have to.'

I didn't need to explain that I required Hartlaub

to cover my retreat if it became necessary, he'd already got that. He'd also realised that I was trying to divert him from his prime objective.

'You know they're not up here, Hunter,' he said. 'I'll follow you down. Don't worry, though. I'm here for Cain, but not at the expense of your sister-in-law. We get her, and then we do Cain.'

I acquiesced silently and we slipped out from between the containers and looked for a way below decks. We moved between hulking machinery, cranes and hoists primarily, and found a large piston-controlled hatch. We ignored that way inside because it would be too noisy and very likely led into another open storage area anyway. In front of us were a few shed-like structures, but because none of them boasted windows I assumed that they contained further machinery that required protecting from the elements. We found a metal stairwell adjoining the upper deck containing the bridge. We didn't want to go up, so I led Hartlaub under the stairs and there we found a door that would give us ingress. It was a heavy steel affair, with a handle that required pressure to open it. If the rest of the ship was anything to go by, the door hinges would be ill maintained and the resulting squeal of protesting metal would be an instant giveaway. Shaking my head at Hartlaub I moved away. There was a soft clunk, and I turned quickly. Hartlaub was peering in through the open doorway. I tried to show my anger with a flash of my eyes, but the gesture was wasted on him. Anyway, when I paused to listen, the noise of him opening the door was lost in all the other clunks and bangs emitted by the ship as it rode the restless sea. Hartlaub stepped inside and I had no option but to follow.

We were in a narrow vestibule. A door on our right led into an antechamber, and two to our left into the forward deck. Directly ahead there was a railing and I moved to it, saw that it marked the beginning of a stairwell leading down into pitch blackness. Last time I fought Tubal Cain I had to descend steps into a similar pit of blackness, and I hoped that this time it didn't lead to such a hellish place as Cain's ossuary at Jubal's Hollow. Cain had decorated the entrance to his bone chamber with archaic symbols, and I was glad to note that a sign on a nearby bulkhead was only written in Cyrillic. It was nowhere near as weird here, but I still experienced a wave of trepidation at what I could find below. When I'd found John, pinned to the walls of Cain's chamber with iron spikes and the skin of his back split open to expose his ribcage, I'd almost lost my ability to fight; God help me if he'd done the same to Jenny.

No, strike that. God help Tubal Cain.

I pushed ahead.

CHAPTER 40

He'd just got off the satellite phone and Cain wasn't very happy. He knew that the CIA man was stalling and even though he'd threatened to start dicing up Jennifer, Walter Hayes Conrad hadn't been moved to hurry the process along. Conrad swore that John Telfer was on his way, but it was beyond his power to organise his transfer in anything below five hours. Cain doubted that; he could have had Telfer bundled on to a military jet and transferred from anywhere in the US within half that time.

'You have one more hour,' Cain had said. 'If Telfer isn't there by then I start cutting.' The fact that Cain himself wouldn't be at the rendezvous by then was academic; he wouldn't allow Conrad the three extra hours he'd pleaded. Those three hours weren't in order to arrange John Telfer's arrival but something else.

Cain knew that the CIA were resourceful enough to have pinpointed his location by now and would be organising some sort of assault on the ship. He had warned the CIA man of what such action would bring. First sign of any kind of military presence, he promised, and he would slaughter his captive. Cain was pragmatic enough to guess that he was a more valuable prize to the CIA man than the life of a nobody from England. The assault would be coming and it was time to move. The location where he'd requested John Telfer to meet him was equally dangerous, but so long as he got his blade into Telfer's body before the attack began he'd be happy enough. He didn't fear death, but he did fear dying without taking his nemesis to Hell alongside him. His legend depended upon it. To the world Tubal Cain, the Harvestman, was a hapless fool by the name of Robert Swan who'd died in the Mojave Desert. It was time that the ridiculous lie was rectified and *everyone* knew the truth. Slaughtering Telfer under the watchful eye of the world would ensure that he would finally earn the credit he was due.

Before leaving the bridge, he smashed the satellite phone repeatedly against the control panel of the ship's guidance system, breaking both. Light crackled and pulsed from the starred radar screen. The damage assuaged some of the anger he felt towards Walter Conrad. A stairwell led down through the tower to the lower decks, and he went in search of Baron and the crew members who'd given him their service since their old captain had perished. Down there he hoped that they'd readied the equipment. Captain Grodek had been a filthy-minded wretch, and he'd delighted in filming his own skin flicks that were uploaded directly to the World Wide Web. Well, it wasn't only human-trafficking pornographers who could use digital technology to spread their message via the click of a mouse. Cain had discovered the room where the girls had been abused, found the cameras and wi-fi compatible laptop computers, and realised that he too could televise his own prime time show.

He found Baron waiting for his return.

'Everything's in order?'

'Everything's in chaos.'

Baron's lips pinched, having no idea what he was alluding to. No, there was only one Prince of Chaos here, maybe even in the entire world. It didn't matter; Baron was still a valuable ally.

'Jennifer Telfer, she's ready?' Cain looked past Baron, peering into the room beyond. It was the ship's galley, the place where the crew had spent their downtime, and was as ugly as anywhere else on the ship. The air was putrid with the stench of old grease, hand-rolled cigarettes and the fumes of strong spirits. Sailors allegedly drank rum, Russians vodka, but it appeared that this crew enjoyed anything as long as it was alcoholic. There was a double row of tables down the centre of the room, chairs parked under them, and at the far end a separate table at a right angle to all the rest. The captain's table was as grimy as the others. Behind it sat Jennifer Telfer, staring back at him, the whites of her eyes stark in the dim light.

Baron neglected to answer: what was the need?

318

Instead he anticipated Cain's next question. 'The crew are readying the lifeboat, bringing the video equipment you requested and loading it before we take her up. Some of the idiots are grumbling about how you intend paying them once this is over with. They didn't anticipate abandoning the ship and are afraid that you're going to renege on the deal first chance you get.'

'Then they're more astute than I thought,' Cain smiled. 'Don't worry about them. If it takes killing a couple as an example I'll do that. The others will beg to be allowed on the lifeboat.'

'Why are we even taking them?'

'The currents are notorious around here. Who knows where we'll end up? If we're marooned on a desert island I want to make sure we've got something to eat.'

Baron blinked.

Cain grinned, showing even white teeth. 'I'm joking, Baron. Jeez, don't you ever laugh?'

'I'll laugh when we're off this damn ship and I know that Joe Hunter's out of the picture. I owe that bastard. When he killed Hendrickson he cost me a lot of money, not to mention shooting me. He ruined everything I'd built up, and it's going to be a long time before I can recoup my losses.'

'You've picked up the reins of Hendrickson's organisation, you've probably gained a thousand times what you lost.'

'But with Hunter around, how long will I hold on to it?'

'He's remorseless, I'll give him that.' Cain touched the scar tissue in his throat. 'I owe him, too. But I'd rather kill his brother. You can have Hunter all to yourself, Baron.'

This was no magnanimous gesture. Cain doubted that Baron was man enough to stop Joe Hunter, but he'd slow him long enough to let Cain finish his own task. Then he would turn his surgical skills on Hunter. Christ but he hoped that both brothers would appear for the final showdown.

Baron shook his head. 'Remorseless. Yes, but I'm not afraid he'd hunt me down, Cain. It's just that I couldn't concentrate on setting myself up again if I was distracted by him. This way I can finish things once and for all.'

Cain didn't think that Baron would ever become an underworld boss. Even if by some miracle he did take Hunter down, Cain wasn't going to let Baron walk away intact. The Harvestman had coveted something of him since the first time he'd looked on his smooth face and wondered how delicate the lines of the skull beneath were.

'You are both going to die.'

Cain turned to the source of the voice. Jennifer was staring at him, her expression that of a she-panther protecting its young.

'Be quiet, will ya? You should be afraid of what's going to happen to you if Hunter does show up.'

'I've known fear for years,' Jennifer said. 'What makes you think you can terrify me any more than all the others?'

Cain dipped his hand into his pocket and came out with a small plastic bag. He walked the length of the galley and tossed it on to the captain's table, then flipped it open and dumped the contents on the pitted surface. Grimy pink lumps scattered across the table, and Jennifer recoiled from the collection of fingers and toes: mementoes from the crewmen who'd refused a new captain. Her shriek of disgust was loud but driven by anger. She swept Cain's trophies from the table with her forearm and they were distributed in a horrifying pattern on the floor.

'Would you just look at the mess you've made,' Cain said, as if he was scolding a child.

'You are sick!'

'You'll be sicker,' Cain said. 'Pick them up.'

'No.'

'I said to pick them up.'

'No. I won't touch the filthy things!'

Cain placed both hands on his hips. 'Hmmm. Then we have a problem.'

Jennifer didn't see him move before he'd snapped his left hand around her wrist and dragged her forward. He was already drawing his Bowie knife before self-preservation kicked in and she tried to flinch away. She screamed, understanding what he intended, and tried to wrench Cain's grip loose, but she might as well have been attempting to rip a tree up by its roots. Cain shook her savagely. 'Sit still,' he snapped.

Baron swayed in the wings as he watched with

fascination. Cain glanced over at him. 'Get over here, Baron, and hold her down while I replenish my stock.'

Baron took hold of Jennifer's other arm. Jennifer hollered, tried to fight the men, but all she achieved was a laugh from Cain. He bore down on her arm, crushing it to the tabletop. Then he guided the Bowie to her fingers. Jennifer scrunched her hand in a tight fist, but it was no deterrent to Cain. He jabbed the tip of his knife between the knuckles of her index and ring fingers and instinctively her hand shot open. Cain transferred his grip, holding her hand flat as he positioned the cutting edge of his knife over the second joint of her little finger. 'Are you afraid yet?'

Jennifer screeched. She bucked and squirmed in their grasp. Both men grinned.

'I see some things do make you happy?' Cain said and Baron winked back at him.

'You like pain, huh, Baron?' Cain switched his attention back to the woman. 'What about you, Jennifer? Do you like pain?'

Cain grunted as he pressed down on the blade, and Jennifer's eyes widened in disbelief as the tip of her finger shot away from her trailing a thin ribbon of blood. 'Oh, God! Oh, God! *Oh, my God!*'

'As good as sex, eh?' Cain said, retrieving the dismembered joint and stuffing it in the plastic bag. 'Pity we didn't have the cameras rolling, we'd have been an instant hit on You Tube!' Jennifer doubled her efforts to escape, but Cain wouldn't release her hand. He placed the knife over her second finger. 'One down, nine to go.'

'Let me go!' Jennifer went wild, and even made it out of her chair, Cain struggling to control her until he swung the Bowie towards her face. The tip slid into the flesh just below her right eye, and the pain was enough to halt her in her tracks. She stood, her chest heaving, but it wasn't for fear of being blinded.

'Do anything you want to me,' she said. Her voice was an octave below menacing. 'But where's the bait for your trap then?'

Cain loosened his grip, nodding at Baron to also let go. Jennifer slumped in the chair, cradling her injured hand. Blood trickled from the stump, pooling in the cup of her palm, but it went unnoticed by both men.

Her release wasn't a show of pity. Cain had heard something even over the din in the galley.

The bland-faced man had heard it too.

'Gunfire.' Baron grinned, looking like a leering sideshow freak.

Cain addressed Jennifer. 'Get up, and no goddamn nonsense this time.'

Jennifer's face was an empty plane formed from shock.

'You said that Joe Hunter would come,' Cain said. 'It seems you were right, after all. Let's go up on deck and meet him, shall we?'

CHAPTER 41

We took it easy as we descended into the bowels of the ship. I took point, with Hartlaub moving slowly behind me, watching back the way we'd come. He had his gun in a two-handed grip, pointing it at every shadow. I chose to carry my gun propped against my hip, a preferred method for shooting in confined spaces. At each landing, we opted to continue down. If Jenny was being held, it would be far from prying eyes and ears. The first two decks were mainly given over to work space, and I believed that Cain – or whoever was in charge of the ship – would want his prisoner nearer the crew quarters where she could be kept an eye on.

'Hunter. Over here.'

Hartlaub was peering through a porthole in a door. His whisper was very low, but his words held enough urgency to send a chill down my spine. I looked through the dirty glass at what lay within. Even in the dimness I could make out the forms of bodies stacked in the otherwise empty room.

Dear God, no!

I pulled open the door and stepped inside,

fearing the worst. The coppery smell of congealing blood made the air viscous. Now that I was inside, I relaxed. The bodies were all male. There was no need to check to see if any of them had survived, because as well as bullet and knife wounds, they'd had fingers and toes removed and none of them still bled. A man with epaulettes at the shoulders of his once-white shirt had had his throat opened up, but his killer hadn't stopped there. The shirt had been ripped open and I could see a deep cleft in his chest where a rib had been carved out. That was all the proof I needed that Tubal Cain was up to his old ways.

Hartlaub muttered under his breath, and I hushed him with an upraised hand. Gesturing him back out of the room, I hurried after him. Outside in the corridor I leaned close to his ear. 'It's Cain all right. But at least Jenny isn't in there. We still have a chance.'

'This Cain's a real piece of work.'

'He's a monster.'

He nodded sharply, swung his head to peer along the corridor. We'd both heard a cacophony of high-pitched screams emanating from further back towards the rear of the ship. Hartlaub took a step in that direction, but I rushed past him, taking the lead.

We came to the cargo hold that we'd forgone when on the top deck and entered it warily. It was an open space that echoed to our footsteps, and groaned with the movement of the ship. I almost fancied that the ship was a living breathing thing. We traversed the hold, heading directly for a door at the far side. We hadn't reached it when we heard more screams. But closer to us were the voices of men. They spoke foreign languages, Russian being the dominant one. Having been a soldier after the Cold War, I wasn't schooled in Russian, but I'd learned enough in my time to judge that the men were almost as disturbed by the screaming as I was. That didn't make them my friends, but I wondered how much these men were involved in Cain's schemes and if they deserved to die. Fuck 'em, I decided, they were human-trafficking scum all the same.

Plus, they were between me and saving my loved ones.

I spurred across the hold to the door and eased it open.

Directly outside was another stairwell, one that must have exited via those sheds I'd earlier discarded as a way inside. Above me on the stairs were two men, hauling armfuls of computer equipment. As long as they continued upwards, they weren't a barrier to us, but it looked like both men had paused there, waiting as they discussed the screaming which came from farther back in the ship. Every second they stood there, Jenny was suffering. I came out the door, drawing my Kabar, intending finishing them in silence.

I took the first step gently, but both men must have felt my presence and they turned my way. I could still get to them, take them down, and their deaths would be covered by Jenny's screams.

The problem was, in my urgency, I'd missed the third man on the stairs below. He too was carrying something – a case of some kind – but in his other hand he held a gun.

'*Derzhite yego!*' the man yelled. I didn't need a translator to tell me he was commanding me to hold it, but his next words were lost in the rush of action. '*Kto ty? Chto vy zdes' delaete?*'

Hartlaub was an undercover CIA agent; his grasp of Russian was better than mine. He said, 'We're here to kill all you pricks!'

Everything went to hell. The two above me dropped their loads, going for concealed weapons inside their jackets at the same time as the first swung his gun towards Hartlaub. Shit! I'd wanted to do them quietly.

Hartlaub shot the first man. I didn't see it, just heard the bang of his gun and the corresponding howl and crashing fall. I was too busy dropping into a crouch while over-handing my Ka-bar at the man nearest me. Up the stairs the man furthest away brought his gun to target and fired. Luckily my drop had caught him out and his bullet went over my head, but my knife hit his friend in the gut. The wounded man forgot about his own weapon as he tried to pull the six inches of steel from his body. It was the opportunity I needed to snatch out my SIG and shoot him in the head.

Hartlaub fired again, but he was making sure

the one he'd hit stayed down. I still had another armed man to contend with. He was yelling gibberish to my ears, what I guessed was a Russian curse of some kind. He fired, but he couldn't decide which of us he wanted to kill and his bullets missed us both. I came out of my crouch, levelled my gun at his central mass and squeezed the trigger. The first shot took him in the solar plexus, and it would have proved fatal in itself, but I shot him two more times higher up in his chest. There was no more cursing after that, and the sudden silence rang in my ears as heady as the sharp tang of cordite in my nostrils.

That only lasted as long as it took for me to round on Hartlaub. 'Jesus Christ!' I hissed. 'Do you think you can try to be a bit quieter in future? Cain will know we're coming for him.'

Hartlaub offered a shrug. 'Would you rather I'd let that punk get the drop on you?'

My anger was misguided. My frustration wasn't at Hartlaub's lack of subtlety but at the knowledge that any chance of getting Jenny free was now going to be a hundred times more difficult. That was if Cain didn't slaughter her immediately. Judging by the screaming, he had started already.

Stealth now wasn't the issue: it was all down to speed and aggression. I charged away from Hartlaub, heading for the back of the ship. The screaming had stopped abruptly, hopefully because of the intrusion of gunfire and not because Jenny was already dead. The corridor I followed ran straight as an arrow's flight, doors on each side, but I ignored them all, just headed for the far end where I could see another door with a round window in it. For the briefest moment I thought I saw a face at that window, a pale blur. Perhaps it was just a trick of the light, but I wanted to find out quickly. My haste was almost my undoing.

A man came out of a door on my left. He was shorter than I, but stocky, with a weightlifter's arms and shoulders. He wrapped me in a bear hug, lifted me off my feet and slammed me bodily into the door opposite. The door was no barrier and crashed open under our combined weight, and we spilled into a small cabin with a bunk and chair. His momentum carried us across the floor and we rammed up against the base of the bed. The man was on top of me and he bore down with his weight, crushing my shoulders to the ground as he raised a meaty fist to pound my head. Would have been fine if that was all he intended, but then I saw the meat cleaver. I snatched at him with my left hand, bucked up with my hips, making a bridge of my spine, and the man was bumped off me so that the meat cleaver veered away from my head and clashed on the metal floor. I still had my SIG but was in an awkward position to shoot, so instead I back-handed it at him and slammed the butt into his chest. A few inches higher and I'd have got his chin, but the strike to the chest still hurt.

He snapped something at me, and for the first

time I saw that his pinched eyes had nothing to do with his anger, but with his heritage. He looked Mongolian, perhaps Siberian, with his round features, narrow eyes and dark saffron skin. Didn't matter that he was a long way from the Russian steppes, he was determined to protect his territory with his life. He struck at me with the meat cleaver again. Luck intervened, the mattress on the bed having slipped off and got in the way of his aim. While he twisted the blade free of the mattress, I got an ankle under my opposite leg and flipped on to my side. He reared back for another cut and I jammed my right knee into his side. As he cut down, I dropped my gun and grabbed at his arm, even as I brought my left leg up and booted him in the chin with my heel. If he'd have reared back then he'd have probably got me, but he'd no real concept of ground fighting. Retaining hold of his arm, I pushed my left leg all the way past him so I could hook his throat in the crook of my knee, and I once again arched my spine. His arm was hyper-extended, and the fulcrum point of his elbow was over my pubis.

People familiar with the reverse cross-body lock know to hook their extended arm with their opposite hand and to power their opponent off the floor. They then dump their opponent on the crown of their heads and put them out of the picture. This man had no understanding of ju-jitsu and made the mistake of attempting to fight the pressure with brute force. I torqued my body so I was facing the floor and now my entire weight was centred on the fragile make-up of his elbow joint. There was no contest. The joint was wrenched apart and the cleaver flew from his hand. My opponent pitched belly down on the floor, writhing in agony. I held the position, levering up on his forearm for good measure. The man screamed and I pulled free with my legs to give him a couple parting shots with my heel as I scrambled away from him and snatched up my gun.

As I came to my feet, there was movement behind me. Hartlaub had finally caught up. 'Here. Let me.'

Before I could do or say anything to stop him, Hartlaub fired a single shot into back of the man's skull. Life went out of the Russian like a doused candle.

'Looks like saving your ass is becoming a habit.'

Heaving air into my constricted lungs, I said, 'I had him.'

'Sure you did.'

Pushing past him, I rushed out of the room. 'Stay close, Hartlaub. I might need you again before I'm finished.'

Back in the corridor I headed for the door where I'd seen the face. There was a rumble of movement from behind and I spun to see Hartlaub dropping to one knee and aiming his gun back the way we'd come. He fired twice, but there was a corresponding volley of bullets from the far end.

Hartlaub swore, went over on his side. He was still shooting, and now I could see another man running at us. He was a scrawny little thing, but the gun made him dangerous. He fired as he came and that was a mistake. If he'd held his position, aimed and fired we'd probably both be dead, but his running steps only caused his bullets to hit the walls and ceiling. I drew a bead on him, squeezed the trigger and my SIG barked. The man went down.

Taking a quick glance over my shoulder I checked for movement beyond the circular window. Couldn't detect any, so I ran back to Hartlaub and hauled him over.

'Goddamn it! I've been hit!'

Hartlaub had one hand slapped over his left hip. Blood was leaking from under his fingers. There was no sign of an exit wound, which was a very bad sign. It looked like the shooter had been using soft-nosed slugs. The bullet would have flattened on impact, split into shards and then ricocheted round inside his pelvic girdle. There would be untold damage to his internal organs.

Cursing under my breath, I pulled his hand from the wound for a better look, but without ripping off his jumpsuit I couldn't make a decent inspection. I grabbed his hand, pushed it hard on the hole. 'Keep pressure on it or you'll bleed to death.'

Hartlaub went through another round of curses, but he could be forgiven the bad language. 'Shit. I'm not going to die, Hunter.'

'We need to get you help.'

'No. I'm not going to fucking die.'

'No,' I lied. 'No, you still have a chance. C'mon.'

I helped him to stand, which wasn't the best idea because it would only help him bleed out all the sooner. But I couldn't leave him there in the corridor like that. Not when other crew might come across him at any second. Injured, he'd no way to defend himself. Propping his arm around my shoulders, I supported him to the door and he grunted with every step. Taking a quick glance through the window, I saw only an empty hall. I shoved through the door, searching for targets with my gun, but luckily no one was in sight. The hall here was very similar to the one we'd just come from, only the doors were heavy metal things with letterbox-sized slots, like you see in some old jails. This must be where the women were confined when the boat was at sea. There were at least half a dozen holding rooms, but the doors were open and none contained any occupants. I wondered if Jenny had been held here, and didn't like what I saw: a chair from which hung leather straps.

I was concerned about Hartlaub, but my focus shifted back to Jenny. When he'd come along on this mission Hartlaub knew that injury or death had been a probability, whereas my sister-in-law had been an unwilling participant from the word go. There was a tenet of the armed forces that I'd been raised upon, though: you don't leave a colleague behind. That made things very difficult for me.

Hartlaub must have guessed what I was thinking. 'I'm only gonna slow you down, Hunter. Go on. Forget about me. I can look after myself.'

'Thanks, Hartlaub,' I said. 'But no can do. I'm getting you somewhere safe first.'

'Joe,' he said, the first time he'd used my given name, 'you were right. Saving your sister-in-law is more important than killing Cain . . . or saving my ass. Go save hers. I'll manage to make my way back up on deck and cover for you from up there. I've still got one good leg, two good hands and a head for thinking. I'll be OK.'

I was torn, but he was right. Dragging him around the ship would get us both killed. At least if we split up there was a chance I could save Jenny. I had to leave him to his fate. 'At least let me take you to a staircase so you can get out,' I said.

Hartlaub nodded, and even that action was enough to make him almost pass out. He was leaking more blood than he had the capacity to hold in, leaving a wide smear of it behind as we hobbled along the corridor.

There was another door at the end, and I propped Hartlaub against a wall while I checked that all was clear. There was a stairwell like the one we'd fought the crewmen on, but this one was empty. I helped Hartlaub up the first flight. He'd only another set of stairs to manage by himself and he'd be back on the main deck.

'You sure you can make it from here?'

He grimaced and waved me back down the stairs. 'Don't worry about me, for Christ's sake! Go get Jenny out of there.'

I placed a hand on his shoulder. Looked him steadily in the eye. 'Hartlaub. Despite the real reason Walter sent you, you're a good man.'

'Yeah, but you're still an ungrateful bastard.' He grunted out a laugh. 'Listen, to me. There is no hidden agenda. I'm here to cover your ass, and I'll continue to do that. I don't intend dying in this crap hole. But if I do, I'll make sure I take some of these bastards with me.'

'You're not going to die under my watch.'

'Go on,' he said. 'I'll be out here waiting for the two of you.'

'Thanks, Hartlaub.' I doubted I'd see him alive again. I turned away before he could see the shame burning in my cheeks.

CHAPTER 42

Cain was assailed by mixed feelings.

He was happy that Joe Hunter had arrived: he could repay the bastard for everything he'd suffered at Jubal's Hollow, and for the many months he'd spent cooped up in a cell at Fort Conchar. In fact, he was ecstatic to find the Englishman was as remorseless as he'd warned Baron, because it meant all his preparations had been worth the time and effort. An eye for an eye, a frickin' throat for a throat.

On the other hand, he was angered that Hunter's younger brother was a no show. All of his plotting, his escape from prison, his wild goose chase to Montana, the trip he'd taken to the UK and then on this ship had all been to find and finish things with John Telfer. Now it looked like the search wasn't over.

First things first, though. He'd warned Walter Hayes Conrad what would happen if anyone tried anything stupid. Well, Hunter and his mysterious friend coming aboard the *Queen Sofia* could be classified as such.

On hearing the brief gun battle, he'd left his

hostage in the capable hands of Baron, made his way along the hall past the cells and peered through the porthole in the adjoining bulkhead door. Hunter, he was certain, had seen him before he ducked back into the shadows, but then one of Grodek's crew had attacked Hunter. Cain had recognised the burly man, a Siberian who'd greeted the death of his captain with a shrug. It seemed he didn't care who his commanding officer was, so long as he was rewarded handsomely for his service. Cain approved of the Siberian's weapon of choice – the meat cleaver. They were both men of the blade. He didn't think it would avail him against Joe Hunter, though, and wasn't surprised to hear another short gun battle a while later. By then, Cain was already on his way back to slaughter Jennifer Telfer.

As he'd been ordered to, Baron had led the woman up another set of steep stairs, taking her to the upper deck and the motor launch that the crew had prepped. Cain found the stairs and went up them, as nimble as a cat. Coming out on the deck, he found he was faced by the towering stacks of freight containers, and the loading mechanisms looming like misshapen giants against the night sky. Unsurprisingly, he couldn't see Baron or his charge. The launch was to the front of the ship, and on the opposite side of the towers. He'd been below decks for some time now, and the cold wind tugging at his hair and clothing brought an unwelcome chill to his body. Overhead, the sky was shrouded by heavy clouds and he felt the first patter of rain on his upturned face. He shivered, thought back to the warm desert he loved and wondered why the hell he was here in this freezing, horrible place. Chaos: that was the answer. It had its way of upsetting the natural order of things. But he was a Prince of Chaos and it was also his ally. It would hinder his enemies more than it would thwart him. As if in agreement with his thoughts the clouds gave up their burden and rain lashed the decks.

He dodged between the freight containers, following narrow paths as though he'd wandered into the Minotaur's labyrinth. There he was spared the fury of the rain, but there was no avoiding a soaking because mini-waterfalls teemed from the containers above.

Without power, the ship was at the sea's whim, and it drifted on the currents, lifting and falling as the rainstorm kicked up whitecaps. All around him the containers moaned like living things, and he wondered if his short cut had been such a good idea. If any of those containers should shift, he'd be ground between them and all thought of revenge would be finished. He quickly slipped out on the port side of the ship, searching the deck for any sign of Baron and the woman. The storm was coming from the north-east, having skirted Virginia before sinking south-west again towards the North Carolina coastline. There, by the port rail, he was blasted by the wind shrieking across the deck, and had to bend his back to avoid being thrown off his feet. He shuffled along, eyes searching for movement ahead. Through the billowing spray he caught sight of an indistinct shape and, as he approached, it metamorphosed into the small group he'd been seeking. One of Grodek's crewmen had joined them.

Jennifer read the menace in his features. She twisted past Baron to place him between Cain and herself. Baron grasped her by the neck of her blouse, pulling her back towards the lifeboat where the other crewman took hold of her, ready to throw her aboard.

'Leave her,' Cain said. 'She's not coming with us.'

The crewman was a tall, thin man with receding hair and pale blue eyes. Another Russian, Cain guessed. He wouldn't understand his command, so Cain decided to show him instead. He stalked forward, lifting his Tanto, and went to grab at Jennifer, but came up short as Baron gripped him round the wrist. Cain stopped, and peered into the man's bland face. 'Release me or lose your hand,' he warned.

'Don't do this, Cain.' Baron's voice too held a note of warning. His gun was only a second away from Cain's gut. 'You're angry that Telfer hasn't come. I understand that, but the woman's worth far more to us alive than dead.'

'Let. Me. Go.'

Baron slowly unfurled his fingers, but he didn't

step aside. 'We can still use her, Cain.' This time he tried to reason with Cain's better sense. 'Hunter and who knows who else is on board. We might need her as a shield.'

'You still expect to use her as a bargaining chip? That's finished with. If Walter Conrad sends anyone now, it won't be John Telfer . . . it'll be a full strike team.'

'Hunter might be working under his own power. Who's to say the CIA even knows he's here? You can still use Jennifer to get what you want, Cain . . . but not if she's dead.'

Cain fumed. 'You know something, Baron? You're right.' He flicked a command to the Russian crewman. 'Well, what are you waiting for? Get her on the boat.'

Jennifer had taken the opportunity to move a few steps away while the men had been caught in the tense moment. Now, as the Russian turned for her again, she shook her head adamantly, refusing to get on the lifeboat.

'Do not try me, woman!' Cain roared. 'Baron has just won you a reprieve. Now get on the goddamn boat before I change my mind again!'

'Fuck you, Cain,' Jennifer said with equal ferocity. 'And fuck you, Baron. You aren't using me to murder my husband!'

Then she threw herself over the rail and into the storm-ridden sea.

Despite himself, Cain lunged after her, but it was a fruitless task. She was gone and that was, that.

'No!'

The shout burst unbidden through the night.

But it wasn't Cain's yell of frustration, or that of Baron or the Russian.

Cain turned slowly, and watched the man materialise out of the pouring rain, a gun in his hand.

CHAPTER 43

Going door to door, I checked every conceivable place that Cain could have hidden Jenny, but I had no luck. Part of me was relieved, because if she was in any of those rooms, then she would be dead already. No, Cain must have taken her with him. I was positive that it was his face I'd seen through the porthole just before the crazy man with the meat-cleaver attacked me. Seeing his opportunity, Cain must have ushered her away to another part of the ship. I doubted he'd go deeper into the bowels, now that he realised a rescue party was on board. A stronger likelihood would be that he had taken her up; to use Jenny as a hostage. That was the theory, but I'd still to continue my search.

A set of double doors opened into a galley. The place stank of spoiled food and unwashed bodies, and nicotine-laden stains coloured everything a deep tan. Though not somewhere I'd like to sit down and eat, it was still one of the cleanest rooms I'd come across on the *Queen Sofia*. My vision flashed to a stain on a distant table. Moving quickly, I went to check and saw something that brought bile into my throat. There was a fan of blood on the table, punctuated at the narrow end by a shallow nick in the tabletop. I could guess what had happened there, but didn't want to think who had lost a digit to Cain's blade. I had the sudden urge to kick the table over, to demolish it beyond recognition, but what purpose would that serve? Better that I go find the bastard who had made Jenny suffer.

My boot scuffed something: a severed finger. I scanned the floor and there was another. Over by the wall was yet another, and something tiny that could have only been a toe. In my time I've seen many horrific sights, but there was something so disturbing about the presence of those scattered digits that I almost vomited. I headed for the nearest door and was surprised to find a narrow vestibule, and a set of stairs leading upwards. On the third stair up there was a droplet of blood, more blood on the next step. It appeared that Cain had taken Jenny that way, and that she was still bleeding. The son of a bitch *had* hacked off one of her fingers, and my only grateful thought was that the other digits on the floor had been too thick and long to have belonged to her.

I went up the stairs warily, my SIG held poised to shoot. Last time we'd fought Tubal Cain he'd been in hiding and had ambushed Rink. Only Rink's supercharged reactions had saved him from having his throat opened wide by Cain's knife.

The scar on Rink's chin was a sore reminder of how close he'd come to death, though.

The droplets of blood led me upwards, like the breadcrumbs in some insane version of the Hansel and Gretel tale. In that story there'd been a cannibalistic witch plotting to devour children, but even the old hag was nowhere near as much of a monster as Cain. Throwing caution aside, I went up the stairs three at a time and banged out of a door and on to a rain-swept deck.

In front of me were the towers of stacked containers, behind me the aft of the ship. I swung round, seeking movement, but the downpour made it difficult to see far. I headed forward, following the wall of the steel containers along the starboard rail. Any second, I thought, and I'd find Cain. My nerves were strung taut, and adrenalin began to flood my senses. I had my game face on.

'Where the fuck are you, Cain?' I whispered, confident that I wouldn't be heard over the drumming of rain and the groaning of the shifting containers.

Then, a second thought struck me. What had become of Ray Hartlaub?

CHAPTER 44

The man approaching with his gun extended in both hands didn't look like he'd the strength to support the gun much longer. His face was smeared with grease, but looked very pale between the streaks, and blood pooled on the deck beneath his boots. He was dying but he could still drill the three of them full of bullets before his strength gave out.

Cain had no clue who the man was, but he'd a good idea why he was here. He was a friend of Joe Hunter who'd come to help save Jennifer from the nasty Harvestman. Cain shook his head. Hell, a few moments earlier he might have even stood a chance. The old *chaos factor* had definitely kicked in.

'Drop your fucking weapons!'

Cain held his hands out to his side, allowed the Tanto to fall on to the deck. He nudged it away with the toe of his shoe. Baron wasn't as happy to relinquish his gun, and the man jabbed his barrel at him. Finally Baron allowed the gun to fall to the deck. It clattered on the metal, sliding away as the deck pitched on a high wave. The sudden surge meant the gunman also staggered, and Cain noted that his left leg could barely sustain his weight.

'Which one of you motherfuckers is Tubal Cain?' the stranger asked as he shuffled closer.

Cain understood what would happen should he reveal his identity. He jabbed a finger at the tall Russian. The man glanced at the crewman, but he was not taken in. He returned his attention to Cain, looked him up and down. The man could barely focus, being so close to fainting. 'What's up, Cain? Too much of a coward to man up to who you are?'

Cain chuckled.

The man lowered his head slightly, peering at Cain from under heavy brows, and suddenly his gaze was fixed. 'Try laughing this off, asshole.'

The man fired.

Cain jerked, but it was at the scream of the tall Russian as he took the bullet in his gut. The Russian fell to his knees, both hands grabbing at his wound.

The stranger pointed at the mortally wounded man. 'See, that's how I feel right now. I'm in the same kind of pain as he is, and that thoroughly pisses me off. So if I were you, I'd stop the fucking wisecracks before I do the same to you.'

Cain wondered why the man hadn't simply shot him. 'You're Walter Conrad's man?'

'Was, but I see things clearly now. I came here to take you back to Fort Conchar.' The man grimaced in agony. 'But I've changed my mind.'

'So what's the alternative? A clean death?'

'That's right.'

'For me or for you?'

'You, asshole.'

'Wrong!' Cain yelled.

From out of the shadows to the stranger's right came another figure and he too had a gun raised.

Confused by Cain's shout, the stranger reacted too late. He was now faced by three targets and had no idea which one of them to shoot first. He should have chosen the newcomer.

It was the driver, Pete Eckhart, who'd come with Cain from Baltimore. He stepped up close to the stranger and shot him in the side. The bullet hit like a heavyweight boxer's punch to his ribs and he staggered. His left leg buckled under him and he went down on one knee. Eckhart swung the gun to shoot again, but even mortally wounded the guy still had some fight in him. He brought round his own gun and fired, taking out Eckhart's groin. Eckhart screamed and dropped his gun, then went down on the deck, the blood pooling around him so viscous that even the pouring rain failed to dissipate it.

'You goddamn . . .' The stranger tried to target his gun again.

Cain was already on the move. But so was Baron. The man flew like a hawk, his hand reaching under his belt as he swooped towards the injured man. Before the stranger could fire again, blue light crackled as Baron jammed the Taser in the hollow under his jaw. The stranger shuddered, a long scream rising from his lips that stuttered in time with the electrical charge racking his body.

Cain came up with his Bowie, and drove in past Baron, plunging the heavy blade between the man's ribs and into his heart. Some of the charge from Baron's Taser crackled up the hilt and into Cain's hand, but he held tight, grinning manically as the light went out of the stranger's eyes.

Finally both men stepped away, Cain withdrawing the blade with a harsh sucking noise. 'Well, Baron, that was a bit of a buzz.'

Baron didn't catch his quip, or if he had, was as unimpressed as usual. Cain tried again, 'Let's finish off this pain in the neck.' He stooped down and jammed the Bowie into the base of the stranger's skull, then sawed the tip back and forth. He looked up at Baron for approval, only to see that the man had merely busied himself with clipping the Taser back on to his belt. 'Sometimes I wonder why I bother,' Cain muttered.

He left the Bowie in the corpse, like it was a marker on the man's grave. He stood, looking around at the three dead or dying men. The Russian would take a little time to die, but Cain wasn't the type for pity. After retrieving his downed Tanto, he just knocked Baron's elbow. 'Come on. Joe Hunter's still here. I think it's time to go and say hello.'

'Yeah.' This time Baron did laugh.

CHAPTER 45

I heard the gunshots and knew the answer to my question.

Hartlaub was in no fit state to take on Cain, so at the cessation of gunfire I had a horrible feeling what I would find. It spurred me with even more determination. Cain had caused untold suffering to people I cared for, and now I suspected that I could add Hartlaub to that tally. If there was any justice in this world, I'd make Cain suffer . . . tenfold.

The ship pitched and then yawed to starboard. The deck went from under my feet for the briefest of moments and I almost went over the side. I wondered if Lassiter and Terry would still be around to fish me out of the water. If they were even a fraction as loyal as Hartlaub had turned out, then there was no question. Steadying myself, I headed for the port side, seeking the source of the brief gun battle.

The most direct route was between the towering stacks, but as the ship rose and fell, I could detect movement in the upper levels that I didn't like. It seemed that the ship's ill maintenance was a factor everywhere, and I didn't trust that the containers had been secured as firmly as they should be. The last thing I wanted was to head through one of the narrow walkways only to find a thousand tons of steel falling on my head. I went quickly towards the front, where I recalled the collection of machine rooms were, as well as an exit from the lower decks. As I progressed, I thumbed the button to release the clip on my SIG, took out a fresh one and slapped it in place. It was the old Boy Scout in me: be prepared.

The rain didn't let up for a moment. Earlier I'd worried that the sea water dripping from our clothes would give Hartlaub and me away; that was no longer an issue, but the rain had caused me other problems. It had wiped out the trail of blood I'd followed until now, and also covered any trail Cain might have left behind.

Coming across the machine rooms, I used one as cover while I peered over towards the port-side rail. There was a lifeboat hanging on winches, and it looked like it had been prepped for launching. Were Jenny and Cain already on board? If they were then they were being very quiet. Was Cain holding a knife to her throat and threatening to kill her if she made a sound? Or worse: had he silenced her permanently? There was only one way to find out. I snuck out from behind the machine room, heading for the boat.

I saw the jumble of corpses and my breath caught in my chest. Two of the men I didn't know.

But the third, the one in the black jumpsuit lying face down on the deck with a Bowie knife savagely plunged into the base of his skull, was Ray Hartlaub. He looked dead, but impulse drove me to check. There was no pulse. I drew my fingers away from his cooling flesh and they were smeared with Hartlaub's blood. I swore: I owed Hartlaub both Imogen's and my life, but now I'd never be able repay that debt. No, I corrected, I could repay him by killing the man who'd murdered him.

There was a groan. The nearest man was a corpse. His groin had been torn away, as had half of his lower spine. So I looked at the third man and saw him move slightly. The clothing at his abdomen looked black with the copious amount of blood he was losing. The man had no weapons I could see, and he didn't have the strength to lift one even if he had. Still, I couldn't take the chance he'd try to kill me in his dying moments, so I approached him slowly, my SIG pointing directly at his face.

'Where is the woman?' I demanded. 'Where's Jennifer?'

The man rolled pale eyes my way, and I could tell from their unfocused stare that he was moments from death. He probably didn't even know that I was there. Keeping an eye on the lifeboat above, I nudged him with the barrel of my gun. 'The woman. Where is she?'

'*Ona ushla . . .*' the man said. '*Ona umerli.*'

'Speak English, goddamn you,' I said.

'*Ona umerli . . . ona umerli . . .*'

'What are you trying to say?'

'He says that "she is dead",' a voice whispered in my ear. 'Just like you are.'

I spun, aiming an elbow at the skull of the man leaning over me. But the strike never reached its mark. Before I'd even made it halfway round he thrust something against the nape of my neck and I was assaulted by a charge of electricity that simultaneously stiffened my entire body and sent my SIG spinning out of my grip.

He must have pressed the trigger again, because I got another whack of power through me, and I almost bit off the tip of my tongue as I fought against it. Somehow, I ended up on my back, lying against Hartlaub's corpse, staring at the shadow leaning over me, and he must have released the trigger because I was now shivering only from the residual effect of the charge through my body.

'You!'

'Bet you weren't expecting your old pal, Baron, huh?'

He was just about the last person I ever expected. I'd gained the impression the smarmy prick had set the police on me and Harvey in that hotel in Virginia, then gone to ground under whatever rock he'd originally crawled out from. There was I thinking that if I survived this latest round with Tubal Cain, I'd have a devil of a time finding Baron. His turning up here wasn't a pleasant surprise.

My SIG was five feet away from me. It lay close to the dying Russian, but the man didn't seem inclined to come to my rescue. I thought about snatching for my Ka-bar from the sheath in my boot, then remembered I'd left it sticking in the corpse of the first Russian I'd killed on the stairwell.

Baron stooped close to me. He held what I could now see was a Taser in his left hand. His right, he touched to his ribs. 'I owe you big time, Hunter. You shot me back at Hendrickson's place. Worse than that! Do you know how much money you have cost me?'

'Oh, right, I remember now. You were only there for the money, weren't you?' I spat at him. 'What a load of crap. You're a fucking sadist, Baron. It's as simple as that.'

Baron's lips pinched together. Then he nodded as if conceding a point. 'I suppose I am.'

He jabbed the Taser into my chest and gave me another zap.

I shuddered and thrashed and went part way on my side, my body jammed up against Hartlaub's.

Baron straightened, stood there with the rain plastering his hair to his pale forehead. 'You know, Hunter, I could keep this up all day.'

'No . . . no more!' I held up my open right palm, warding him off.

'Actually, there's plenty more,' he said, and dipped in for another blast.

'No,' I said, and rolled on to my back, the knife

353

so recently spearing Hartlaub's neck clutched in my left fist. Baron blinked down at me, raindrops shivering on his lashes. Then he lunged at me with the Taser. There was nothing I could do to stop the contacts striking me, or to halt the electric charge shooting through my body, but I swung hard with the hilt of the Bowie and got him directly in the centre of his face. His nose was crushed under the blow and he staggered back. I swarmed up and went after him. Now it was him who was stunned, and as I backhanded the hilt of the knife across his jaw he went down on his arse on the slick deck.

'You've been a little too handy with that fucking thing,' I said as I stood over him. 'You should've checked the charge, Baron, 'cause it isn't strong enough to stop an able-bodied man now.'

Baron looked at the Taser. He'd depleted most of the power the first time he'd hit me; second time it was enough to cause me to spasm but that was all, third time, all I experienced was a tingle. Fuck, the anger I felt towards him hurt more. When I'd checked Hartlaub's throat for a pulse, I'd noted the faint red marks on his skin. At the time I hadn't recognised them for the localised burns caused by the Taser, but as soon as Baron introduced me to it, I'd known. The piece of shit had used it on Hartlaub before he'd died. Maybe he'd used it on others on the ship, too, the way he had when torturing Rink.

'You know something, Baron? I promised Rink

354

that I'd save him a piece of your arse.' I hit him with the blade this time, leaving an inch-deep slash in his skull. 'But I'm sure he'll forgive me for keeping you all to myself.'

Baron fell on his side and the Taser clattered away from him. He was concussed at least, perhaps brain damaged, but he still had some life in him. His super-quick draw was pretty feeble though. He inched his hand towards the gun holstered on his hip. I stooped, picked up my SIG and languidly shot him in the skull, once, for Jenny. Then I fired three times into his body – once for Hartlaub, once for Rink, then once for myself. There were others I could have punished him for – not least Louise Blake – but that would have been overkill.

Then I went back to the Russian and kneeled close to his head. His face had taken on the colour and texture of molten wax and his eyes were practically the colour of cataracts. 'You said that the woman is dead?'

He was almost gone, but he still had enough strength to lift one hand and point towards the rail. He jabbed his finger, and I understood. She'd gone over the side. Then the Russian's arm flopped and he lay there, just another corpse among the pile of dead men.

No, that wasn't the entire truth. One of those was a dead friend, and I went to him. I rolled Hartlaub over on to his back, looked down at his relaxed features. In death he looked decades younger. Whatever the man's motive for being here, he'd given his life to help me. It was another burden I'd have to carry, but I wasn't about to waste his sacrifice.

I lifted my face to the storm. The rain pelted me and I opened my mouth, letting the water pool on my tongue. Then I spat it out, and raised my voice in competition with the roaring wind.

'Tubal Cain,' I screamed. 'You piece of shit! I'm going to tear your fucking heart out!'

CHAPTER 46

E ven over the tumult of the storm and the crashing of waves against the hull, the ominous moaning and the bangs and clicks of the ship, Cain heard the gunshots.

They came in a single harsh crack, followed by silence, then another trio.

They had brought him to a halt as he'd moved along the starboard side of the ship, retracing his steps towards the stairs to the galley. He turned, listening for more gunfire, but knew that those final rounds, so controlled and spaced, were punctuation marks in a very definite statement. The last was the full stop.

You should have kept a gun, he told himself. But he wouldn't let the fact that he'd foregone his firearms in favour of his blades trouble him. He had all the weapons he required, plus one very special addition. Actually, he relished meeting Joe Hunter with only the simple tools of his trade. It would be far more satisfying showing Hunter that the last time they'd met had been a fluke. Hunter had brought guns that time, but their fight had still ended blade to blade, and it would be the same here. Someone once claimed you didn't bring a knife to a gunfight. OK, you didn't: not unless you were Tubal Cain, the Father of Cutting Instruments.

He heard his name, the shout challenging the level of the rainstorm, and he smiled. It sounded like Joe Hunter had indeed survived his meeting with Baron.

'You piece of shit! I'm going to tear your fucking heart out!'

A poor choice of words from someone who had almost lost his heart to Cain's blade.

I'll show him the error of his ways, he thought. It was one thing killing a baron, quite another taking on a prince.

He chose the Tanto for setting up this kill. It had proven itself before and it would serve him well until he elected to show his ace card. Gripping the Tanto's hilt, he carried the blade braced against his wrist and crept slowly across the deck to the port side.

There was a rumble somewhere to the east. Thunder?

Let the storm build, it would add atmosphere to the drama about to play out. He knew the roar from the heavens was a sign that Chaos favoured his actions and that today would be his.

Kill Hunter.

Take his trophy.

Move on.

He had a more important reckoning to see to,

and that was with Hunter's brother. Big bad Joe was simply a stepping block in the right direction.

He'd lost Jennifer to the sea, but he'd been seconds away from killing her anyway. Once Hunter was out of the way, who'd know that the woman was no longer under his control? He could still draw John Telfer to the prearranged meeting. It would be an even sweeter reunion when Telfer found out he'd come too late to save his wife.

Cain wiped the rain from his eyes. There on the port side, the full fury of the storm was once again in his face. Wind tore at his clothing, as though trying to strip it away, leaving him naked, and in his most natural, feral form. For the briefest moment he even considered helping the wind in its mission: tearing off his clothing to meet Hunter the way nature had designed. But that would be stupid: in this weather hypothermia would kill him as readily as would Hunter's gun.

He moved slowly, but surely, towards the area where the lifeboat hung on its winches. Though he was still too far away to make anything out, he thought he saw movement through the drifting spray. He batted more rain from his eyes, thankful that he hadn't discarded his clothes in that moment's madness, because he needed the sleeve of his jacket to keep his vision clear.

The ship tilted, and he grabbed at the rail for support.

Again came that rumble from the east.

Was it thunder . . . or something else?

He searched the storm-tossed sea but couldn't detect anything; even so, this time he knew that it wasn't a product of the storm. That was a goddamn engine revving as a boat fought the waves.

Hunter and his friend must have arrived here by boat. They hadn't just teleported aboard the frickin' ship like this was a cheap TV sci-fi show. So, who the hell was out there? Jared Rington, the Jap who'd gone and spoiled everything last time? He hoped so: two birds with one stone, and all that.

Forget what's out there, he told himself. Concentrate on Hunter.

He continued, steadying himself with one hand on the rail. Through the shifting veil of rain he saw the bulky outline of the lifeboat as it swung on its ropes. It thumped against the wall of the ship with a resounding boom. On the deck directly to the right of it he could see the pile of shattered humanity, all the dead sprawled in various poses, as though positioned by the hand of a deranged choreographer of violence. Standing over the pile of corpses was another figure. Dressed in a black jumpsuit, an equally dark cap pulled over his hair, there was no mistaking him. He looked strange, a stark shadow amid the spray, shoulders hunched, his fists clenched by his sides, swaying with the pitch of the deck as he peered down at his dead friend's corpse.

Cain moved closer.

The man had his back to him.

Perfect.

Cain allowed the Tanto blade to swing forward and held it primed for a killing rush.

He was ten feet away now, and Cain held his breath. He wanted to leap in, but he recalled Hunter's catlike reflexes and thought he'd only make it halfway before the man twisted round and shot him dead. He squeezed rain from his eyes.

Another step.

Another.

Then Cain could no longer contain the urge for slaughter, and he launched himself at Hunter's back. He looped his left arm around the man's neck, driving the Tanto under his ribs with all the weight of his body behind it. He twisted the blade, seeking the liver, howling a shout of triumph in Hunter's ear.

He stepped back, pulling out the knife, and readying it for another plunge.

Hunter didn't fall.

He didn't even react.

He just swayed with the motion of the ship.

Cain wasn't one for swearing, but he couldn't stop himself.

'What the fuck?'

Then he saw it, the thin wire supporting the man, and he followed it up to where it was fixed to one of the overhead cranes. He looked at the back of the corpse's skull, saw where he'd recently jammed his Bowie knife through it.

Down on the deck, the other black-suited figure sat up and pointed his gun at Cain's face.

'Drop the knife, Cain,' Joe Hunter snapped.

CHAPTER 47

Using a friend in that way seems callous, but I believed that given the choice, Hartlaub would have said to go ahead. He'd given me his life, and now the means to draw Cain into a trap. The idea had come to me when I'd shouted my challenge at Cain. He was the type who couldn't refuse an easy kill when my back was turned. I'd seen the winch and the hook and had fed it under Hartlaub's armpits and hauled him off the deck. I'd positioned him so that he looked like a man stooped in grief, and it seemed to have done the trick.

It was difficult lying there among the dead, waiting as Cain crept forward, and more than once I'd wanted to leap up and shoot the bastard before he could reach Hartlaub. The ruse would only last so long, and I hadn't honestly thought he'd spring on to my dead friend's back like that. I'd waited, held myself lax, ready for my moment.

And then it had come.

'I told you to drop the fucking knife,' I said.

Cain shook his head sadly as I came to my feet. I stood with my feet planted, one slightly in front of the other, toes turned inward to grip the deck, the butt of my SIG supported in my opposite cupped palm. Only ten feet away, I could shoot Cain in either eye without stirring his lashes.

'That wasn't very sporting,' Cain said. 'Tricking me like that.'

'It isn't a game.'

'Oh, but it is. Don't say you don't agree. I know what you're like.'

'No, Cain. You don't. You can't begin to imagine what it's like to be me. You aren't human.'

'I'm not?'

'No. A human has a soul. Your soul died the day you picked up a blade and became Tubal Cain.'

'Maybe. But we're alike in so many other ways.'

'I'm nothing like you are, you murderous bastard.'

'Sigmund Petoskey. Kurt Hendrickson. Need I continue the list?'

'They deserved everything they got.'

'Where's the difference? You enjoy killing, I enjoy killing. There's this Hemingway quote I'm fond of. It goes something like, "Those who've hunted armed men long enough and liked it, never care for anything else." That's us, Hunter. We're both hunters of armed men. We *are* alike.'

'No, Cain.' I shook my head. 'You don't care if they're armed. You hunt anyone . . . including defenceless women.'

Cain's gaze slipped to the rail. 'Aah, I see now why you're pissed with me. But I had nothing to do with that. Jennifer chose her fate. She jumped overboard, I didn't push her. You can't blame me for that.'

'I can,' I said. 'And I will. Now drop the knife.'

He dropped the Tanto.

'And any others you're carrying.' I wiggled the gun barrel to show him I wasn't taking no for an answer. 'Take it real easy, Cain. The rain's making my finger a little slippery on this trigger.'

He sighed, then dug in his pocket and pulled out what looked like a Stanley knife. He tossed it away from him.

'Anything else?'

He shook his head. 'You can search me if you want.'

'Isn't going to happen, Cain.'

'So you're just going to execute me? Just like that?'

'Yes.'

I held the gun steady, aiming for the point directly between his eyes. Give him his due, he wasn't a coward like many notorious killers turn out. He didn't flinch, just stood there. Maybe I'd been correct: what did a man whose spirit had already been slain have to fear? I drew the moment out, and finally I noted his gaze slip slightly.

'So what are you waiting for?'

'Before I kill you I want to tell you something you might not want to hear.'

'Oh, God! Save me the sermon, will ya!'

'Don't worry, I'm not going to play psychiatrist.

You're a sick-headed bastard, we know that already.'

Cain snorted, but the derision was tinged with humour.

'John's dead,' I stated.

The words sounded wrong even to my own ears. But it explained Walter's reticence every time my brother's name was mentioned, and why John hadn't come to bait a trap as I'd requested. I'd denied what common sense had been telling me all along, but to voice those thoughts was still an alien sensation.

'Liar. I've been speaking with your old pal, Walter Conrad. He told me that John was on his way.'

'He was lying to you, Cain. The way he's lied to me since Jubal's Hollow. You remember what you did to my brother there? How could he survive *that*?'

'The medics saved him, the way they saved me.'

'So why isn't he here?'

'Because Conrad sent you instead.'

'We've both been played along. John's dead.'

'You're only saying that so that I stop chasing him.'

'No, Cain,' I corrected him. 'That isn't necessary. Not when I'm going to kill you. I'm telling you so that you realise what a total fuck-up all of this has been. You've been chasing a trophy that you'll never get your hands on. All the pain, all the suffering that everyone has gone through, it's been for *nothing*.'

366

'Lies.'

'Truth,' I countered. 'You're going to Hell with the knowledge that you'll never get to John. You already missed your opportunity.'

'Nooooo . . .'

Everything about him changed in that instant. His shoulders rounded, his head dipped, and he flicked out with his right arm. From his sleeve projected the item I was certain he'd disclose at this last moment. The fiendish bastard had been busy during his downtime aboard the ship, whittling and paring the rib bone taken from the ship's captain. Cain had planned to spear me with it, the way I'd rammed a rib bone through his trachea back at Jubal's Hollow. Well, I'd also something to pay him back for: my brother.

I allowed him a moment, and he took it. He launched himself at me.

Calmly, I shot him.

His forearm was shattered, and the horrifying weapon went spinning across the deck alongside chunks of his arm.

Cain kept on coming, teeth bared like a wild beast's.

I shot him again, this time through his left thigh.

He staggered against the rail. Clawed hands held him upright. He twisted to look at me, his eyes squinting as I shoved the gun away, replacing it with the Bowie knife I'd jammed down my belt. I thought it only just that I use his own weapon to punish him. He watched me load up like a javelin thrower, and barely reacted as I swiped the blade across his face with all the power I could muster. His jaw shattered under the force, and he stood there with a glazed expression, blood spewing from the open wound. He tried to say something, but it was difficult speaking with a mouthful of broken teeth and blood frothing between his lips.

'Save the sermon,' I taunted, and backhanded the knife across his chest.

His jaw was opened up, his chest gushing, but still he was alive. Good, because I'd intended that the slashes of the knife were debilitating without taking his life. The knife was his weapon, mine was the SIG. I lifted it. 'This is for John, you piece of shit.'

I aimed directly between his eyes.

I fired and his skull snapped backwards, and his body went with it. He collapsed over the rail, then very, very slowly his weight eased forward and he slipped over the side and into the night. Over the roaring wind, I heard the slap of his body as he smacked the waves.

Normally I feel no satisfaction in killing.

But Cain had been right about one thing. There was nothing in the world like the hunting of armed men like *him*. I cared for nothing else than to see *them* dead. A long time ago Tubal Cain had been slain in the spirit; now he'd been slain in the flesh and I couldn't have been happier.

I stood alongside the railing where he'd gone

over, watching the pale blur of his corpse as it rode the pitch-black tide. Within seconds, a wave rolled him over on to his back, and he sunk beneath the surface, his wide open eyes staring accusingly at me. They were like they'd always been: dead and soulless.

CHAPTER 48

Hartlaub was my first priority. I unhooked him from the winch and laid him out on the deck, away from the other dead men. His eyelids had peeled apart, and I gently pressed them shut with the pads of my thumbs. All the while, I listened for anything that would warn me of an impending attacker. As far as I could tell, though, everyone here was dead, and the *Queen Sofia* was indeed a ghost ship. Looking down on the dead agent's face, I whispered my stepfather's wise words, 'Mocking is catching, Hartlaub.'

They weren't exactly true. Hartlaub hadn't invited bad luck, it had been forced on him the moment he'd turned up at Imogen's house in Maine. From that time on his days had been numbered. It's what came of being dragged along in my undertow.

I loaded him into the lifeboat and set the winch-motors running so that it was lowered to the sea. The fury of the storm had passed by then, and the boat only made a faint knocking sound against the hull of the ship. I went down a rope ladder. Before I could start the outboard, a different engine roared and from around the stern of the *Queen Sofia* came another vessel. It was low in the water, with inflatable cushions and a single cabin perched near the front.

'Hunter! Over here, buddy!'

I recognised Terry's voice. I stood up in the lifeboat and watched as he steered the inflatable boat towards me. Someone was at the prow; at first I thought it was Lassiter, but then I noted there were two heads watching from inside the illuminated cabin.

I looked again at the figure in the prow, and couldn't believe my eyes. Standing there, hugging a hand to her chest, was my sister-in-law. Lassiter and Terry had done exactly as promised: they'd been there waiting for when Jenny got off the ship, and had plucked her safely from the water.

I'm not a praying man, but at that moment, I closed my eyes, leaned back and thanked God in heaven for all of my good friends, old and new.

Terry steered the inflatable alongside the lifeboat, and I pulled them close and tied the boats up to each other. I scrambled over the side, to be greeted by Jenny as she threw herself into my arms. We held each other for a long time, and it wasn't just Jenny who cried.

'I'm so, so sorry,' I said to her. 'I wish I could have got here sooner.'

'You came, that's what's important,' Jenny said. Something in her voice told me her words held a deeper meaning. 'If he could have, John would've come too,' I said.

She looked up at the freighter towering over us, as if expecting John to come scrambling down the ladder at any second.

I took her face in my hands and tilted it up. She had a cut under her eye, but it was the least of what she'd gone through. She had suffered enough for now – or for any lifetime – and I decided to spare her my conclusions about John's fate. I just looked at her, and by the way her face folded in on itself she knew. I pulled her into my embrace, whispering in her ear, 'John told me he still loved you and the kids, Jenny. Very much.'

She sobbed against my chest, and I allowed her to. I would have cried as well, but the tears wouldn't come again, maybe because the truth had been troubling me for so long now. Perhaps Jenny was crying for her children, that they'd never again see their father, or maybe, for all that he'd put her through, she still loved John too. After a while she stood back, mopping her face, but it was awkward for her. I took Jenny's hand in mine. I was very gentle, because she was in pain. 'Cain did this?'

She'd swaddled the stump of her finger in a dressing supplied by one of the crew. Her bottom lip trembled, but her eyes were drier now. 'He told me that he'd go after my children. For them, I'd have given both my arms.'

'I know,' I said. 'So would John given the chance.'
'I know that, Joe.'
I kissed her on the forehead, gave her a hug.
'C'mon. Let's get you home to your kids.'

CHAPTER 49

After her wounds were tended to and she'd undergone a thorough debriefing, Jennifer went home to Jack and Beatrice and I would have preferred to have gone with her. I owed my parents that much: they should hear from me that my younger brother was dead, not from some anonymous cop turning up at their home. Of course, I had to face the music in the US first, but I promised Jennifer that I'd follow in a few days' time, supposing I wasn't locked up for the next fifteen years.

The Navy and Coast Guard, ATF, FBI, CIA: they all wanted a piece of the action concerning the *Queen Sofia* and they were welcome to it. Grodek's ship was towed to port at Hampton Roads and the official line offered to the media was that the suspected human traffickers on board had been involved in a power struggle that had erupted into violence. Jennifer's name was never mentioned, but then again neither was mine or Hartlaub's. Also left out of the story was the inclusion of a certain Tubal Cain. That didn't surprise me, and I was happy to play ignorant. Jeffrey Baron disappeared too, literally.

It struck me that a mystery surrounded the nearby Roanoke Island, where once an entire community of settlers disappeared: it was an enduring legend, and now others had slipped from the face of the earth and no one would ever have a clue as to their passing. Another myth for the conspiracy theorists to fret over.

There was nobody left alive who would attest to my involvement in the deaths of either Sigmund Petoskey or Kurt Hendrickson and their passing would remain an equally contested mystery. The fact that both my and Harvey's fingerprints were discovered at the motel where we'd holed up after the assault on Hendrickson remained, but without Baron's evidence, all they had were charges of dangerous driving, theft of an automobile and criminal damage, and they were covered easily enough. The weapons we'd used had already been spirited away into the same empty place where everything else of consequence went. I have often railed against the fact that Walter has kept me on a loose leash, and manipulated me for his own ends, but, what was the alternative? I was lucky to have him covering my arse. Yes, I owed him, but he had some explaining to do before I'd ever trust him again.

When the naval helicopter touched down outside Walter's fishing cabin, I had a small crowd waiting to greet me. Some of them I didn't know; they were officials working with Walter to tie up all the loose ends, a job I didn't envy them. Then there were the people that mattered to me. First to come forward was Rink, who bulled his way past the others and grabbed me in a bear hug. I was glad to find that his shoulder wound wasn't troubling him as much now, judging by how tightly he squeezed me. When he put me down, his eyebrows worked like a couple of thunderheads.

'He's really dead this time. You're sure, Hunter?'

'I shot him in the head and watched him sink to the bottom of the ocean.'

'Good, it's what the frog-giggin' sumbitch needed. What about that other asshole, Baron?'

'I got him as well, Rink. I got them all.'

'I'm glad, but I wanted Baron for myself.' He knuckled me in the chest. 'You shouldn't have run off like that, goddamnit! You should've given me a couple hours to get my shit together and I'd've come with you.'

'That's exactly why I left when I did. You were in no shape, and if I'd told you I was going you'd have never stayed behind. I'm happy to see that Rene Moulder worked her magic on you.' The veterinarian was standing in the crowd, but she hadn't come forward. I winked my thanks at her and she smiled.

Rink leaned close to my ear. 'It was me that was working *my* magic, brother.'

'So rank's no longer an issue?'

'No, man. Now Rink's the issue.' He laughed, and I gave him a nudge with my elbow.

Harvey was there as well, but he just stood

quietly, regarding me with calm eyes. He dipped his head in a slow nod of respect that I could only reciprocate. We'd been friends for some time, but lately our bond had grown even tighter; that's what comes of fighting for your life alongside someone. Like Rink, he'd have preferred to have accompanied me on my final fight against Tubal Cain, but he also knew the reason why I'd chosen to leave him behind.

Standing at Walter's shoulder were new hard-faced bodyguards, replacements for the men who'd died alongside Bryce Lang. One of them was the guard who'd been at the back door of Walter's cabin that first day I arrived, the one who'd given me the knowing look. I wondered how much he'd known at the time, about how Walter, the man I saw as a surrogate father, had been lying to me. Walter had his unlit cigar clamped as usual between his teeth.

'Let's go inside, son.'

I followed him towards the cabin.

Behind me, Rink grunted a curse. He hadn't been invited, but he wasn't staying out of the loop. He followed close behind and damn the consequences.

Once we were inside Walter dismissed his bodyguards. This meeting was personal. I regarded Walter like I was seeing him for the first time.

'I've done everything I can for you, son,' Walter said. His voice was flat, and held little strength. 'For now you're off the hook for the killings. But

I can't promise that something won't come back to bite you on the ass further down the line. You might still be brought to book at some point.'

'I knew the consequences of going rogue. If I have to, then I'll pay my dues.'

'We're talking murder, son.'

'Don't forget I've also outstayed my visa,' I said. 'I don't even have a green card. What're the chances that I'll be kicked out of the country as an illegal immigrant?'

'You can joke at a time like this?'

'I've cried all the tears I'm going to, Walt. I've none left to shed.' I hadn't wanted to believe that Walter would lie to me about my brother's death. I'd suppressed the doubts, the way I'd suppressed the tears. The only ones I'd allowed were those I'd shared with Jennifer on the boat, and when she'd finally boarded her airplane home.

Walter hung his head, but it wasn't from genuine shame. 'I should have come clean about John. I'm sorry.'

'Sorry doesn't cut it, Walter. When did it happen?'

'Three days after Jubal's Hollow.'

Three days. A long time before I was sent after Luke Richard, before I foiled Carswell Hicks' and Samuel Gant's racist plot to detonate a dirty bomb in Manhattan. On both those occasions Walter had used me and I'd gone along with him through loyalty. Well, wasn't I the misguided fool?

Walter noted the anger building in me.

Misreading the signs, he tried to appease me. 'He didn't suffer, son. John never regained consciousness and despite the best care he died from complications. I wanted to tell you . . .'

'But then you'd have had nothing to hold me on,' I snapped. 'I felt indebted to you while I thought you were protecting my little brother. Fuck sake, Walter! Why didn't you just tell me?'

'It wasn't my decision, son. I was ordered to keep his death from you.'

'Who ordered you, Walt? Your Arrowsake bosses again? Or was it *just* the CIA this time? There must be a shortage of assassins if you've to keep me around like a fucking attack dog.'

'I'm sorry, son . . .'

'Don't,' I said.

He blinked up at me, incomprehension plain on his wide face.

'No father would treat his son like that.'

'Joe, if there was any way, I'd have changed things.'

'You'd have saved John over Cain, would you?'

'You know I would have, goddamnit!'

'So tell me the truth. What was the real reason for sending Hartlaub this time?'

'Extra protection for you, help to get Jennifer free, what else?'

'I think he was there to bring Cain in alive, and that makes me wonder who would have been sacrificed to ensure that. Luckily, Hartlaub proved to be a better man than that.'

'I can't believe that you'd even suggest that . . .'

'Walter. Hendrickson was dead. Even if he wasn't, the case against him wasn't going to go ahead, because you knew all along that your star witness couldn't testify. If all you wanted was Jennifer safe and Cain dead you could have sent in an entire team of Navy Seals. Instead you chose to send me and one of your own men. Like I said, Hartlaub was sent to protect Cain, not kill him. Hartlaub witnessed first hand what Cain was capable of and realised – in wanting to keep him alive – what kind of monsters he was serving. Thankfully he chose to disobey his orders . . .'

'You're deluded, Joe, but if that's what you think then there's nothing I can do about it.'

'It's just the way it is,' I said.

Suddenly, Rink rounded on Walter and I thought I'd have to step between them. But it was Rink himself that was hurting. He was feeling the betrayal as much as I was. 'That ain't right, Walter. You can do something . . . a goddamn apology wouldn't go amiss.'

'I've said I'm sorry,' Walter said.

'No, Walter. You just repeated what you've been *ordered* to say. Just like you always do.'

Walter shook his head sadly. He knew that Rink was right. His face reddened, in itself proof of his guilt. I was too wrung out to push him further but Rink wasn't finished with him yet.

'Even if Joe's wrong about you, you still brought this on everyone. You realise that Cain wouldn't have needed stopping if you'd admitted that John was already dead. Son of a bitch! Hendrickson wouldn't have got him outa prison, and all of those people wouldn't have died as a consequence. Bryce, Hartlaub, Louise . . . everyone! I hope you're fucking proud of yourself, Walter?'

The old man looked around the cabin, taking in the plastic sheets and the chemical smell, and that was a more potent lesson than any Rink could fire at him. He sat in his chair, pulled out his cigar and dropped it on the floor. Then he folded at the waist, placed his face in his hands and began to weep.

We left Walter to grieve alone.

CHAPTER 50

This latest episode of my life had begun with me standing over the headstone of a loved one, and it had come full circle. On that first occasion Imogen had been by my side, and she was this time as well. The difference now was that we weren't in the freezing north but out on the West Coast in a graveyard bathed in warmth and sunlight. It didn't make the place any less depressing. I stood there, round-shouldered, as I peered down at the forlorn grave marker. Imogen had slipped her hand into mine, and she held on, her pledge that she'd be there to help carry the burden fulfilled. I welcomed her presence, because I'm not sure how I would have handled things if she wasn't there.

'I don't believe this,' I said.

'Can't you have it changed?'

'I could probably force the issue with Walter, but what good would it do? It would just cause more heartache.' In my other hand I was carrying a small wreath, but it seemed pointless placing it on this grave.

The headstone was a plain marker devoid of

embellishment; there were no other floral tributes, no one had been by to tend the grave and it was now strewn with weeds. A name had been chiselled into the rough granite, but that was all. The name did not match that of the man buried below it, and that's what hurt the most. When Tubal Cain supposedly died that first time, the CIA needed a body to fill his coffin. They had lied about the identity of the Harvestman, placed all the blame on the illegitimate brother of Martin Maxwell, and marked his grave accordingly. But it wasn't Robert Swan who was in that grave, it was my little brother.

Imogen squeezed my hand. 'Have you thought about having him exhumed and given a proper burial back home in England?'

'No. I wouldn't like to put my parents or Jenny and the kids through that.'

'It would offer them a sense of closure,' Imogen said, 'and you, Joe. At least you'd have somewhere to go and show your respects. Instead of this . . . this mockery.'

'No, Imogen, it's not going to happen. Arrowsake will never allow the truth to come out.'

'We could tell everyone, though. Who could stop us?'

'They could, Imogen. I know now what lengths they'll go to hide their dirty secrets. We would never be safe. I don't want you to go through anything like this again. It's like you said back in the Adirondacks, it's behind us. Let's leave it there. Let's leave *everything* there.'

'You're sure, Joe?' She looked at me expectantly. 'Everything?'

'I'm sure, love,' I said and pulled her into my embrace.

When we walked away, I was still carrying the wreath.

EPILOGUE

Two days earlier . . .

The storm that had hit the North Carolina coast caused little structural damage, but all along the beachfronts of the Barrier Islands, residents were out cleaning the sands of the unsightly aftermath. They picked driftwood and rubbish off the beach, carting away the flotsam and jetsam on trailers and undertaking the minor repairs to windbreaks and fences with the spirit of camaraderie that came from such work. Community spirit was always at its highest following times of travail, and once the work was done, their triumph over the elements would be celebrated with barbecues on the beach. But that would come later.

For now, they scoured the sands, hauling away the trash, calling out to each other when they found something beyond the ability of one person to lift, and hurrying to lend a hand. The shouts were a regular feature.

Along the beach another yell went up, this one tinged not with joviality, but trepidation. A woman beckoned her neighbours down to the waterline, while she clutched at her throat with shaking hands.

A group gathered around her, eyes wide as they studied what the storm had thrown at their feet.

One of them took out a cellphone. They couldn't deal with this alone; the emergency services were required. They didn't call the police . . . this man needed urgent medical assistance if he was going to survive his horrendous injuries.

Branch	Date
TS	12/11